BONES

OF

CALLALEY

BEST WISHES

Colin Youngman

Colin Youngman

The Works of Colin Youngman:

The Ryan Jarrod Series:

Bones of Callaley (Book 8)
The Tower (Book 7)
Low Light (Book 6)
Operation Sage (Book 5)
High Level (Book 4)
The Lighthouse Keeper (Book 3)
The Girl On The Quay (Book 2)
The Angel Falls (Book 1)

**

Other Standalone Novels:

The Doom Brae Witch

Alley Rat

DEAD Heat

**

Anthology:
Twists*
Incorporates the novelettes: DEAD Lines, Brittle Justice, The Refugee and A Fall Before Pride (all available separately), plus a BONUS READ: Vicious Circle.

Colin Youngman

This is a work of fiction.

All characters and events are products of the author's imagination.

Whilst most locations are real, some liberties have been taken with architectural design, precise geographic features, and timelines.

Seaward Inc.

ISBN: 979-8-39144-890-7

Bones of Callaley

DEDICATION

To

Trevor

*Whose 'discovery' beneath his floorboards
inspired this tale.*

(It was all very innocent, honest guv.)

And To

The residents of the 'real' Callaley Avenue who are nothing like those portrayed
here.

I hope.

**

In Memory of

Jennie

1

'Family quarrels are bitter things. They're not like aches or wounds; more like splits in the skin that won't heal because there's not enough material.'

F. Scott Fitzgerald

'One cannot and must not try to erase the past merely because it does not fit the present.'

Golda Meir

ONE

'You're looking at the home of your dreams.'

That's what the Front Street estate agent promised as she pored over the brochure with the excited couple. Five months later, Ivor and Marina Hickson remained unconvinced.

The move had been fraught with problems. Firstly, the buyer for their Moor Court apartment overlooking Grandstand Road and the Town Moor itself pulled out of the deal. The Hickson's plan to fund the purchase of their new home with the proceeds of the sale lay in ruins. Instead of making a cash offer, they were left seeking a mortgage provider willing to accept them in a time of recession.

Secondly, weeks into the process, they discovered the solicitor they'd hired for the conveyancing was the husband of the estate agent. The conflict of interests worried Ivor. Ivor agreed a settlement payment for the work already undertaken by the solicitor before the Hicksons picked themselves up, dusted themselves down, and started all over again.

By the time contracts were ready for exchange, their new home had stood empty for over two months. When they revisited the property, they discovered a severe winter frost had burst the pipes resulting in a bathroom flood which brought down part of the kitchen ceiling. The ensuing disagreement over who bore responsibility for the reparation work dragged on between the legal teams for months until, again, Ivor Hickson relented.

Ivor and Marina finally took up residence in March. A month later, the three-bedroomed house overlooking the Derwent Valley was not yet the promised dream home - but at least it was no longer the house of nightmares.

Or so the Hicksons believed.

Marina pulled at loose tresses of dark hair trailing from her straggly bun with one hand. In the other, she held a metal scraper which cast trails of poor-taste wallpaper onto the bare floor like drool from a boxer dog's lips.

She looked out the kitchen window and shook her head at the sight of Ivor and his latest 'project.'

Her husband sat astride a hired mini excavator with not a clue what he was meant to do with it. The rear garden sloped away from the house at an upward angle towards a towering mass of Leylandii screening Callaley Avenue from the neighbouring Woodpack Avenue.

'The lawn's going to be a bugger to cut,' Ivor had declared when they'd first seen it. 'I think it'd be improved if I levelled it or, even better, terraced it.'

'How the hell do you propose to do that?' Marina scoffed.

Ivor shrugged. 'Where there's a will, and all that.'

'Is it worth it, darling?'

'I think it is, yes. We only moved here so we could have more space and a garden. Might as well make the most of it. Besides, he'll love it when he gets older.'

'Or she,' Marina pointed out.

'Ah, well - that's the beauty of adoption, isn't it? We can have whatever we want.'

'I'm not sure it works quite like that.'

Ivor scowled. 'Doesn't it? Well, it should.'

'Depends how long we're prepared to wait. You wanted us to start a family pronto, didn't you?'

'Oh yeah - blame me, why don't you? Of course, I forgot. It's always my fault.'

Marina felt a part of her die inside but she didn't let it show. She never did. 'Anyway, back to the point - how are you gonna sort the garden?'

Ivor scratched his head. 'Well, I'll flatten out one section. Dig into the bank, level out the next strip...'

'And how do you propose to stop the bank collapsing in the meantime?'

'Easy,' Ivor said with a triumphant gleam in his eyes. 'Dry-stone wall. See, I've thought of everything.'

'Who's going to build this mythical dry-stone wall?'

Ivor paused. 'Hmm. Never thought of that.'

Marina had thrown a damp dish cloth at him and he retaliated by scooping up soap suds from the sink and depositing them on top of her head where they sat like a pyramid.

They'd fun-fought, laughed, and wrestled each other to the floor where they made love on the cold tiles of their forever home.

Now, Ivor looked as if he was making love to the excavator as he frantically battled to start the damn thing. Marina tapped on the kitchen window.

'Coffee?' She mimed the act of tipping a mug into her mouth. The excavator chose that moment to fire up and take off like a bucking bronco in slow motion. 'I'll take that as a no,' she chuckled to herself.

Instead, she topped up the wallpaper steamer and waited for it to hiss and gurgle before carrying it to the cloakroom. Her knees crackled as she bent to steam the last remaining strip of paper.

Marina began humming 'Our House' while she stripped away the sodden wall covering. Through the fug of steam, she noticed a scratch on the wall. Moved the steamer away from her for a better look.

It wasn't a scratch. It was a paint mark. A few inches lower, another mark - a black line and an inscription. '15/3', it read. Marina looked up at the higher mark and spotted a similar inscription '17/9.'

She used her fingers to peel away a stubborn strip of paper. Another mark, more numbers. '10/2.'

Marina felt a sense of comfort well up inside her, a warmth which surprised her, when she realised the marks were height measurements.

'A child lived here,' she thought, before deriding herself. The house was more than forty years old. Of course there'd have been children. Still, it was good to know their child wouldn't be the first to live there.

Marina's knees popped again as she stood, job complete. She cocked her head to one side, looked at the measurements, noticed they stopped around four feet from the floor, and wondered where the family had moved to. She began inventing stories about the child. Pictured him - or her - married with kids of their own, possibly in a house just like the one she stood in.

Marina became aware of a silence outside. Ivor had, somehow, successfully brought the excavator to a halt. She knew what that meant. Coffee and biscuit time.

She ran her hands under the tap, filled the kettle, and prepared the mugs to the accompaniment of her high-pitched rendition of 'Sweet Home Alabama.'

Marina sensed movement behind her. 'Kettle's on, love.' When she received no acknowledgement, she pressed on.

'I said, *'Kettle's on.'* She half-turned. 'Ivor?'

He stood in the doorway, shivering.

'Is it cold out there? You just need to work harder,' she smiled.

Ivor stared straight ahead.

'What's up? You look like you've seen a ghost.'

He blinked. Shook his head as if he'd only just realised she was there. 'What did you say?'

'Doesn't matter. Coffee's nearly ready. That'll warm you up.'

'Fuck the coffee.' His voice was barely a whisper.

'Is there any need?'

He nodded. Short, sharp inclinations of his head.

Marina continued to look at him, waiting.

'I've found a body.'

**

'Don't come any closer.'

They were outside, Ivor staring down at a dome-shaped object poking through the soil. When he looked up, Marina was heading towards the excavated trench. 'Go back inside,' he warned.

'Don't be stupid, man. It'll be a cat or something. Kids will have wanted their cat buried close by.'

'It's not a cat.'

'A dog, then.'

'It's not a fucking dog, either.'

Marina made to turn back to the house then quickly leant sideways so she could peer around him.

She stepped back at the sight of the crown of a skull and a few scattered bones. Her finger trembled as she pointed at them.

'My God. What's *that*?'

'It's what I said it was.'

'It's a skull!'

'I told you but you didn't believe me. You had to come and see for yourself, and now I'll have to put up with your hysterics all bloody day.'

Her eyes remained locked on the skull. Something in her brain shifted and her eyes softened. 'You know what, I reckon it's a Hallowe'en decoration. I've seen them before. Folk lay them out like it's somebody escaping from a grave. That's all it is. They'll have forgotten about it. It's plastic. Look.'

Before he could stop her, Marina reached down into the trench. The moment her fingers brushed against it; she shot back as if electrocuted.

'Shitting hell. It's bone. It's real! It's really real.'

'That's what I've been telling you.' He took her by the arm. 'Let's get that coffee and think this through.' He marched his zombie-like wife back to the house.

Marina collapsed into a chair. This was the last thing she needed, just when she'd started feeling more like her old self.

'It's awful. What do you think it's doing there?'

'Not a lot, by the looks of it.'

'You know what I mean. *How* did it get there?'

Ivor shrugged. 'I doubt it buried itself.'

Marina sipped her coffee. Screwed her face at its bitterness. 'It might be a relic of some sorts. You know, a monk or something. Or, maybe, a warrior killed in battle centuries ago.'

'This is Whickham. Not Lindisfarne or Flodden Field. Besides, it wouldn't be so close to the surface if it was ancient.'

Marina puffed out her cheeks. 'We'd better call the police.'

Ivor looked pensive for a moment. 'We don't have to.'

'What? Of course we do! You've found a body.'

A plan began to form in the firmament of his grey matter. 'A body nobody knows is there. A body no-one is looking for. I could just cover it up again. Nobody would be any the wiser.'

She breathed hard. Tried to suppress the tears.

'Listen,' Ivor said. 'It'll be fine. You don't want to upset yourself. Not now, not after everything. Why don't you take yourself off to bed? Take a couple of your pills.'

Marina snorted a laugh. 'Don't think a couple of pills will help, somehow. The full bottle might.'

Ivor stood. 'No! You're not going down that road again. Let me go outside and fill the damn hole in. Let sleeping dogs lie. What do you say?'

'It's not a dog. You said so yourself.'

Ivor sucked in air. Spoke softly. 'Honey, we're just getting things back on track. If we report it to the police, we'll be straight into negative equity. It'll knock thousands off the value. We'll have all sorts trampling through our garden, treading mud all over the house. Who knows, they might want to pull up the floorboards, dig up the drive. Once they start, they'll never stop, that police lot.'

'It's not right.'

Ivor changed tack. 'What about the adoption agency?'

'What about them?'

'Do you really think they'll want to place a child in a house where someone's been murdered? It'll be the end of your…of our…dreams.'

'How do you know they were murdered?'

He rubbed an eyebrow. 'Marina, who buries their maiden aunt in the back garden rather than a graveyard? Of course it's murder.'

'Then, we've got to tell the police.'

Ivor shrugged his shoulders to relax them. 'What if whoever killed them still lives nearby? If they know we've found something; know it's us who reported it - they might come for us.'

Marina's eyes flitted from side to side, as if studying the neighbours through the walls. 'But whoever the poor soul is, they deserve a proper burial on consecrated soil not our bloody back garden.'

Ivor scratched the back of his neck. 'Must you always be a goody-two shoes?'

She stared at the ceiling. 'It's either that, or the bottle of pills.'

With an impatient grunt, Ivor Hickson reached for his phone and dialled 999.

TWO

The excitable puppy found the lamppost enthralling. So much so, his leader became wrapped around it like tinsel on a Christmas tree. Ryan Jarrod laughed as he struggled to unwind it, only for the dog to cock his leg over the post - and Ryan's hands.

Jarrod laughed again. He'd done that a lot recently; laugh. When he first joined the ranks of the City and County police Major Crimes Team, he'd done it for the challenge and the excitement of the chase, not to mention a get-out from the mundane paperwork of the civil service.

Ryan never thought he'd welcome the quiet routine of the last few months, a few months of innocuous community detective work. It was the equivalent of a journalist working the hatched, matched, and despatched column yet it served its purpose.

After the attempts on his life by a drugs baron named Benny Yu, the short secondment arranged by his Superintendent, Sam Maynard, enabled Ryan to rediscover his mojo - or, as DCI Stephen Danskin described it, to get his shit together.

Now, his shit WAS together. Life had returned to normal and he was ready for the cut-and-thrust of working the city again. Just another three weeks as Detective-in-Charge at Whickham village police station, and he'd be back amongst it.

'Howay, Kenzie. Nearly there. Come on, boy.' Ryan slapped a palm against his thigh and the German Shepherd pup he'd named after a fallen colleague bounded towards the young Detective, its ears seemingly permanently erect as it took in the world around him.

Ryan knocked and walked straight into the house on Newfield Walk. 'Your day guest's arrived, Dad,' he called as he unclipped Kenzie's leader.

'Aal reet, son?' Norman Jarrod asked through a mouthful of greasy bacon.

'Never better. He's been fed,' Ryan said, pointing to the dog turning circles at Norman's feet. 'Not as well as you, mind.'

'Give ower, man. This is just a snack. I'll have me breakfast in a bit,' Norman joked. 'What time will you be picking him up?'

'Six-ish, I reckon. As per usual.'

'Oh aye. Still cannot get used to you working regular hours.'

'Not for much longer, though.' Ryan checked his watch. 'Right, I'd best get off. It's canny being able to walk to work these days. I'll miss it from next month.'

Norman belched and rubbed his stomach. 'Aye, we all need exercise.'

Ryan couldn't tell if he was being serious or taking the piss. 'That's good 'cos Kenzie will need a decent walk around eleven.'

Norman rolled his eyes, and Ryan knew it was the latter.

The spring sun seemed to follow Ryan like a spotlight as he made his way down Glebe Avenue towards Front Street, where traffic noise drowned out birdsong. He nodded 'hello' to a few villagers, waved at an old mate across the road, sent a WhatsApp message to his sometime girlfriend Hannah, and smiled at her humorous reply.

He'd reached the Front Street veterinarian's, a couple of hundred yards from the station, when a squad car zoomed by, its lights ablaze and siren sounding.

Ryan reached the station's walled entrance and stepped back as traffic stopped to allow another police car out of the gates. Ryan just had time to mouth 'What's up?' to the uniformed officers inside before it sped away.

His phone vibrated in his pocket. Hoping it might be Hannah Graves, he looked at the caller details. The screen read, *'Rick Kinnear.'*

'Ryan, where are you?'

'I'm just at the station now. What's going on? There seems to be a bit of activity this morning.'

'Aye, there is,' Kinnear replied.

DCI Rick Kinnear was, nominally, overseeing Ryan's activities in Whickham from City and County's base in Newcastle city centre. In truth, there'd been very little contact between them. Kinnear knew Ryan was competent enough to be left alone, and Ryan knew Kinnear was all for an easy life.

Rick was a canny enough bloke, but there was a reason Stephen Danskin headed the Major Crime Team and not Kinnear. The fact Rick was calling now unnerved Ryan.

'Are you gonna give us a clue, then?'

'Might be nowt, but there's reports of a body find.'

'That doesn't sound like nowt to me,' Ryan shot back.

'Well, thing is, it's an old body.'

Jarrod sucked air between his teeth. 'Do you mean it's the body of someone old, or the body has been there for a while?'

'Sorry, Ryan. I should have been clearer. It's been there a while. A good while. So long, in fact, it isn't a body anymore. Just a few bones.'

A car moved forward from the parking bays in front of the station building. Its lights flashed, and PC Eric Ross - one of the local plod - beckoned Ryan towards him from the driver's seat.

'When did it turn up?' Ryan asked Kinnear.

'About nine. Some bloke working in his garden found it.'

Ryan was due to start his shift at ten. He checked his watch. Ten past ten. 'Why the delay?'

'I don't think there's any mad rush. The golden hour hardly applies. Probably not even the golden year.'

Ryan allowed himself a laugh. 'True enough.'

'So, I alerted forensics first. Thought they could have first dabs at it.'

'And?'

'Don't know yet. Too early. Thought you might check it out for me.'

'*Yep. That's about right,*' Ryan thought. 'Okay. I will do. Eric's got a car ready for me now,' Ryan cradled the phone under his chin as he clambered in and fastened his belt. 'I'll take a neb and let you know what's what.'

'Good lad.'

'Where we headed?' Ryan asked.

'Callaley Avenue,' Rick Kinnear and Eric Ross replied in unison.

**

'Do you know this place?' Ross asked as he turned left off Thistledon Avenue.

Ryan gave a silent nod.

'Good, 'cos I've only been around these parts a couple of times. Not much call for us down this end of the village.'

Ryan said nothing.

'So, where's the house?' Eric Ross continued.

'It's fairly obvious, isn't it?' Ryan peered up at a property bordered by blue and white cordon tape which fluttered in the air like the unease in Ryan's stomach.

Eric pulled up behind a patrol car parked sideways on, presenting as a makeshift barrier. Ryan continued to stare at the house with unblinking eyes. He'd never been inside it, yet he felt he knew every nook and cranny hidden by its brick walls.

Ryan realised Eric was speaking.

'You'll want a look, I guess.'

Ryan nodded as Eric handed him a pair of latex gloves and shoe covers from the glove compartment. Jarrod took a deep breath and stepped outside.

PC Blair recognised him immediately. 'Morning sir,' Blair said, holding up the tape for Ryan to pass beneath. Ryan offered a curt smile and took the side path to the back of the house where, despite the daylight, floodlights were being erected. Looked like it would be a long job.

'What have we got?' he asked the Scene of Crime officer.

'Skeletal remains. They were uncovered by an Ivor Hickson, the owner of the property. He purchased it recently and was doing some work in the garden when he saw them.'

Ryan knew the answer but he had to ask. 'Definitely human?'

'I'm nee expert but I know a skull when I see one,' SOCO replied.

Ryan smiled grimly. 'How long have the bones been there?'

'Like I says, I'm nee expert.'

Ryan glanced towards the kitchen window. A woman stood with her back to it, rocking back and forth. An ashen-faced man stared out at the scene, watching intently. 'Is that Mr Hickson?'

The SOCO followed Ryan's gaze. 'Aye, him and his missus.'

'Her name?'

'Marina.'

'How long they lived here?'

'I just told you, man: recent. They've only moved in and they're still doing the place up.'

Ryan stared up at the house. 'They should have left it like it was.'

'Sorry?'

Ryan shook his head. 'Nothing. It's nowt. Anyway, we need to know how long he's been buried here. Get me that expert you were on about.'

A voice came from behind the floodlight scaffolding. 'That'll be me, I take it.'

'Aaron, man!' Ryan grinned. 'I didn't think the expert I'd get would be quite so expert as you.'

He went to shake hands with his friend Dr Aaron Elliot before he remembered the dangers of cross-contamination. He swiftly retracted his hand.

Elliot's scowl morphed into a smile. 'Remembered just in time. My, and you've remembered your gloves and shoes, as well. I am impressed.'

Ryan ignored the veiled sarcasm with the hint of a smile. 'Reet, what can you tell me?'

'Far too early to tell you anything yet, Sherlock. In fact, it would help if you could find out a couple of things for me first.'

'Shoot.'

'If you could find out what was on the land before the houses went up, and when the estate was built would do for starters...'

'1980 or thereabouts.'

'Wow. Clever boy.' No sarcasm this time.

'And before that, farmland.'

'Sure?'

'I'm sure.'

Ryan looked back at the house once more. He almost told Aaron Elliot how he was sure.

Almost, but not quite.

Now wasn't the right time.

He needed to let it sink in first.

THREE

'Mr Hickson?' Ryan tried to focus on the man in front of him, but he couldn't prevent his eyes from scanning the kitchen in which they stood.

'I'm Detective Sergeant Jarrod, City and County CID. This is PC Ross,' he indicated Eric who nodded an acknowledgement. 'You say you've found a skeleton?'

'Aye. Knocked us for six, I can tell you.'

'Can you describe it for me?'

Ivor Hickson looked puzzled. 'Well, it was like a skeleton. Couldn't see most of it. It was still half-buried, but I definitely saw a skull.'

Without looking outside, Ryan said, 'Nice location here. Right on the edge of the estate. Lovely views over the valley.'

'Yes. That's one of the things that first attracted us, or my wife in particular, to it.'

'It's quiet down here,' Jarrod said.

'Is that a question or statement, Detective Sergeant?'

'An observation,' Ryan clarified. 'Did you touch anything?'

'I did. I'm Marina. Ivor's wife.' Her voice was mouse-like.

'That's fine, as long as we know what you touched.'

'*It*. I touched it. The head.' Her mouth curled in distaste.

'It was only for a millisecond,' Ivor clarified. 'You only brushed it didn't you, honey?'

Marina seemed to shrink into herself as she nodded.

'You weren't to know,' Ryan reassured her. 'Now, I'll leave you with PC Ross here and join my colleagues outside. Try to relax if you can. PC Ross - Eric - will look after you and if there's anything else I need, I'll pop back in after I've spoken with the forensics team.

He left Ivor and Marina with Eric. When he glanced back from outside, Marina and Eric were nowhere to be seen. Ivor stood by the window, watching.

Ryan found Aaron Elliot knelt on the edge of a half-dug trench, an abandoned mini excavator perched at a precarious angle alongside him. Without looking up, he told Ryan the bones were human and almost certainly those of a child.

'How old is he? Or she?'

'Impossible to tell from the skull alone. We'll need to get the rest of the remains out first. At a guess, I'd say no more than ten or eleven, possibly as young as three or four.'

'There's a helluva big difference between a three-year-old and an eleven-year-old. Surely you can do better than that, Aaron?'

Elliot swung around so he faced Ryan. 'And there's a helluva big difference between me telling you something off the record and suddenly finding it being quoted as fact. I'll let you know when I know.' Elliot's voice was kindly, but there was no hiding the fact Ryan Jarrod had received a ticking off.

'Fair enough. Any idea how long it's been there?'

Elliot gave the matter some thought. 'Soft tissue is long gone but, in a temperate climate like ours, it could take anything from four weeks to several years for total decomposition.'

Ryan blew out his cheeks.

'There's no obvious trace of material or fibres on the exposed bones,' Elliot persevered. 'And it takes significantly longer for clothing to break down. Go to any landfill you choose and you'll see tons of the stuff. It lasts nearly as long as plastic bags.'

Ryan scratched the back of his head. 'So, are you saying these are bones of antiquity?'

'Not exactly. I won't know whether there's any fibres elsewhere on the remains until we've uncovered the rest of the body. Same goes for sexing the deceased. Probably need the pelvic girdle to determine that with any certainty.'

'Which will take how long?'

'This won't be a priority back in the lab so it'll take as long as it takes, even once we've got him or her out. Besides, you wouldn't want me to miss or disturb anything, would you?'

No. Ryan wouldn't. 'Okay. I'll leave you to it and have another word with the owners.'

Aaron Elliot stood. Wiped the palms of his hands against his protective suit. 'There is one other possibility.'

'Yeah?'

'That the victim's clothes were removed in one location and the body placed here separately.'

Ryan scratched his neck. 'We don't have a victim, we don't have an age, we don't know where the crime occurred. We don't even know if it is a crime. Thanks, Aaron. Thanks a bloody bunch.'

'My pleasure,' Aaron Elliot smiled.

As Ryan trudged back to the house Elliot shouted after him. 'But you do know I'll get you the answers given time, don't you?'

'Be quick with it, yeah? I need this solved in three weeks. I want to get back to HQ. To Forth Street. Fun though it's been, I don't want my arse stuck in Whickham forever.'

'One more thing to complicate matters, Sherlock. Just because it can take a number of years for body tissue to decompose, it doesn't necessarily mean that's the amount of time it's been here.'

'Thanks again,' Ryan moaned.

'In fact, if the body was buried here with clothing, we could be looking at anything up to thirty-five years.'

Ryan stumbled, a black mist in front of his eyes; a mist which clouded his vision - and one which threatened everything he thought he knew about himself.

Thirty-five years?

'Please God, no,' he muttered to himself.

**

Back in the kitchen, Ryan peeled off his overshoes and stamped his feet for good measure to ensure he didn't trample mud into the carpet. He filled a glass with tap water and noticed his hand shook as he drank.

Marina invited him into the lounge where he addressed the Hicksons. 'The forensic team have established the bones are indeed human, almost certainly those of a young child.'

Ryan watched the couple closely. Marina Hickson's hand covered her mouth, while her husband nodded sagely. He couldn't read anything into their actions so he continued.

'We won't know any more until the forensic team have studied the remains in the lab but I'm sure I needn't explain the potential seriousness of what we have here.' The Hickson's gaze sought the floor. 'I have a couple more questions if you don't mind. Just to confirm a few facts, like.'

'Of course,' Marina whispered.

'Are you alright? You look a bit pale,' Ivor asked Ryan. 'Like you've seen a ghost or something.'

The Detective ignored him. 'What were you doing when you found the remains?'

'I was terracing the garden. At least, trying to. You'll have seen I haven't got very far with it.'

'How long have you lived here?'

'Just moved in. March, it was. It's stood empty for four or five months before that, though. We had a few problems, let's say.'

Ryan glanced between Ivor and Marina Hickson. 'Personal problems or logistical ones?'

'Logistical, financial, just about everything you can think of.'

'And the folk who lived here before you?'

Ivor shrugged. 'I'll have their names somewhere if that'll help. It'll be in the paperwork, no doubt.'

'Yes, please.'

Ivor reached across and took Marina's hand. Ryan thought

he saw her wince slightly as he did so. 'Can it wait? My wife's really shook up by this.'

'Of course. I'll leave you in peace for now. Plenty for me to do outside,' Ryan added cheerfully. 'Tomorrow would be good for the names. Oh, and in the meantime, don't go anywhere near the excavation site. Not until we've finished examining it and removed the body.'

Ivor Hickson nodded. Ryan closed his notebook and signalled for Eric Ross to follow him outside.

'What do you make of them?' Ryan asked.

Ross was noncommittal. 'Hard to tell. I'm not usually party to cases like this. I don't know how folk are expected to react. You don't think it could be something innocuous? Like, ancient, I mean?'

'I don't think so. More importantly, neither does the pathologist. No, I'm sure we'll find it's fairly recent.' Almost silently, he added, 'In the last thirty-five years, for sure.'

Ryan walked around the side of the house, examining the footpath, squinting up towards a patterned bathroom window, then to the roof. He stumbled slightly, fingers grazing the wall.

Eric Ross reached out to support him.

'I'm aal reet, man,' Ryan admonished. 'I can manage.'

The two walked to the front of the house. Neighbours rubber-necked their every movement, a woman across the road leant on her garden gate, a youngster had even scaled a tree in his efforts to see what was going on.

PC Blair was still on duty out front, maintaining the cordon as though his life depended on it.

'See if we can get some screens put up,' Ryan requested of him. 'Keep the neighbours at bay until we properly know what's gannin on. Besides, I've no doubt the press won't be long getting here. That's the last thing we need.'

'I'm on it, sir.' Blair gave a mock salute and reached for his radio.

Ryan felt for the gate with trembling fingers. He held it open for Eric Ross. As they walked towards the car, Ryan stopped. He turned his back and stood where he could take in the full view of the house.

Eric watched him quizzically whilst opening the passenger door for Ryan. Jarrod made a wheeze-like noise as he took his seat. He was so fixated on the Hickson's house he struggled to buckle the seatbelt.

Eric squinted at Ryan. 'Are you sure you're okay, Sarge?' When he got no reply, he assumed Ryan's thoughts were on the case. 'If it is a murder, it's not going to be easy to solve, is it? Not if it's as old as you say it could be…'

'Thirty-five years.' Ryan said. 'Thirty-five years to the month, I believe.'

'I don't follow.'

Ryan lay back against the headrest and closed his eyes. 'It's thirty-five years this month.'

'What is?'

'Since they moved out.'

'I'm still not with you.'

Ryan's eyes snapped open. He let them linger on the house on Callaley Avenue.

'Me Mam and Dad lived there. They moved out thirty-five years ago.'

FOUR

Ryan lay in the darkness of the bedroom, arms behind his head, staring up at the ceiling. The silence seeped into his very being, gobbled him up, and spat him out in a venomous spew of self-doubt and an unnerving fear of what may lie ahead.

It was almost three in the morning, and he'd not slept a wink since climbing into bed. Deep down, he knew the fears he harboured were irrational, yet…

He felt for his phone on the bedside cabinet. The voice which answered the call was slurred and confused.

'Eric, it's Ryan. You asleep?'

'What? Yeah, I mean, no. What time's it?'

'About three.'

Ryan heard sheets and duvet rustle. He pictured Eric Ross sitting bolt upright in his bed.

'What's up?' Ross asked.

'The bones in Callaley Avenue. I need you to document everything I - we - did. Who we spoke to, what we touched, what was said.'

Eric yawned his reply. 'That's standard procedure, man. I've already done it. Why ring me at stupid o'clock to tell me my job?'

'Because I want my arse covered on this. We need to be scrupulous in our approach to the case. Nobody must doubt our input.'

'Jesus, man. It's a heap of bones. Just a pile of bones from yonks ago. Are you like this with every case?'

Ryan hesitated. 'No, but this one is different. I have a connection, no matter how remote, to this crime scene. I don't want to become part of the investigation.'

Eric Ross rubbed his eyes. 'I get that. Now, can I get me heed doon again?'

'Aye, you can.' He paused again. 'Just don't tell anyone about my family and the house. Not yet. Not until we have confirmation of how long those bones have been buried there.'

'Ryan?'

'Yeah?'

'If there's a case which comes to court, you need to disclose your connection to the property. It might prejudice…'

'Who's telling who their job now, PC Ross? I know protocol, don't worry about that.'

Ryan ended the call. Ross needn't worry about it. Ryan Jarrod was doing enough worrying for the pair of them.

**

Nikki Reid switched on breakfast TV and immediately felt her jaw sag open.

'Yes, Charlie,' the reporter was saying, 'You can see I'm in the outskirts of a sleepy village across the Tyne valley from Newcastle. This is a leafy, suburban location with a low crime rate - and, certainly, not somewhere you'd anticipate finding the skeleton of what police suspect is that of a child.'

Nikki gasped. 'Andy. Andy! We're on the telly!'

A muffled voice replied from the kitchen as Nikki peeked through the window blinds.

'They're right outside! It's about all the palaver next door last night. They've found a body!'

Andy Reid dashed into the room, a slice of toast half in his mouth, half in hand. He chewed noisily as he listened to the report.

'I gather police have not yet ruled out a suspicious cause of death but, at present, the focus is on identifying the remains. I spoke to Detective Chief Inspector Rick Kinnear earlier who told me they are searching missing person files going back several decades but, until forensic reports are filed, they are making no other comment on the matter.'

'Do we have any indication how old the remains may be?'

'No Charlie, we don't - but the fact that the police are looking at historic records seems to indicate this may be a long, protracted, investigation.'

'Yes, indeed, Megan. Not what you expect to find when doing a spot of gardening.' He swung his arm from the back of the sofa and turned to camera. 'Now, the time is...'

Andy Reid muted the TV. 'Whey ya bugger. Who'd have thought it?'

'Eee, I know. I said it must be something big last night, didn't I?'

Andy looked at his wife, head to one side. 'You don't think it could be...?'

'They said it was a child.'

'*Probably* a child, she said. It'd be an easy mistake to make.'

'Surely not? Not after all this time.'

'How long's it been?'

Nikki's brow wrinkled. 'We've been here, what, twelve years? Must be at least nine since it happened.'

'I think we should tell them.'

'Won't they be doing door-to-door? We could mention it when they knock. Don't want them thinking we're nosey neighbours.'

'Says her with her sneck stuck out the blinds.'

Nikki laughed. 'Shut up. It's exciting.'

A serious look masked Andy's normally laid-back features. 'It will be if it turns out to be her, that's for sure.'

**

Ryan's phone lay alongside him as he tied his shoelaces. The screen lit with a message.

'*I take it you want me to keep the mutt again?*'

He typed out a reply. '*Aye. Was busy til late yesterday.*'

The reply wasn't long in coming. '*Could have let me know you weren't coming for him* 🙁. *Bring some scran this time. Had to give the bloody thing me sausages yesterday.*'

'*Other things on my mind.*' Ryan deleted the message. Instead, he typed, '*I'll pop round with some food for Kenzie and poo bags for you. Think it'll a late one again.*'

A few moments later, Norman Jarrod's reply appeared. '*Ok. See you soon. Don't need the poo bags though. I can still make it to the bog in time.*'

When he didn't laugh, Ryan realised it was the moment he had to get the sodding skeleton and its links to the former family home sorted once and for all.

The Peugeot pulled up outside Norman Jarrod's house less than three minutes later. The morning was mild and calm. Daffodils opened their arms to welcome the burgeoning sun and birds gave a cheerful song as they foraged for nesting material. Kenzie appeared at the window, ears forming perfect triangles, tail like windscreen wipers in a storm, as he watched Ryan clamber out the car.

The only downer on the day was the black cloud suspended over Ryan Jarrod's thoughts as he pushed open the front door.

'I've got Kenzie's food,' Ryan announced. 'It's not defrosted yet.' He popped the pouch of raw food on the kitchen bench. 'How's your fettle?'

'Okay, I guess,' Norman replied from behind the pages of the Carabao Cup final programme.

Ryan rubbed his top lip. 'Seen the TV this morning?' seemed a less than subtle opening gambit, but those were the words which escaped his mouth.

'Nah. Can't be arsed with it. Might put Sky Sports News on in a bit.'

'Okay.'

A silence hung over them, an awkward one in Ryan's mind. Norman didn't seem to notice.

'Sorry I left you in the lurch yesterday,' Ryan said, pulling at a rope toy clenched between Kenzie's jaws.

'I'm used to it by now, son.'

Another silence as Ryan pondered how to raise the subject. 'It was a bit of a day, yesterday.'

'You seem to have a lot of 'em in your line of work.' Norman's eyes scanned the programme notes. 'Can't believe you paid a tenner for this. I was there in seventy-six and it was only summat like twenty pence. Mind, we still got beat, as usual. Wor time will come, though - I just hope I'm here to see it.'

Ryan ignored his bumbling. 'Dad, you and Mam lived in Callaley Avenue at one time, didn't you?'

The crown of Norman's head bobbed behind his reading material. 'Yonks ago.'

'It's just the case I'm tied up on, it's on the same street.'

'Oh aye.'

Ryan watched his father carefully. 'In fact, it involves your old house.'

'Lot of water under the bridge since we were there. Not the happiest of memories.'

This was Ryan's opportunity, though he dreaded asking the question. 'Why's that, Dad?'

Norman set down the magazine. ''Cos it's where your Mam and me started out. I don't like thinking back to those days.'

Ryan thought he saw a tear glisten in his father's eyes. Despite his bluff exterior, Norman had never fully recovered from the loss of his wife. Ryan was in his early teens at the time, his brother - James - a nipper. Norman brought both boys up alone. It'd been hard. Very hard. Ryan knew only too well how hard it had been. But he had to plough on.

'Did owt odd happen while you lived there?'

'Odd? What's that supposed to mean?'

Like a body in the back garden, Ryan thought. 'I dunno. Just something strange. Anything a bit 'off', if you like?'

'Son, man, it was donkey's years ago. You weren't even born.'

Ryan took a deep breath. 'It's just that the current owners of your old house dug up a skeleton in the garden yesterday.'

Norman's eyebrows shot up from his forehead like a pair of startled birds. Norman cast his eyes at the floor at the same time as Ryan's stomach plummeted towards his scrotum.

He had his answer.

Norman Jarrod knew something about the house on Callaley Avenue.

FIVE

'Kinnear wants you to give him a call.'

Ryan screwed up his eyes. 'This early?' He gave Eric Ross a suspicious glance which asked, *Have you told him?*

'Ryan,' Rick Kinnear said. The warmth in his voice relaxed Jarrod. 'Thought I'd let you know Elliot's given me a prospective timeline regarding the examination of your remains. He reckons it'll be about two weeks before he gets round to it.'

Ryan sighed. 'Can't he fast-track it?'

''Fraid not. Up to his eyeballs.'

'There must be someone else who can do it. I want this sorted before I re-join DCI Danskin's team. It doesn't give me much time.'

'Relax, man. One of my lads will pick things up for you if necessary.'

'No; this is my case!' Ryan snapped. Then, more calmly, 'Sorry, sir. I didn't mean to be short with you but I feel a connection to this one.' He saw Eric Ross give him a quizzical look. 'Being my home village, an' all,' he added.

'Then I suggest you stop arse-farting around and get yourself back to the scene. Who knows, you'll probably find something which proves there's nowt for us to involve ourselves with.'

Some bloody hope, Ryan thought. 'Yes sir, I'll take PC Ross along with me. He can have a word with the neighbours while I see if the Hicksons have anything more to say for themselves.'

He ended the call, nodded towards Ross who grabbed the car keys and made for the station's exit.

The first thing Ryan asked Eric about was the paperwork.

'It's all in order, as you instructed. Most of it was done already but I've gone through it with a fine-toothed comb. Everything's there. Who we spoke to, what they said, what we saw.'

Ryan nodded. 'Good. It's important.'

'You should tell someone. About your connection to the case.'

'No, I shouldn't.'

Eric shook his head. 'You know, you arrived with a bit of a reputation. A maverick, they said, but a bloody good detective. *One of the best*, folk said.'

Ryan stared out the windscreen as they drove by the Gibside Arms. 'And?'

'And they were right about the first bit.' Eric glanced sideways at Ryan. 'I hope, for your sake, they are about the second.'

'Don't get above yourself, Ross.' He paused. 'But, for what it's worth, I hope they are, too.'

Police tape still hung listlessly around the Hickson's home. A police car guarded the exterior, a uniformed officer by the door and another at the rear of the property where a yawning cavity betrayed the former resting place of the bones; now safely ensconced in Aaron Elliot's 'office', as the pathologist liked to call it.

The TV crew had evaporated into the ether, and the street was mercifully empty of journalists. Despite this, high white sheeting had been erected on two sides of the garden. It served to give the remains a modicum of respect while the forensic team hoisted them from their resting place. It also frustrated the neighbours who were left with only their imagination.

Ryan saw curtains twitch as he and Eric Ross wandered to the front of the house. A few doors down, a middle-aged man brazenly stared at the Detective from his front garden. Directly opposite, an elderly woman leant on her garden wall before retreating up the path when Ryan gave her his look.

The front door of the house next door opened, exposing its innards. Nikki Reid smiled and waved at the officers from the hallway.

'Bloody hell, you'd think they'd just won the postcode lottery,' Ryan muttered.

Eric laughed. 'Right. Who do you want me to talk to first?'

Ryan gave the question a moment's thought. 'Change of plan. We're doing this together.'

'That'll take twice as long, man.'

'Aye, it will. But I didn't call you at three in the morning for nowt. I need my arse covered on this. We do it together.'

'Okay - and I know the score. I'll document everything.'

'Too bloody right you will.'

'So who do we start with?'

'We start here.'

He looked up the drive leading to the house of Ivor and Marina Hickson.

The house which had once belonged to the Jarrods.

**

Marina sat in the same seat as yesterday. She looked as if she'd been there all night. Dishevelled hair, no make-up, ghostly pallor. A man - not Ivor - sat alongside her, stroking her palm with his fingers.

'How are you today?' Ryan asked her while studying the stranger.

She shook her head. 'Awful.'

'It's been tough for her,' the man said.

Ryan studied him. He was stocky erring on the edge of flabbiness, stern-faced, yet gentle eyes. 'I'm sorry - you are?'

'I'm Morris. Morris Chaplin. I'm Marina's brother.' Ryan glanced between them, checking for similarities. 'Half-brother,' Morris added as if he followed the Detective's train of thought.

Ryan introduced himself and Eric to the brother. 'Mrs Hickson, I have some more questions for you. Just routine, but we must go through the motions. Is your husband here? It'll save us going through everything twice and…'

'He's at work,' Morris snapped.

Tetchy, Ryan thought. 'That's okay. We'll talk to him later. Now, Mrs Hickson - Marina - you've only just moved into the property, is that right?'

'You already know that from yesterday,' Morris jumped in.

'I told Morris about the conversation we had,' Marina explained.

'So, you see, there's no need to ask her again,' Morris Chaplin continued.

Marina wrapped her other hand around her brother's. 'I'm sorry. Please excuse him. It's not every day his sister finds a skeleton in her back garden. It's come as a shock to us all.' Marina spoke to Morris. 'Get the policemen a cup of tea, please.'

Chaplin harrumphed and made for the exit.

'Can you tell me anything about the previous owners?' Ryan asked after the man had left them alone. 'You said you'd have their names ready for us this morning.'

'Did I? Sorry, I forgot. Been a bit of a time, you know? We never met them. All contact came via our solicitor but, when I think about it, I reckon it was something foreign sounding. A French name. Chambeau, or something. The Estate Agent will have the details.'

'How long had they lived here?'

Marina looked at the floor. 'How would I know? The neighbours might. You should ask them.'

'We will.'

Eric Ross stopped documenting the conversation and asked, 'Was the house empty when you bought it?'

'Pretty much, yeah. A few bits of junk we sent to charity shops. Old clothes we gave to one of those Cash for Clothes places. Nothing else springs to mind.'

'But nothing that seemed unusual?'

'Apart from bones in the garden, you mean? No, not that I noticed.'

Ryan took up the baton again. 'Depending on what forensics come up with, we might have to take a closer look for ourselves.'

Marina shuddered. 'Do you have to? That's what Ivor was afraid you'd do. He didn't want me to tell you.'

Ryan felt Eric Ross's eyes burn into his face. He gave a slight nod to let his colleague know he'd picked up on it.

'Your husband didn't want you to tell us there was a body buried in your back garden?'

Marina picked at the skin alongside her thumbnail. 'He didn't want our dream home ripped apart. Ivor said you'd turn it into another Cromwell Street.'

Ryan sucked air noisily. 'Do you believe we might find more bodies in your back garden?'

She shook her head and began to cry.

'What have you said to her?' Morris's voice from the lounge doorway.

'Just making a few enquiries, sir,' Ryan reassured.

'What sort of enquiries?'

Ryan fixed Morris with an icy stare. 'Relevant ones.'

Morris set down a tray of drinks with a heavy hand. Brown liquid sloshed from the cups and stained the tray's surface.

'Don't say a word, Marina. They'll twist anything you tell them.'

'Mr Chaplin, please, these are all just general questions. Nothing to worry about. We don't even know a crime's been committed yet. All we're doing is collecting background information, but we also have to check out everything we're told.'

'And what HAVE you been told, Detective?', his eyes no longer gentle.

Marina sobbed loudly. She reached down to her handbag. Pulled out a small bottle of pills, tipped a couple into her hand, popped them into her mouth and tilted back her head. 'Gentlemen, I'm not feeling too well. Could we do this when my husband is here, please?'

Ryan remained silent. Slowly, he rose to his feet. 'Okay. Please, let us know as soon as he gets back from work, won't you?'

'I will. Thank you. I'm sorry to hurry you away.'

'You've nowt to apologise for,' Morris said, taking her hand. 'You're doing the right thing. You don't want to be telling the likes of them owt.'

Back on the street, Eric Ross puffed out his cheeks. 'That didn't get us very far, did it? What now?'

'We talk to the neighbours. See what they can tell us about the previous residents. Oh, and do me a favour - ask Rick Kinnear to get one of the lads to run checks on a Morris Chaplin.'

**

The old woman invited Ryan and Eric into a house with better days behind it. Before they took a seat, Ryan looked out the window and noticed it offered an uninterrupted view of the house opposite.

'I wondered when you'd come calling,' she said.

'Par for the course, Mrs…?'

'Douglas. Nancy Douglas.'

'DS Jarrod and PC Ross. Have you lived here long, Mrs Douglas.'

Her laugh sounded like sandpaper. 'You could say that.'

'And I bet you've seen some comings and goings in that time.'

'I refer the gentleman to the answer I gave a few moments before.'

It was Ryan's turn to smile. 'I've seen you a couple of times in your garden, watching us. I'm wondering if you've seen anything unusual?'

'How long do you want me to go back?'

Ryan didn't want to think too far back. 'Let's start with the previous owners of the house opposite.'

'They weren't here long enough to get to know. Nine months, if that. Paul Chevrier and his wife, Teresa.'

'Were they foreign?'

'From Durham, if that's foreign enough for you. No, they weren't foreign.'

'Did they have children?'

Nancy Douglas shook her head, strands of grey falling from beneath a headscarf.

'And before them?'

Nancy smiled. 'Lovely couple, the Mowdens. They had children, before you ask. Boy and a girl.'

'How old were they? The kids, I mean.'

'One had just started at the Comp. Eleven, I think he'd be. The lassie probably five or six. They were never any bother.'

Eric Ross scribbled in his pad like a toddler painting by numbers.

'What happened to them?'

'Emigrated. Canada, I think.'

Ryan's gaze had drifted to the window and the house across the road. He snapped his mind back onto the job. 'Did the Mowdens live there long?'

The woman picked up a pile of knitting and started clacking away. 'Canny few years. Think the lad was just a toddler in reins when they came.'

Ryan thought for a moment. 'Were they keen gardeners?'

Nancy's laugh again. 'Not really. Alan - that's Mr Mowden - called it a busman's holiday. Worked for the Cooncil. Did some of the Britain in Bloom displays around the village.'

Ryan saw Ross draw a circle around the name *Alan Mowden*. 'Yet, you never saw him take on any projects at home?'

Nancy's knitting needles picked up a ferocious pace. 'Most of the garden's at the back so I couldn't be sure, but I don't think he did.'

'Okay,' Ryan said. 'I know it's going back a while, but can you remember who lived here before the Mowdens?'

Her face took on a sad appearance. 'That'll have been Aggie.'

'What can you tell us about her?'

'She killed herself. She was found hanging in the garage.'

Ryan blinked. This house had some history.

'Do you know why she'd do such a thing?'

'It was all very tragic. Her husband traded her in for a younger model. On top of everything else, I reckon it got too much for her.'

'You said *'On top of everything else'*. What else?'

She looked between Ryan and Eric. 'You're the coppers. You should know.'

'Pretend we don't. Tell us what else.'

'She lost her son.'

Stay calm, Ryan told himself, though he knew this could be the breakthrough he wanted. 'When was this?'

Nancy made a whistling sound as her eyes drifted to the ceiling in thought. 'About, what, fourteen years ago? Maybe more.'

'How did he die?'

'Oh, he didn't die. I said she lost him. He went missing. Disappeared into thin air, he did. All very, very sad.'

'What was his name?'

'Graham Waitrose. Like the shop. He'd only be about eight or so. No, I tell a lie - he was ten. I remember the balloons on the door for his birthday.'

Ryan felt his heart thud against his rib cage. This was it; he was sure. But he had to cover all the angles. 'What about the owners before Aggie?'

Nancy stopped knitting again. 'Now you're asking. Think it stood empty for a while, if memory serves me right. Not sure who had it before Aggie, but there were a couple of queers, if you know what I mean, in for a short while at some point.'

'Jesus. David Olusoga would have a field day if he based one of his series on this house,' Eric Ross said.

Ryan shushed him with a glare. 'Why don't you interview the owners of the house next door to the Hicksons?' he said to Ross.

'But you said…'

'I know what I said, but this is taking too long.'

Eric's brow furrowed. 'You know you shouldn't be doing this, don't you?'

'Just go.'

Eric Ross snapped shut his notebook and went.

The moment he left, Ryan asked Nancy how long, exactly, she'd lived there.

'Thirty-five years.'

He shifted uncomfortably. 'Can you remember the couple who lived in the house opposite at that time?'

Nancy thought for what seemed like minutes. 'Yes.'

Ryan's mouth felt like the floor of a budgie's cage. 'What do you remember of them?'

'They were pretty nondescript as far as I remember.'

'Nothing unusual?'

She shook her head. 'No. I lost my husband around that time so I was a bit pre-occupied, if you know what I mean. I went to stay with my younger brother and his family in Bournemouth for a few months. When I got back, they'd moved. They were just an ordinary couple. Not long wed. No, I tell a lie. Must have been married a while, I think.'

Ryan released the breath he seemed he'd been holding ever since he despatched Eric Ross across the road. There was nothing to tie his family to any crime which may have occurred in the house. *Nondescript,* Nancy Douglas had described his parents. Plain old everyday folk.

Ryan stood to leave. 'Thank you, Mrs Douglas. You've been very helpful.'

'You know,' Nancy said, deep in thought. 'I can't remember the couple's names yet I often wonder what happened to their child.'

Ryan felt himself sway.

'She had the most beautiful eyes.'

SIX

Ryan thrust his hands deep in his pockets as he marched across Callaley Avenue. He gave the Hickson residence a cursory glance as he took the stone steps up to the front door of the neighbouring house.

A woman answered, early forties, probably. He showed her his warrant card. 'I'm DS Jarrod.'

'Your colleague's already here...'

'I know.'

Ryan recognised Eric's voice from behind a door. He opened it and walked straight through. 'Anything?' he asked.

'I've just started obtaining Mr and Mrs Reid's background details.'

'Okay. We're going.'

'What?'

'We're going. Sorry to have intruded on you, sir. Ma'am. We may be back but that's all for now.'

Ryan frogmarched Ross outside.

'Howay, Ryan. What's going on, man?'

'We've more important things to do.'

'Such as?'

'Running checks on previous occupants of the house, that's what. Turns out Old Mother Hubbard's memory isn't all she makes out. We need something more reliable than her word.'

Eric rubbed his chest with the palm of his hand. 'You asked her about your folks, didn't you? That's why you sent me away.'

'What if I did?' Ryan snapped. He sucked in air. 'Sorry. Yes, I did. She got it all wrong about them, so she's probably off-key with all the other shite she told us. That's why I'm calling this in. Let's see if Forth Street have any resources spare.'

Eric shrugged. 'If that's what you want.'

'Aye, it is. Now, you chase up on Morris Whats-his-face. I've some calls to make.'

As soon as Eric slipped inside the car, Ryan pulled out his phone. His finger hovered over Rick Kinnear's number. Instead, he called someone else. Someone he trusted with his life.

'Hi. It's me. Can you do summat for us?'

'Hmm. I always get a sinking feeling when I hear you say those words,' DS Hannah Graves replied.

'Is that a yes?'

He visualised her eyeroll as she said, 'Go on.'

'I want you to do some background checks on a property for me. See if there's any history of incidents. Domestic abuse, mispers, anything at all. I've been told you might find a couple of things but let's just say my source doesn't seem the most reliable.'

'Fire away. What's the address?' Hannah made a note of it. 'Are we talking a year? Five years? Ten?'

She made a good point. Ryan had to think carefully. He trusted Hannah, but some things were best left hidden. 'Go back twenty years. No further.'

There was a silence on the line.

'Did you get that, Hannah?'

'Yeah. I'm just wondering, that's all.'

'Wondering what?'

'Why me? We haven't worked together for yonks. The Super would go bananas if she thought we were working together.'

'We're not *working together*,' he made verbal air quotes. 'I've asked you to run a few checks for me, that's all.'

'Aye. And I ask again: Why me?'

Ryan made something up on the spot. 'Because I don't want Kinnear thinking I can't handle this on my own.'

Hannah sighed. 'Okay. Consider it done.'

'Good. I owe you one. Let me know as soon as you find owt.'

He ended the call and smiled wistfully. Hannah was a good 'un. Too good for him, that was for sure.

**

Ryan called at Norman Jarrod's home on the way back. He felt awkward and foolish suspecting his dad had any involvement in the events in Callaley Avenue, so he didn't hang around. A quick chat about the Toon's chances at the weekend, a brief catch-up on how his brother James was getting on with his odd-ball girlfriend, and a bit of roustabout with Kenzie before he clipped the lead onto the dog's collar and set off across The Glebe.

There was a nip in the air, but puffball clouds drifted lazily in an ice-blue sky. Ryan unleashed the German Shepherd and tossed a tennis ball for the pup to chase.

Kenzie's genes were inherited from his police dog father and, already, the pup responded to basic commands. The dog lolloped after the ball when released and obediently dropped it at Ryan's feet on recall.

Ryan smiled. His previous dog, Spud, would have ripped the ball to shreds, urinated against the goalposts, and had a dump on the cricket field. Chalk and cheese, they were. Like Ryan and his brother.

He kicked the ball away. Kenzie pawed the ground anticipating the 'Fetch' command, and the dog sprinted after it when the word came.

Ryan had his phone in his hand by the time Kenzie returned. 'How you doing, wor kid?' he asked.

'Not bad. You?' James countered.

'Oh you know, busy.'

'I thought you said work was a piece of piss now you were at Whickham?'

Ryan laughed. 'It was but there's a bit more pressure to wrap things up now before I go back to Danskin's troupe. Or Kinnear's, if that's where they decide to put me.'

'Will Hannah have to move teams if you work for Danskin again?'

Ryan shrugged. A pointless gesture considering James couldn't see it, but it was the only answer he gave. 'How's your lass?' he said.

James breathed through his nose. 'A bit down but she goes through these phases. She'll pick herself up again.'

'Are you sure it's working between you two? I mean, this Emo culture isn't really your thing, is it?'

'No, but that doesn't mean Muzzle and me can't get on.'

Ryan ruffled the fur on Kenzie's neck before clipping the leader to his collar as he left the sports field and headed onto Millfield Road. 'That's okay, James. Just making sure you're both happy.'

'As a matter of fact, we are. Which is more than I can say aboot you and Hannah so take care of your own love life and I'll look after mine.'

'Ouch. Below the belt there, mate.'

James sighed. 'Aye. Sorry, Ry. Just I get worried about Muzzle sometimes. You know, with her background and such like.'

Ryan took a right and a sharp left onto the green in front of the old, terraced houses on Southfield Terrace. He almost trod on a dog turd some lazy owner hadn't been arsed to pick up. He stripped a bag from a roll and carefully scooped it up.

'Dog shit,' he muttered. 'Do something special for her.'

'How's dog shit gonna cheer her up?'

'No, man. I've just stepped in some. I meant treat her to summat. A night out, a concert, anything to take her mind off stuff.'

There was a silence at the other end of the line.

'You still there, James?'

'Aye, I'm here. You've just given me an idea. Cheers, bro: you're a genius.'

'Pleased to be of service,' Ryan said, but the line was already dead.

**

Kenzie lapped at his food bowl voraciously. The bowl slid over the kitchen floor like a curling stone but the dog's nose never left its interior. He continued to sniff and lick long after he'd devoured the last morsel.

Ryan, meanwhile, nibbled on a cheese and chutney sandwich with less enthusiasm. He had less than three weeks to resolve the Callaley Avenue mystery, and he didn't yet know whether he was looking at murder, concealment of a body, or no crime at all.

He switched on the TV and swigged from a Heineken can. After a few minutes channel hopping, he called Eric Ross. 'Is Ivor Hickson home yet?'

'His wife hasn't called so I guess not.'

Ryan chewed on a lip. 'Odd. You'd think he'd want to support his missus. I think we'll give them a knock first thing tomorrow. What about our Morris Chaplin? Found anything on him yet?'

'No, boss. I haven't started on it.'

'Why the hell not? It's a priority.'

'More of a priority than covering up for you, do you mean? Right. Fine. I'll stop writing up the report and go through the database.'

Ryan softened his tone. 'Sorry, Eric. You weren't to know but Nancy Douglas was able to put me mind at rest. My folks aren't involved. I'm more relaxed about it after talking to her.'

'Hang on a sec. You said her memory wasn't to be trusted, yesterday.'

'I know. There were some things she said which were totally bonkers but others rang true. I'm not going into details with you, but she remembered my Mam and Dad as the ordinary folk they are. While I still don't want their occupancy to be public knowledge, I'm not as worried about it as I was. So, leave the paperwork for now and see what you can find on Chaplin.'

Eric Ross sat back in his chair and twiddled a pen between his fingers. 'Suits me. How long have I got?'

'It shouldn't take more than fifteen minutes max to find out if there is anything. If there is, then take as long as you need to research your findings. Is that okay?'

'It is. I'll get onto it now.'

**

Someone else was getting onto it, too.

In the Forth Street HQ of the City and County Police, DS Hannah Graves trawled through police records for any mention of Callaley Avenue.

She stumbled upon details of several residents, long-since relocated, with records of no real significance. Still, she made a note, if only to keep Ryan happy.

'Are you busy, Graves?'

Hannah jumped at the sound of DCI Stephen Danskin. Ever formal, he insisted on calling his stepdaughter by her surname, the same as he did all others under his charge.

'Researching a couple of things, that's all.' She brushed an errant curl from her forehead. The movement hid her lying eyes, but her smile was a thin disguise which she hoped would be enough to satisfy Danskin.

'Anything I should know about?'

'No. Just a run-of-the-mill case.'

Danskin frowned. 'If it's run-of-the-mill, it should be Kinnear's territory.'

'I haven't much on so I'm happy to help, as they say in Asda.' She smiled again, more genuine this time.

'Okay. Good. Carry on. Mind, I'm off for a meet with the Super so if she's got anything for us, you'll be off that job.'

'Sir.'

She sighed as she watched Danskin disappear into Maynard's room. Lying didn't come easy to Hannah.

She resumed her search. Twenty minutes in, and she found something a little more interesting. She took a screen-print, cross-referenced it with newspaper archives, and printed out the relevant articles.

Ten minutes later, she stumbled across something else. Let out a whistle and sent more documents to the printer. She filed them with the others.

She looked around. The silhouette of Stephen Danskin remained clearly visible through the blinds at Superintendent Maynard's office window.

Hannah continued with her research. Became lost in it as she uncovered more information she hoped Ryan would find useful.

She checked her watch. She'd give it five more minutes, then she really must get on with *'proper'* work.

'Bloody hell!'

Hannah jumped from her chair and bolted down the bullpen.

SEVEN

The car entered Callaley Avenue at a snail's pace. Ryan wanted Eric to go over the backstory of Morris Chaplin one more time before he confronted Marina Hickson.

'It's like I said: he was interviewed about a domestic dispute six years back. His ex-wife called the cops, then retracted her statement. Nowt more happened.'

'You've tracked down the ex-wife?'

Eric nodded. 'Aye. She's still living in the same place. William Street, tucked in behind the Brandling Villa. Do you know it?'

'I do, actually. Well, the pub, I do. Had the odd pint in it when I worked up the road at the Ministry.'

'Anyways, we've never heard of her before or since.'

'Pull up a minute.'

When Eric applied the handbrake, Ryan spoke almost to himself. 'Let's run over what we know. Ivor Hickson digs up a skeleton. He tells his wife not to report it to us. When she eventually does, we arrive to find Marina Hickson with Morris Chaplin. She sends us packing, then fails to let us know her husband's returned. And now, we find Chaplin is a perpetrator of domestic violence.'

'Alleged,' Eric Ross corrected.

'And his ex-wife refused to press charges,' Ryan continued without acknowledging Eric's comment. 'You then drop the bombshell on me that Chaplin isn't related to Marina Hickson at all. Not a half-brother, stepbrother, brother-in-arms nor nowt.'

He turned to face Eric. 'You are one hundred percent sure of that before I go mouthing off in there?'

'Absolutely, Sarge.'

Ryan opened the door. 'Okay. Time for me to *'mouth off'*, methinks.'

Marina answered the door still wearing her dressing gown. 'Is he in?'

Marina looked blank for a second. 'Oh. Yes. Sorry. I forgot to tell you, didn't I?'

Ryan brushed past Marina who stood aside to allow Eric Ross entry.

In the living room, Ivor sat on a sofa, ringing his hands. He looked up. 'Can we help you, Detectives?'

'Why did you ask your wife not to tell us about the remains?'

Ivor sat back. 'Cut to the chase, why don't you?' He looked down. 'Okay. I panicked. I wasn't thinking straight, you know?'

'Mr Hickson, that doesn't explain anything.'

Ivor looked at Marina, back to Ryan, then to his wife. Ryan noticed Marina dip her head, briefly.

'Alright. Here goes. It might sound pathetic, but it's the truth, yeah? We moved here for the location and its outside space. We want children. Marina wants a child above anything else in the world. That's why we came here.'

Ryan waited for Ivor Hickson to continue. When he didn't, he said, 'That doesn't answer my question.'

Ivor sighed. 'Marina can't have children of her own.'

'I've had a hysterectomy,' Marina explained. She spoke with her eyes closed. 'I have - I had - severe endometriosis. Do you know what that is?'

Ryan hadn't a clue. He admitted as much.

'It's a condition where tissue normally confined to the womb grows elsewhere in the body. In my case, it was my fallopian tubes, and it caused me unbearable pain. I mean, excruciatingly unbearable, yeah?'

'We could hardly have sex,' Ivor jumped in.

'Ha! Trust you to think of that first. I assure you, Detective, that was the least of my worries.'

'I still don't understand…'

Marina held up a hand to silence him. 'I fell pregnant, eventually, but the pregnancy was ectopic. I miscarried at ten weeks. Ten weeks, five days to be precise.' Marina Hickson fell silent.

'It broke her,' Ivor picked up. 'Marina had a… I suppose you'd describe it as a breakdown. We couldn't go through that again so we decided to ask about a hysterectomy.'

Marina opened her eyes. 'YOU decided to ask. Not us. YOU.'

'Okay, I asked. So, that's why Marina and I can't have children.'

Ryan's face creased in confusion. 'Yet, you told me you came here so you *could* have children.'

'Adoption,' Ivor explained. 'Marina wants to adopt. We'll have more chance in a home like this, with outdoor space, and countryside on our doorstep. What isn't in our favour is that we have a dead body buried in the garden. Now do you understand why I was reluctant to report it?'

Ryan did. At least, he said he did.

He turned to Marina. 'Mrs Hickson, the man who was here yesterday - Morris Chaplin. Tell me again about your relationship to him.'

**

'Well, that was a load of bollocks,' Eric Ross commented once they were outside. 'Nothing I've read about Morris Chaplin indicates he was ever a psychotherapist.'

'I agree,' Ryan added.

'So, they're shagging, you reckon?'

'Probably. Why else tell us he's her brother when he's not, or that he's her therapist when he isn't?'

'We should have asked her.'

'Nah. It's not relevant. If she can't have kids, it isn't their child buried in the garden. Besides, they've only just moved in. I think Marina Hickson has enough troubles without making it obvious to her husband that she's playing away.'

'True, but we never asked her why she didn't let us know her husband was home.'

'Didn't need to.'

'Why?'

'Cos she was scared we'd ask her the questions we've just asked her.'

Eric let the explanation circle his brain until it made sense. 'Oh aye. I get it.'

'You said I interrupted you before you'd had a chance to really talk to the neighbours. Howay, Eric - let's have a quick word with next door before we go. See if they've any light to shed on things.'

**

Andy and Nikki Reid had no light to shed, only more shade.

They knew nothing about the Hicksons, and little more about their predecessors. They'd barely spoken to any of the local children lately and, despite having lived in Callaley Avenue for well over a decade, they only really knew the woman opposite, old Nancy Douglas.

Nikki Reid, though, seemed delighted by the fact two police officers, one a Detective Sergeant no less, sat opposite her in the pastel shades of her tastefully furnished lounge.

'I saw all the carry-on the other night and, when I saw what you'd discovered next door, well - we couldn't believe it, could we, Andy?'

'Not really, no.' Nikki Reid's husband, clean shaven and wearing a Ralph Lauren polo shirt over cream chinos, seemed less overjoyed with their presence.

'To sum things up, then,' Ryan said, 'You haven't seen anything suspicious in the last few years?'

'Nothing that springs to mind, no. There again, I sometimes forget what I go into the kitchen for so I might have missed something.'

'Do you remember a Graham Waitrose? A young boy who went missing.'

'Oh, hell, aye. I didn't think you were interested in things that far back.'

Ryan scratched his chin, unsure how much he was at liberty to reveal. 'And his mother?'

'She died not long after.'

'Did you know them well?'

'No. Not at all, really.'

Nikki Reid clearly wasn't about to make a revelation. Ryan stood to leave. 'If you think of anything, especially anything relating to the Waitrose boy, please get in touch.'

Andy Reid rose from his seat. 'I'll show you out, gentlemen.'

Once in the lobby, Andy Reid asked, 'You think it's Graham Waitrose, don't you?'

'I don't think anything at present, sir. We're just looking at all the options.'

Andy swung open the door for them. 'It was definitely a child?' he asked.

'We're waiting for forensic confirmation but I'd say so, judging by the size of the bones. That's the pathologist's initial view, too.'

'Okay.' Andy made a sucking sound. 'It's just that…'

'What?'

'It doesn't matter. It's nothing.'

'Mr Reid, everything matters at this stage of an enquiry.'

Reid nodded. 'In that case, you might want to step back inside for a moment.'

**

Andy Reid grimaced as the whisky hit the back of his throat.

'She started coming about ten years ago, I'd say. She'd ask if we had any jobs she could do for us. It was always in June, but it took a couple of years before we made the connection.'

'Connection with what?', Ryan asked, keen for the man to get to his point.

'All in good time. I need to set her visits in context. So, after a couple of years, she started coming at other times. Every month at first, then every week.'

'We felt sorry for her,' Nikki interjected, 'So we indulged her. Gave her bits and bobs to do in exchange for a couple of quid. She was very grateful, yet it only encouraged her to come more often.'

'She became a bit of a pest, to be honest,' Andy continued. Eventually, I told her to try next door because we had nothing left for her to do. Besides, it was a good excuse to pass her onto somebody else.'

'We saw her a few times after that. Always gave us a wave as she passed on her way to the Waitrose's. Then, one day, this bloke came with her. A big guy. Scruffy looking with tattoos covering his neck and one side of his face.'

Ryan checked his watch. 'Could we get to the point, please? PC Ross and I have things to do.'

Andy Reid drained his whisky. 'Okay. I heard him shouting at someone. I think it was the Waitrose lad but can't be sure. I opened the window a bit and he was yelling something about touch his daughter again and it'd be the last thing he did, you know the kind of stuff.'

Ryan did. 'What happened next?'

'The bloke dragged his daughter away and we never saw either of them again.'

Nikki Reid saw Ryan's expression. 'It makes it sound like an awful neighbourhood but it's really lovely. You must understand we're talking about a couple of incidents over many, many years. It's quiet as a mouse round here normally.'

'I'm sure it is,' Ryan said, knowing full well it was the truth, 'But I need names and addresses if you have them.'

'We knew her only as Stacey,' Andy said.

'Address?'

'No idea. Don't even think she had one.'

'Sorry?' Ryan asked Nikki, accepting Andy wasn't big on explanations.

'She was a traveller. A gypsy. That's why, at first, she only came round in June. You know, when the Hoppings fair was on the Town Moor, like. Seemingly, after a couple of years, they parked their caravan semi-permanently. I'm not sure where exactly but I got the impression it was close to Derwent Caravan Park, near the Gibside Estate and Rowlands Gill.'

Eric Ross looked up from his notepad. 'How old was the child?'

Nikki frowned. 'Child? Oh, Stacey wasn't a child. She must have been in her twenties, I reckon.'

Ryan clenched his fist in an attempt to hide his frustration. 'Well, Mr and Mrs Reid, thanks for your time but I don't think this is relevant to our enquiry. We're looking for a missing child, not a woman in her twenties.'

Andy Reid smiled. 'You might be wrong.'

'I don't think so. The bones weren't those of a grown adult.'

'Ah, but you still don't get it. Stacey may have been an adult, but she wasn't grown. She was scarcely taller than a six-year-old. You see, that's why she went to the Hoppings every year. While her mother told fortunes, Stacey was put on display alongside the bearded lady and the world's tallest man.'

Nikki concluded the statement for her husband. 'Detectives, Stacey was a dwarf.'

EIGHT

They took the short journey back to Whickham police station in stunned silence.

Once inside, it dawned on Ryan how much thinking time was spent at the Forth Street HQ simply staring out the window at the murky Tyne and its seven bridges. Many a case had been cracked by DCI Danskin, DI Parker, and even Jarrod himself drawing inspiration from the winding river.

There was no such luxury in the old, two-storey Whickham station. The view from the front aspect offered nothing more than a car park and a stone wall. At least the western offices afforded glimpses of The Orchard and Duckpool Lane. Where Ryan and Eric Ross sat, at the rear of the building, a copse of trees restricted vision so even the few houses which comprised Devon Avenue, a tiny street so secluded many locals didn't know existed, went unseen.

There was no inspiration to be drawn here.

'Eric, I'm going for a wander. See if some fresh air will clear me head. I need to think through what the Reids have told us.'

Ross closed his notebook. 'I'll come with you.'

'No. You stay and type up the notes from this morning while I'm oot. I need to make a few calls. I'll chase up the pathologist, for one; then I'll see if Hannah - DS Graves - has come up with owt of note. I won't be long. We'll get wor heads together when I'm back.'

The sun speared rays through the window blinds so Ryan shunned his jacket. Once outside, he regretted the decision. The air held a distinct chill which belied the clear sky. He buried his hands in his pockets and turned right along Front Street.

The traffic lights at the foot of Broom Lane were out of operation, replaced by three-way temporary lights which caused a tailback almost to the station in one direction and Wetherspoons in the other.

The exhaust fumes from a stationary double-decker made up his mind for him. He hurdled the Bay Horse fence and crossed its almost deserted car park. Drinking on duty was officially off-limits but, providing you were sensible, powers-that-be tended to turn a blind eye. In Ryan's case, there were no eyes - blind or otherwise - who would report back.

He made small talk with Joanne as she drew his pint before he took a seat in the corner of the establishment, well out of earshot from the handful of customers dotted around the open-plan space.

Ryan toyed with a beermat while he deliberated who to call first. He opted for Aaron Elliot. If Elliot could confirm the bones weren't those of a child, anything Hannah unearthed was irrelevant. The skeleton was that of the mysterious Stacey. What's more, if they were those of a child, chances are the remains were those of Graham Waitrose - and Stacey's father was a killer.

Ryan listened to the mechanical plink-plonk music of an AI generated composition while he waited for Elliot to pick up the call transferred by his secretary. Finally, the pathologist picked up.

'Sherlock, my friend. What's new?'

'I was rather hoping you could tell me that. The remains found in the Whickham garden: where are we with them?'

Elliot's voice came and went, accompanied by the occasional metallic chime as he readied his instruments for the next poor sod to cross the slab.

'I don't know about you, but I'm nowhere with them. Like I said, it'll likely be a couple of weeks until I get to them.'

'Seriously? There's got to be something you can do to bump it up your list.'

'Unless you've discovered something to prove it's a murder, or you suspect they're the remains of a long-lost member of the Royal family, the answer's a resounding no.'

Ryan blew out his cheeks. 'Okay. Tell me one thing: you're sure the bones were that of a child?'

Aaron Elliot delayed his reply while he considered it. 'You saw the size of them,' he replied.

'Could they have been from someone short? Like a dwarf, perhaps?'

Another pause. Longer, this time. 'I don't think so.'

Ryan noticed a hint of doubt in the voice. 'But you can't be sure?'

'What is it your DCI says? *'Don't see what you expect to see?'* It's possible that's precisely what I did but, without closer inspection, I can't be sure. No, Ryan - I'm confident the remains were those of an infant.'

Jarrod ran his finger down the condensation on the outside of his glass. 'Yet, you need another look to be sure. Does the doubt bump it up your to-do list?'

Ryan listened as the clink of instruments stopped. 'You're a persistent bugger, aren't you?'

'Yep, I can be.'

Aaron Elliot exhaled loudly. 'Look, this is what I can do. I've an intern come to work for me for a few months. I'll ask him to check it out for you.'

'Ah, come on, man. A student? No way.'

'Rufus isn't a student. He's a qualified doctor who wants to specialise in pathology, that's all.'

'What sort of weirdo wants to specialise in dead bodies?'

'I did.'

'Exactly.'

Elliot guffawed at the other end of the line. 'Anyway, what do you say? Rufus has only been with me a couple of weeks but he seems sound. I promise I'll look over his report with a fine-toothed comb, if you excuse the mixed metaphor, before

I forward you it. It's the best I can do if you want anything quickly.'

'How quick is quickly?'

'Three or four days. He isn't at your beck-and-call, I'm afraid.'

'I suppose that'll have to do.' Ryan heard a distant swish of a door open and a rumble in the background.

'My next guest has just arrived,' the pathologist said. 'It would be rude to keep her waiting. I'll get Rufus's findings to you as soon as. 'Bye for now.'

Aaron Elliot ended the call before Ryan had a chance to respond.

He took a swig of beer. 'Right, Hannah Graves. I guess it's over to you, now.' Her number was on speed dial and he wasted no time in calling her.

'Ryan, hi.'

'Howdy pardner…'

'I'm not your partner.'

Ryan rolled his eyes. 'Aal reet, be like that, then. Listen, I was wondering whether you've had a chance to check out that stuff for me?'

'I've found a couple of things but I've other things to do as well, you know.'

She was in one of her moods, Ryan could tell, so he decided it best not to hit back. 'Okay. I appreciate it, Hannah.'

A small group of customers huddled around a table beneath a TV showing a music channel with the sound muted. Ryan thought it defeated the object and, as peal of laughter rose from the table, he wondered if they'd read his thoughts.

'Where are you?' Hannah asked.

'I'm in the pub. I needed to get out the station to consider a few things.'

'Right. In that case, I'm not sure we should discuss this now…'

'Hannah, man, it'll be okay…'

'If you'd let me finish, I was going to suggest we meet later for something to eat.

Ryan hadn't been expecting that. His spirits rose.

'Oh, umm, yeah. That'll be great. I've heard good things about 1771. It's at the bottom of the bank, Swalwell way. Mainly does Italian but, if there's nowt on the menu you fancy, we could go for a curry. It's not a kick in the pants away from Jashn.'

Someone unmuted the TV. A grainy black and white image of The Animals in tightly buttoned dark suits and black polonecked sweaters. Eric Burdon's vocals filtered through the air.

'I was thinking more of cooking something,' Hannah said over the background noise.

Ryan fought to contain the smile from reaching his voice. 'Oh, even better. Yeah, I could get to Jesmond if you like. What time?'

'I was thinking about seven-thirty?'

'Brilliant!'

'But not at Jesmond. Not at mine. Or yours, for that matter.'

'I don't understand.'

'We'll meet at Stephen's.'

'DCI Danskin's? Bloody hell, man, you don't need a chaperone with me.'

Hannah laughed, somewhat coldly. 'He wants a word with you. You're due back in a couple of weeks and the DCI wants you up to speed before you get back. I thought it'd kill two birds with one stone.'

This wasn't what he'd hoped for after all, but it was better than not hearing Hannah's update - and he'd get to see her. A start to mending their relationship, perhaps.

'Yeah, okay. That's fine. See you tonight, then.'

Burdon's voice cut through the farewells of Ryan and Hannah.

'I'm just a soul whose intentions are good
Oh Lord, please don't let me be misunderstood.'

NINE

Ryan pulled his Peugeot into an off-street bay thirty yards from Stephen Danskin's apartment. The dashboard clock showed 7:40.

Ryan stepped onto the Great Park estate in a darkness illuminated by a full moon and prepared for his date with the only woman he'd truly loved. And her stepfather.

'Great,' he muttered to himself, steeped in irony.

He rang the doorbell and heard Danskin shout 'Come!' as if granting access to his Forth Street office.

Once inside, Ryan's nostrils flared at the heady perfume of lemongrass, chilies, garlic, ginger, coconut milk, and spices.

'Thai cooking, eh?' Danskin greeted him with. 'One of the greatest kitchen smells ever. Come in. You're late but Hannah's kept it warm for you.'

Hannah poked her head from the narrow kitchen's doorway. 'Aboot bloody time,' she grinned. She was ruddy cheeked with the kitchen's heat, sweat beading her forehead, her curls scraped back behind a bandana.

She removed it, tossed her head to release her curls, and Ryan fell in love with her all over again.

She fully opened the door with her hip and emerged carrying plates as if she were a MasterChef contestant entering the tasting room.

Noodles. Ryan hated them, and Hannah knew it.

'*Back to earth with a bump,*' he thought to himself.

Hannah poured herself a glass of wine, the DCI a mineral

water, and Ryan a stubby bottle of Bud while they made awkward small talk.

'Mmm, this is good, Hannah,' Ryan said as he forked ginger pork between his lips. 'Apart from the noodles, like.'

She pursed her lips. 'You're not the only one here, you know. I'm not gonna make three different meals.'

'It's fine,' Ryan said, suitably chastised.

'I thought I'd get you here to talk about your return to proper duties,' Danskin announced.

'Sure. It makes sense. Before we do, though, I'd like to hear what Hannah's found out for me about my case on Callaley Avenue.'

Danskin frowned. 'What? You've been calling on my resources to help on one of Kinnear's cases?'

'Shit.' Ryan had forgotten Hannah had sworn him to secrecy.

'Relax,' Danskin grinned. 'I know all about it. Mind, only cos I had to prise it out of Hannah here. She didn't volunteer the info, if that's what you're thinking.'

Ryan wiped a sliver of sauce from his lips with a paper towel. No such thing as a napkin in Stephen Danskin's house. 'Thought I'd dropped us in the clarts there,' Ryan winked at Hannah.

'Messy,' she winked back. Ryan feared he'd melt when Hannah's dimple puckered her face beneath her cheek bone as she smiled at him.

'So, what have you found out?'

'Well, nothing much on the current occupants. Ivor and Marina Hickson aren't known to us at all, but I guess you know that already.'

Ryan mumbled his confirmation through a mouthful of pork.

'And I suppose you know she can't have children, but is looking to adopt?'

Ryan nodded. 'I'm impressed. I thought you'd only check on criminal records, not do a full background history.'

'You know Hannah,' Danskin said. 'She's nothing if not thorough.'

'There's nowt much on anybody, if I'm honest.' She beamed triumphantly. 'Apart from the fact a child was reported missing several years ago.'

'Ah. That'll be Graham Waitrose.'

'You knew?'

''Fraid so.'

'Then you'll also know his mother committed suicide.'

'Yep. I don't know anything about the father, though.'

'Malcolm Waitrose. Lives in Easington Village now with a dental assistant young enough to be his daughter.'

Ryan picked at a piece of meat wedged between his teeth. He studied the stringy morsel between his fingers before setting it aside on the edge of his plate. 'I take it he was cleared of any involvement in the boy's disappearance?'

Hannah nodded. 'He was away on business. The official report confirms it.'

'And the mother?'

'Agatha, known to all as Aggie. Regular churchgoer until her son went missing. Apparently, she lost her faith as well as her son and husband.'

'I take it she has an alibi?'

'Sort of.'

'What's that supposed to mean?'

'Well, she'd popped across to check on a neighbour. When she got back to the house, Graham had gone. She was only away about ten minutes. The records show the neighbour corroborates her story, and the neighbour said Aggie was in such a tizz when she discovered he was missing, she couldn't possibly be putting it on.'

Ryan sipped from his bottle. 'The neighbour was?'

'A Nancy Douglas.'

Ryan considered for a moment. 'Interesting. I've already spoken to her and she didn't mention that bit. I'd better have another word.'

Hannah ran her fingers up the stem of her wine glass. Ryan had to look away before he became dry mouthed. 'Any mention of a dwarf?'

Danskin laughed. 'That's a bit left-field, son.'

'It's just someone mentioned that a dwarf went missing soon after. Her dad threatened Graham Waitrose.'

'Whoa. News to me,' Hannah said. 'No record of that on file.'

'I didn't think there would be. She was a traveller. A gypsy, if you like. All I know is her name was Stacey. I don't have a surname, or her father's name.'

Stephen Danskin clicked his tongue against the roof of his mouth. 'Doubt we'll ever trace 'em after all this time. What do you make of it, Ryan?'

'I'm not *seeing what I expect to see* until Aaron Elliot or one of his cronies has completed an analysis of the bones but, if you pushed me, I'd say the bones are most likely those of Graham Waitrose. The only problem I have is the ages of those involved.'

'How come?'

'Graham Waitrose was ten years old; Stacey in her twenties. Would he really be worldly-wise enough to threaten a woman - even a small woman - like Stacey?'

Danskin considered Ryan's words. 'Not beyond the realms of possibility, though.'

'In which case,' Ryan said, 'We NEED to trace the Romany family. Stacey's father remains the most likely suspect.'

Hannah set down her glass. 'What were the nature of the threats he made against the lad?'

Ryan shrugged. 'Summat about the Waitrose lad touching up this Stacey. The Waitrose kid was only ten. I doubt he'd know what to do with it at that age, yet I've a witness who says the father threatened the lad in no uncertain terms.'

'I wonder,' Hannah mused.

'Are you onto something?'

She fingered her glass again. *'Do you know what that's doing to me?'* Ryan thought.

'Well, if this Stacey was indeed sexually assaulted, we have another suspect.'

Ryan stared at Hannah, open-mouthed. 'What? Who?'

'A Des Waddell. He's a registered sex offender - a relatively minor offence, but one that's relevant in the circs - and he still lives in Callaley Avenue.'

She told him the house number. Ryan tried to think back to the night the bones were discovered. Something jarred in his memory.

'You know, I think that's round about where a bloke was giving me funny looks when I first turned up in the street. I'll pay our Mr Waddell a visit tomorrow, as well.'

**

Hannah ferried empty plates - apart from one laden with untouched noodles - back to the kitchen.

'You ready to hit Forth Street again?' Danskin asked.

'Aye, I am. I appreciate the fact you and the Super stationed me at Whickham while I got over the Benny Yu thing, but I'm more than ready to up the stakes again. Mind, I want to put this case to bed first.'

Danskin steepled his fingers. 'I get that.'

'I suppose I don't even know there is a case yet, not until Elliot gets back to me.'

'It's looking more and more likely though, bonny lad. Especially after what you and Hannah have come up with.'

'Time will tell. So,' he said, looking at DCI Danskin, 'You want to fill me in on the latest at the station.'

The DCI pulled a face. 'Not a great deal, really.'

'I'd like to know if I'm back reporting to you or sticking with Kinnear?'

'How man; I don't let my best men get off my books that easily.'

They heard Hannah rinsing plates and loading the dishwasher.

'Does that mean Hannah will be moving back to Rick Kinnear's mob?'

Danskin rubbed a hand across the crown of his shaven pate. 'I think that's best. Certainly, the Super does. Sam Maynard never liked the potential nepotism that comes from me working with my stepdaughter; nor you teaming up with your girlfriend, for that matter. This arrangement suits everybody and it means we can both still keep an eye out for Hannah without her being farmed off on secondment again, like when Maynard sent her off to the Port of Tyne authority.'

Ryan gave a sage nod. He quite liked the idea.

'Speak of the devil,' Stephen said as Hannah re-joined them.

'I thought my ears were burning.'

Ryan scratched the back of a hand. 'I don't suppose there's any chance of holding back my return until I've got to the bottom of this investigation, is there?'

There was a sparkle in Danskin's eye as he said, 'I've been given that some thought.'

'And?'

'And I reckon I could spare you a hand to help out.'

Ryan looked towards Hannah.

'No, son. Not Hannah. I was thinking more along the lines of Nigel Trebilcock.'

'Won't that leave you a bit light?'

Danskin gave a dismissive wave. 'I can get around that. Lucy Dexter's almost back to her old self. She's been on Kinnear's team to settle back in but he's got her on duties so light she's in danger of floating off. I'll take her back on my team to replace Trebilcock.'

'Kinnear's okay with that?'

'He doesn't know yet,' Danskin snickered, 'But he can hardly object if he's getting a DS in return.' He patted Hannah's hand.

Ryan considered the offer. 'There's no chance I could have Todd, is there?'

'Robson? Bloody hell, man; he's fine for the heavy stuff but this case is more cerebral. Robson's no good at that sort of thing. He's only developed an opposable thumb in the last couple of years.'

Ryan and Hannah laughed. 'Treblecock...sorry, Nigel,'

Ryan said, remembering Superintendent Maynard's order to cut back on nicknames, 'Is okay. I like him, but nah - on balance, I'll stick it out myself. Me and Eric Ross can cover it.'

'Sorry, Ryan. You can't.'

'What do you mean?'

'You can't: that's what I mean. I'm not allowing it.'

Perplexed, Ryan stared at his DCI. 'Why the hell not?'

Danskin met Ryan's stare. 'Because I know. And I'm not having any case jeopardised.'

'You know *'what'*?'

Danskin's cheeks billowed. 'I know about your connection to the house, that's what.'

Ryan stood. 'It's got nothing to do with my folks! It happened way after they left.'

'Aaron Elliot tell you that, did he?'

Ryan fell back into his chair, deflated. 'No. But it stands to reason.'

'I'm sure it does, but it's not a good look for the force, Ryan.'

'For fuck's sake. Are you saying I'm off the case?'

'Think about what I've said, man. No, you're not off the case. I've offered Trebilcock to work WITH you, not instead of you. I've every faith in you but there's a protocol to follow and...'

'Fucking Eric Ross! He promised me he wouldn't say anything to anybody.'

'He didn't, Ry. It was me,' Hannah said, apologetically. 'I discovered it when I looked into the ownership records. I couldn't ignore it. I had to tell someone, and Stephen's the only one I could trust.'

Ryan stood once more. 'You? No, no. You can't have. *'Go*

back twenty years', I said. Not thirty-odd.'

Hannah smiled thinly. 'It's like Stephen said: I'm nothing if not thorough.'

'I can't believe you'd betray me.'

'I only told Stephen to protect you! Don't you realise how this would look if it got out your family had connections to that house, and whatever went on inside it?'

Ryan clenched his fists by his side before flinging open the door. 'I'm done here.'

'I think you're being a bit over dramatic, Ry, aren't you?'

He glared at Hannah. 'In fact, you and me are done!'

The door almost ripped from its hinges as Ryan slammed it shut behind him.

'That went well, all things considered,' Stephen Danskin muttered to the vibrating door.

TEN

Marina Hickson woke like a bear emerging from hibernation, aware of a sickly feeling in her stomach. When she remembered why, she buried her head into a pillow with a groan.

The tiny skull, some already crumbled away, its jawbone almost smiling at her. She shuddered. What with the skull and the issues between Ivor and her, it was no wonder she felt like shite. It wasn't her *'condition'*, as Ivor described it. Nothing to do with her mental state, but everything to do with the skull.

She turned on her side as she remembered the feel of the bones against her fingers as they brushed over it. The sensation had been horrible. It reminded her of death: her mother's, her grandmother's, even the unformed mass of cells which, one day, should have become her own child.

Death triggered too many memories for her. Still, if she'd taken one thing from therapy, it was not to dwell on stuff. With an effort, she flung back the bedclothes, made her way to the bathroom, and turned her face into the soothing spray of the shower.

With the dark thoughts washed away, Marina made her way to the head of the stairs. She heard voices in the lounge. Marina sat on the stairs. Who would call so early in the day? Surely not Morris. Even he wouldn't be that brazen. Whoever it was, she didn't feel like entertaining anyone.

After a few minutes eavesdropping, Marina realised by the tone of the conversation Ivor was talking to a policeman. She breathed through her nose and made her way downstairs, painting a smile on her sallow face as she did so.

Ivor looked up as she entered the room. 'I was about to come and wake you when the Detective called,' he smiled. 'Are you feeling better?'

'So-so, but I thought I'd go mad - like, properly mad - if I stayed in bed any longer.' She looked at the sandy-haired detective. He seemed in a worse state than her this morning. 'What can I do for you this time?'

'Nothing too specific. I've a couple of neighbours to speak to and thought I'd see how you were doing.'

'We're fine,' Ivor said, 'Bearing in mind all we've been through.'

'It's awful,' Marina contradicted. 'I can't get that skull out of my head.'

Ryan smiled though his face remained taught with strain. 'I can imagine.'

She tucked a strand of hair behind her ear and cast a downward glance. 'I've been through worse, though. I'll survive.'

'I'm sure you will. Just a couple of things while I'm here. Firstly, does the name Graham Waitrose mean anything to you?'

They both shook their heads.

'What about a Stacey?'

'I'm sorry,' Ivor said, 'Are these people local? I mean, we've only just moved here so we're hardly likely to know them.'

Ryan ignored the comment. 'I seem to remember you told me you'd had someone in to repair your ceilings before you moved in. I'll need to check them out, if you have a name.'

'I'll have it…'

'…Somewhere,' Ryan finished, knowing Marina's standard response.

'They came highly recommended and did a first-class job. I'm sure they won't have been involved.'

Ryan smiled. 'Probably not, but you'll understand we need to check.'

'Tomkiss. That was the company,' Ivor said. 'It was all done remotely. Neither of us ever met anyone from the company, before you ask. I think they're based in Dunston somewhere but I can't be sure. Definitely not far from these parts, though; that's for certain.'

'Thank you, Mr Hickson. That's very helpful.' Ryan stood. 'You'll be sick of hearing me say this, but if there's anything else you can think of, you know where you can get me.'

'Of course. Here, let me show you out,' Ivor offered.

'There is something,' Marina said. 'Probably not important, but there's some markings in the cupboard.'

Ryan and Ivor both looked at her.

'Paint, I think. It looks like somebody's been measuring a child. You know, as they grew.'

'Could I see them, please?'

'Of course. This way.'

Ryan followed Marina Hickson into the kitchen. She clutched the top of her nightdress as she bent to show Ryan the marks.

Jarrod's ankles cracked as they took the strain when he hunkered down and gazed at the inscriptions.

If the Detective looked as if he'd had a bad night before, he appeared significantly more shaken now.

**

'All by yourself today?' Nancy Douglas said when she opened the door to Ryan.

'Aye. I might be getting someone to give me a hand with the case soon so I've left PC Ross to ensure all the paperwork is in order. That's not my cup of tea.'

'Speaking of which, do you fancy a cuppa? Kettle's not long been boiled and you look like you could do with one, if I'm being honest. Are you not feeling well?'

'Thank you, Mrs Douglas. That's very kind,' he said, disregarding her second question. 'Milk and two, please.'

'TWO sugars? You'll lose all your teeth by the time you're forty, believe me.'

'I usually only take one, if that helps.'

'They might make it to fifty, then,' she said from a kitchen reeking of smoked bacon.

'Am I interrupting your breakfast? I can come back if you like.'

'Nonsense. It's nice to have some company,' Nancy said. She carried a tray containing two cups and a plateful of bacon sandwiches. 'Help yourself.'

'Just the tea for me, thanks. I'm not hungry.'

She gave Ryan a grandmotherly look. 'Hmm. You're not okay, are you?'

Ryan ignored her. 'Do I take it you don't get many visitors?' he asked.

'Not many. What's left of my family live down south. I think I told you about my brother, didn't I? Lives on the south coast. My nephew's fairly local, though. I see him from time-to-time, usually when he wants something. Otherwise, it's just me and the neighbours.'

Nancy used a floral handkerchief to dab at a smear of ketchup on her cheek. 'So, what can I do for you this time, young man?'

Ryan looked out the window towards the Hickson house standing opposite at the top of the stone stairs. 'The new couple - did you see much of them before they moved in? I mean, did they inspect the property while it was empty, for example, or decorate it?'

Nancy pursed her lips. 'Not a great deal, no. They had some deliveries and tradespeople in, a plumber for one, but can't say I saw much of the Hicksons themselves.'

Ryan sipped his tea and set the cup down on a mahogany coffee table next to Nancy's knitting paraphernalia. 'Did you notice any other visitors? Perhaps a neighbour looking after the place?'

Nancy studied Ryan. 'You look familiar.'

He shuffled uneasily. 'I live in the village so you've probably seen me around. So,' he continued, keen to get back on track, 'The house opposite - ever see anyone there who you think shouldn't have been?'

She waved a finger at him. 'None of my business, really.'

'What isn't?'

'Her *visitor*. The fat man.'

'I think we have to describe him differently these days,' Ryan said with a smile.

'Her manfriend. Is that better?' Nancy Douglas's eyes sparkled. 'Her fat manfriend.'

Ryan smirked. He was warming to old Nancy Douglas. 'I take it you mean Morris Chaplin?'

'I've no idea what his name is, but he's portly,' she smiled again, 'And rarely around when her husband's at home.'

Ryan's suspicions about Marina Hickson's relationship with Morris Chaplin were confirmed. 'What about before the Hicksons moved in?'

Nancy watched him over the rim of her teacup. 'You think it's him, don't you?'

'I can't comment on who is or isn't a suspect. I don't even know there's a crime to investigate yet.'

'I didn't mean a suspect. I meant the victim. You think it's Aggie's boy.'

The old woman had all her marbles, that's for sure. 'We'll know more when we get the forensic report. Until then, we're keeping an open mind.'

The smell of bacon finally got the better of him and he picked up a crustless sandwich. 'Speaking of the Waitrose family, you didn't mention Aggie came to you the day her son went missing.'

'Didn't I? Sorry, I thought I had.'

'How did she seem?'

'In a mess. Worried. Confused. A right state, basically.'

Ryan pondered on a thought. 'How would you describe Aggie's relationship with her son?'

Nancy narrowed her eyes. 'I'll just stop your line of thinking right there. I assure you, Aggie Waitrose had nothing to do with her son going missing. The poor woman was distraught. Distraught enough to take her own life.'

'*Or guilty enough,*' Ryan thought. He swallowed a string of fatty bacon, cleared his throat, and moved on. 'Did Aggie or Graham get any unusual visitors?'

'Mind, you're testing my memory now. That was years ago.'

'I know. I'm sorry but do you remember anyone out of place?'

'Such as?'

'For example, did you ever see her husband at the property after they split?'

'No, I haven't seen hide nor hair of him. He wouldn't have been welcome, believe me.'

'Anyone else you wouldn't expect to see?'

Nancy looked towards a cobweb hanging from the ceiling. She thought of Aggie Waitrose hanging in her garage. Suddenly, she clicked her fingers. 'The midget!'

'We call them dwarves these days, Mrs Douglas.'

She waved a hand at him. 'Ah, don't give me all that woke stuff.'

Ryan's eyes widened. Nancy Douglas laughed.

'I learnt that word from my nephew. Down with the kids, I am.' She shook her hand, two fingers extended like a Brooklyn rapper.

Ryan laughed again. He was pleased he'd called. Nancy Douglas had lightened his mood; taken his mind off Hannah's betrayal. 'What can you tell me about the visitor?'

'She was little,' Nancy said with a smirk. 'No, in all honesty, all I know is she popped around now and again. Did some jobs for Aggie and a couple of other neighbours, I think. Not me, though. I never had two ha'pennies to rub together.'

'Did you ever see the woman's parents?'

Colin Youngman

Nancy shook her head.

'Are you sure, Mrs. Douglas? It could be important.'

'I'd remember if I had. We don't get many of their sort around here.' She saw Ryan's face. Shook her head until the skin on her neck quivered. 'I shouldn't say that either, should I?'

'Not really. I'll let it pass, seeing as you've been so helpful. And kind. The sandwich was lush.'

She slid the plate towards him.

'Thanks, but no. I have another couple of calls to make. I'll see myself out.'

'Any time you're passing, feel free to pop in.'

'*Bless her*,' he thought. She reminded him a lot of his grandmother in her better days.

Ryan sighed. If only Doris Jarrod was still in her better days, she'd have been able to set his mind at rest.

**

'Mr Waddell?'

The man stood with arms folded across his chest. 'Who's asking?'

Ryan held out his warrant card. 'Detective Sergeant Ryan Jarrod.'

Waddell rolled his eyes. 'What do you want?'

'A word, if I may.'

'Gan on, then.'

'Inside would be better.'

'Would it?'

'Unless you want all your neighbours to know about your past, I think it would.'

Waddell stiffened and let Ryan into his house.

Inside, the lounge was cold and unwelcoming; out of keeping with its exterior and those of its neighbours. A pile of dirty washing peeped out from behind the sofa. A beer glass and two empty cans, one crumpled by hand the other on its side, lay atop a glass coffee table. Finger marks covered its surface and it had a crack running its length.

Crumbs littered the carpet. The windowsills were coated in a thick layer of dust. An Amazon Prime movie was paused mid-scene, and a laptop computer stood alert on the arm of the sofa.

Des Waddell flicked down the cover of the device as he joined Ryan inside. 'Spit it out. What do you want?'

'I'm speaking to most of the neighbours, Mr Waddell, about the police activity on the street the other night.'

'What activity might that be?'

'The activity you were watching. I saw you when a colleague and I drove past.'

Waddell breathed out. No point in pretending anymore. 'Aye, I saw you. Saw it on the news, as well. You found some bones, I hear.'

'Yep. I'm asking a few questions...'

'You're never going to let it drop, are you?'

'Sorry?'

'Your lot.' Waddell was snarling through lips which barely moved as he spoke. 'I heard what they said on the news. *'Child's bones'*. Straight away you jump to the conclusion that it'll be the pervert on the street. *'Des Waddell'*, you'll have said. *'Let's pin this on him.'*

The man was defensive to the point of bristling. It didn't escape Ryan's attention.

'We're talking to all the neighbours, like I said. What makes you think I'm singling you out?'

'Howay, man. Do you think I was born yesterday? I've a record, haven't I? And you lot know it.'

Ryan deliberately avoided glancing towards Waddell's laptop. 'I'd like to hear your version of events.'

'Okay. Look, I admitted it in court. I watched some kiddie porn. Nowt serious, mind. No videos. Nothing posed. Just kids with no clothes on. Nobody with them, nobody doing nowt to 'em.'

Ryan pulled at his bottom lip. 'Who reported you?'

'The bloody window cleaner. He saw us looking at it, phoned you lot, and you know the rest.'

'You pleaded guilty; I believe.'

'Of course. I had nee choice, did I? You lot had my computer. You went at it like a dog with a bone.'

Ryan backtracked a moment. 'Why do you think this has anything to do with the remains found along the street?'

'I don't. It's got sod all to do with it, but as soon as the remains were found, I guessed bad ol' Des Waddell would be top of your suspect list. Do you know, even the magistrate felt sorry for me during sentencing. He said it was the lowest grade offence of this nature he'd come across. I was fined peanuts, only had to pay me own costs, yet I had to sign the sex offender register.'

Waddell gestured around the room. 'And that's why nobody will employ me and why my beautiful house looks like Blaydon landfill!' He looked down at the threadbare carpet. 'Listen, I'm sorry. I shouldn't take it out on you, but the whole thing boils my piss, you know? And, before you ask, no: I have nothing to do with whatever happened along the street.'

Ryan looked at Waddell for a long moment. Finally, he spoke. 'For what it's worth, I believe you. At least, I do unless forensics find something that links you to the remains.'

'They won't.' Waddell wiped his hands along his thighs. 'Is that it, then? You're finished here?'

Ryan confirmed he was. He left Des Waddell's home with one final house call left on his list.

It was the one he least wanted to make.

ELEVEN

Thick grey clouds scudded across the heavens creating a false dusk in the early afternoon. The vehicles traversing Whickham Bank did so with headlights glowing and windscreen wipers readied for a brewing downpour.

The parked-up cherry red Peugeot rocked in the wind as Ryan scrolled through his messages. Finding nothing of significance, he checked in with Eric Ross.

'Everything up to date?' he asked.

'Just about, aye. I've sorted all the files, checked they reflect the chronology, and transferred the electronic data into an indexed bookmark.'

'Cheers, Eric. I appreciate it. Owt else?'

Ryan heard Ross suck air between his teeth. 'The bloke with the funny name's been on. He reckons he's starting tomorrow.'

'Trebilcock, you mean? It's news to me but he'll appreciate your efforts, I'm sure.'

'What's gonna happen to me, Sarge?'

'Nothing. You're still on the case with us.'

'Really? That's great. I thought I wasn't cutting the mustard or something.'

Ryan chastised himself for not making himself clear to Eric. 'That's my fault, Eric. I didn't explain myself properly. I've had a lot gannin' on but that doesn't excuse it. No, mate, you're doing just fine. In fact, Treblecock - Nigel - will be looking after me, as it were, not you.'

Ryan sensed Eric's bemusement. Finally, the penny dropped. 'Oh, they've found out about you and the house. It wasn't me, honest.'

'It's okay, Eric. I know it wasn't. So, the three of us will be working together for now.' It wasn't a lie - he just didn't know how long the arrangement would last.

He looked up at the building towering above him like a Gothic mansion. The one woman who, at one time, could have provided him with an answer was inside, somewhere. Sadly, Doris Jarrod, forever locked in her own world, was unable to provide Ryan with the reassurance he craved.

He was left with no choice. Plan A, it was.

Ryan started the engine and pulled out of the care home grounds, turning right towards the crest of Whickham Bank.

**

The figure lay sprawled across the sofa, head to one side, mouth open.

One arm dangled over the edge of the seat until the man's fingers trailed against the carpet.

He snored like a congested walrus.

Ryan coughed loudly. There was no response from the somnolent man. He tried again.

Nothing.

Ryan put a hand on the man's shoulder and shook him.

Norman Jarrod shot bolt upright as if electrocuted. 'Fuck me, man! You could have seen me off there. Jesus Christ!'

'You really should lock your doors, you know. I could've been anybody.'

Norman screwed his eyes up and peered at the wall clock. 'What's the time?'

'Just after two.'

'Two? In the morning?'

'No, man. Afternoon.'

Norman rubbed his eyes and yawned. 'You're finished early. Kenzie's around somewhere.'

'That's another thing, he could have gone anywhere. You left the kitchen window open. You know how easily he can get on the bench.'

Norman swung his legs onto the floor. 'Shit, he hasn't

escaped, has he?'

'No. He's having a dump in the garden as it happens.'

Ryan's father smacked his lips. 'Stick the kettle on, man. I'm as dry as Prince Andrew's armpits.' He looked at his eldest son. 'You don't look yersel. Is summat up?'

'I'll get that coffee,' was Ryan's only reply.

He returned from the kitchen with two cups and one excited German Shepherd.

'I've shut the window for you. It's started raining outside.' As if to confirm his master's weather report, Kenzie shook himself dry. Ryan reached down to stroke him. 'It's not fair on the dog, you know. You need to give him more attention.'

Norman lowered the cup from his lips. 'Had on, son. Think yourself lucky I take him every day. He's your bloody dog, remember. Hannah got him for you, not me.'

Ryan knew his father was right, but his mood wasn't conciliatry. Norman Jarrod's mention of Hannah hadn't helped, but that wasn't Ryan's most pressing concern.

'I've been to the house again,' he said.

Norman smoothed down a tuft of bed hair. 'Give us a clue. Which house is that?'

'Callaley Avenue.'

Norman rolled his eyes and winced as he sipped steaming coffee.

'I'm not getting far with the case. Don't even know if there is one yet. We've got a couple of possible leads but they're a bit tenuous, if I'm honest.'

Norman put his cup on the floor. Moved it away from Kenzie as the dog's curiosity got the better of him and gave it a sniff. 'I don't want to know, Ry. You're not supposed to talk about cases, remember? Besides, every time you do, it tends to come back and bite me on the arse.'

Ryan shrugged. 'Just thought you'd be interested, that's all; being your old house an' all.'

Norman flicked on the TV. A standard definition picture of a younger John Nettles appeared on screen. 'Bergerac, for

God's sake.' He skipped channels. An equally dated version of The Sweeney popped up. Another change. Britain's Most Evil Killers took an ads break. 'Daytime telly's shite.'

'See that red button at the top of the remote? Press it. Like magic, you'll find the telly switches itself off.'

The room fell silent as Norman Jarrod took the hint. 'Wor James was on earlier. He sounded a bit nervous. Or excited. Couldn't make out which.'

'Oh aye?'

'Aye. It'll be summat to do with that Muzzle lass of his.'

'I wish he wouldn't insist we call her that, but he won't have us calling her Germaine.'

'It's that gaming culture, isn't it? Everybody uses a handle, or whatever they call it. It's become blurred with reality. Still, if that's what she wants.' Norman slurped his coffee. 'He said you'd given him an idea.'

'*I* had?'

'Yep. Summat about giving his lass a treat.'

Ryan rubbed his forehead. He sensed a headache coming on. He knew why.

'It's got some history, that old house of yours.'

Norman sighed. 'Give it a rest, son. I don't want to be reminded of it. It hurts, you know.'

'Why, Dad?'

'You know I get upset talking about your Mam. She's always with me, in me heed like, but talking about her still hurts. Brings things back to me, her last couple of months...' Norman fell silent.

Ryan understood. He remembered how frail his mother had become when the cancer took hold. The painkillers. The delirium. The constant trail of lovely McMillan nurses. He knew how his father felt because he felt it, too.

'Why did you leave Callaley Avenue?'

Norman shrugged his shoulders. 'Time to move on, I guess.'

'Why?'

'Howay, man. I can't rightly remember, now,' he said, avoiding Ryan's gaze. 'It just felt right.'

'Why?'

'Bloody hell, man - have you regressed to a five-year-old? All these *'Why's'* are doing me heed in.'

'I'm not five years old - but someone in the house was.'

Norman's anger faded. Faded to be replaced by something else. Doubt? Concern? Ryan wasn't sure.

'Probably. There'll have been loads of folk lived there since we moved out. There's probably been dozens of kids lived in the hoose over the years. And, like the news said, a kid's been buried in the back garden. It shouldn't take a Detective Sergeant to work out that there's been kids in the house at some point.'

Ryan held a silence. Even Kenzie sat still. 'Thing is, Dad, we found something beneath the wallpaper.'

'Where's this going, kidda?'

'We found a height chart; measurements, and such like.'

'And?'

'And the chart had been hand painted on the wall.'

Ryan looked long and hard at Norman Jarrod.

'It was your handwriting, Dad.'

TWELVE

Norman Jarrod made a sound more animal-like than human.

It made Ryan's skin crawl. He watched the muscles in his father's face knot and twitch as if a puppeteer worked them from beneath skin which had become parchment-coloured.

Norman clasped his hands together. Squeezed them tight. His leg jumped up and down at a rate of knots. He rocked back and forward on the sofa, eyes clasped shut.

The bestial noise rose again in his throat and Ryan saw his father's nostrils flare as he sucked in air. Finally, he stilled.

He opened his eyelids and stared towards Ryan, though his eyes were seeing something else.

'Sit down, son, and listen. There's something I need to tell you.'

**

'It's your turn to read tonight, love.'

'I know you did it yesterday but do you mind doing it again? It's just that the England match will be on in a bit, and I've had a hard day's graft.'

'Ha! Graft? Sitting on your backside in the office all day? I'm the one who's had the washing and ironing to do, not to mention trailing her round the shops with me.'

'Okay, I'll do it. 'Goldilocks' again?'

'It's her favourite so if you want her to fall asleep quick, she won't get over 'til the end.'

'Puss in Boots' it is, then.'

'Thanks, Norman. I'll make it up to you later.'

'I like the sound of that. Come on, sweetheart. Time for bed. You

can have a nice long lie tomorrow. Make the most of them cos you'll be at school soon. You're a big girl now.'

**

Ryan opened his mouth to speak.

'Shut it! Just listen, okay? This is hard enough as it is. You can ask questions later but don't interrupt.'

Ryan shifted uncomfortably in his chair. Kenzie lay on his lap, doe-eyes blinking at Norman.

'So,' Norman continued. 'I went upstairs just like I always did, made sure she had a wee before bed, tucked her in, and read the story to her. As soon as she drifted off, I came back downstairs.'

'How was she?' your Mam asked.

'Same as normal. Why?'

'I don't know. She's been a bit sleepy all day. When I took her up to Kwik Save, she dragged her feet…'

'It's a canny steep walk for a little 'un, you know.'

'Tell me about it, but she's normally fine. She got a right strop on in the shop. Took a paddy. Stomped her feet and refused to budge. I had to lift her up and strap her in the trolley seat.'

'That doesn't sound like her,' I said.

'I know. She's normally good as gold.'

'Hmm. Maybe she's coming down with a bug,' I said.

'Possibly, but there's no sign of a cough or cold.'

It must have been out of character for her because I remember being concerned enough to switch the match off. 'Was she okay apart from that?'

'Not really,' your mother said. 'She wouldn't eat her spaghetti hoops at dinner time, and she clung onto Harvey most of the afternoon.' Your Mam picked up a fluffy white stuffed rabbit and showed it to me as if I didn't know who Harvey was. 'She seemed to pick up after that, though.'

'I was going to say, she's seemed fine since I got in. Made short shrift of those fish fingers and potato alphabites.'

'True, but if she hadn't had any lunch…'

I thought about how she'd been since I'd arrived back. I convinced mesel' there was nowt wrong. I told your Mam as much. 'She's fine,' I said.

'Probably.' Your Mam didn't sound convinced.

I tried to reassure her. 'Tell you what, if she has a bad night, I'll take a day's special leave and book an appointment at the Cottage docs for her.'

'I can do it, if you like.'

'Nah, it's nee bother,' I said. 'Everybody else at work does it.'

So, that was it. We didn't say anything more about it. I put the telly back on and settled down to watch the rest of the match.

I remember it to this day. It was a World Cup qualifier, Italy away, and as boring as hell - until we heard the bump upstairs.

'What was that?' your Mam said.

'I think she's fallen out of bed.'

I got up to see to her but your mam told me she'd go and I should watch the match.

I did, for about thirty seconds.

I heard a scream. I'll never get the sound out of my head as long as I live.

'Norman!' your mother yelled. 'She's not breathing!! Call an ambulance!'

I took the stairs three at a time. Must have taken me less than three seconds to get from the foot of the stairs to her bedroom. Her face was pale and her lips were already turning blue. She was kind of shaking, not exactly a fit but a lot more than a shiver. Then, she stopped. Just like that. One minute she was moving, the next still as.., well - she'd stopped moving.

It was then her eyes rolled back and I knew she'd gone.'

**

Ryan and Norman sat in silence. Ryan felt a sense of disorientation, almost an out-of-body experience. He didn't understand what his father had just told him, nor did he want to.

Norman's fingers clasped and unclasped the neck of his T-shirt, his eyes shimmered with tears. He gulped a lungful of air and his shoulders heaved.

Kenzie shuffled from Ryan's lap, tail down, and licked Norman's face once before returning to lie against Ryan.

The silence hung in the air for minutes. Slowly, Norman raised his face and offered Ryan a feeble smile before he lowered his gaze to the carpet.

'Who was she?' Ryan asked.

'It's obvious, isn't it?'

'Not to me, no.'

The wounded animal sound escaped Norman again. 'Ryan, she was your sister. The four-year-old sister whose height I measured against the wall of the house in Callaley Avenue.'

'What? No. How? No, no.' He ran his fingers through his hair. 'There's only me and James.'

'I'm sorry, son,' Norman said, a broken man. Defeated.

Ryan shook his head as if trying to rid his brain of the conversation. 'I'm not taking this in. What do you mean: *'my sister'*?'

'You've always joked about me being close to forty when you were born, saying I was a late starter, and all that. Truth is, I wasn't. Your mam and me - we had a little girl before you were born. Long before. After we lost her, we didn't think we could go through all that again - the pain, the heartache - but, slowly, we got our mojo back. We moved - of course, we moved - we couldn't stay there with all the memories; and we started again.'

Norman smiled, warmly this time, and rested his hand on Ryan's wrist. He pulled it away from his father as if it was on a bungee rope.

'Son, you and James - you saved me and your mam. You're all we ever wanted. Sure, I can be an arse at times, but you've no idea how loved, precious; how WANTED you've always been.'

Ryan looked away from his father. Stared into nothingness. 'This isn't one of your bullshit stories is it?'

He saw his father's head shake in his peripheral vision, but he already knew it was the truth.

'You never thought to tell me?'

'I'm sorry, son. Me and your mam swore we'd never say owt to you. We didn't want you to think you were a replacement...'

'A spare, you mean?' he spat.

'If you like, yes; but you were never going to be that. Your mam and me waited so long before we had you precisely for that reason. We had to get your sister's death out of our system so we knew for sure it was you - and James, for that matter - who we wanted. For *yourselves*. Not a spare, as you put it.'

Kenzie jumped to the floor and curled up with his head beneath his bed in denial of the tension around him.

Ryan remained silent for a moment, letting the magnitude of his father's revelation sink in. 'Did you swear Gran to secrecy, as well?'

'She was in on it, aye. She wasn't especially happy about it but it was wor call, and she respected it. Now, of course, she wouldn't be able to tell you even if she wanted.'

'What was her name? You haven't even told me her name.'

'Rhianne.'

A momentary pause. 'You're kidding me.'

'No. We named her Rhianne.'

Ryan whistled through his teeth. 'Bloody hell. Not only have I discovered the sister I never knew existed is dead, but now you're telling me I'm named after her! And you say I'm not a replacement. Do you think I'm daft?'

'It's not like that, son, I promise you. It's just a coincidence. We named her after one of my favourite old songs, *'Rhiannon'*. You were called Ryan after Ryan O'Neal. He was your mam's favourite actor.'

'Do you expect me to believe that?'

'It's the truth, Ryan. We didn't realise the coincidence until your Gran told us what a nice touch it was, naming you after Rhianne. It never even crossed our minds until then.'

'I need a drink.' Ryan moved to Norman Jarrod's drinks cabinet and poured himself a brandy. He hated brandy, but he needed something.

He knocked it back in one, smacking his lips and twisting his face. 'How did she die?' He said it matter-of-factly, as if talking about a stranger. Come to think of it, she WAS a stranger.

Norman closed his eyes again. 'It's still a mystery. The coroner put it down as an unexplained death. SIDS, or summat. Sudden Infant Death Syndrome.'

'Like Cot Death, only older?'

'I suppose.'

Ryan poured himself another brandy. 'I think I might be sick.'

'I know, Ry. It must be a lot to take in.'

'It's not that; it isn't the fact my sister's dead. Not even the fact I didn't know anything about her. It's nowt like that.'

'Then what is it?'

Ryan stared at his father with barely concealed hatred.

'It's because you buried her in your back garden!'

THIRTEEN

'Don't be bloody ridiculous, man! Of course we didn't bury her in the garden.'

'What? You mean another child's skeleton just happens to turn up in the same spot my secret sister, the sister no-one knows about, died? You've got to admit it's a bit of a coincidence.'

'Calm doon, son. People DID know Rhianne. Your Gran, people who lived nearby at the time...'

Suddenly, it fell into place. 'Like Nancy Douglas, the woman opposite. She was right all along. She said she remembered a young lass lived there around the same time as you and Mam. How bloody stupid am I? I tried to convince myself she'd got mixed-up, that there was nothing in what she was saying but, really, my water told me she was right. I knew there was something wrong with all this the moment I pulled up outside your old house.'

'There you are, then. If people knew about Rhianne, we wouldn't just dig a hole and hoy her in as if burying a pet rabbit. She was my daughter. I know you've had a shock but have a bit of respect, for pity's sake.'

Ryan screwed his middle fingers into his temples to ease the headache. 'Where's she buried? Can I see where she is?'

'Sorry, no.'

'Please, Dad, don't deny me that right.'

'I can't, son. We sprinkled her ashes under her favourite tree, over Foxhills way. Rhianne used to collect conkers from under it.'

'Death certificate? You've got to have a death cert.'

Norman shrugged.

'What's that supposed to mean?' Ryan asked.

'It'll be around somewhere. In the loft, probably. I've never been one for paperwork at yem. Your Mam looked after that sort of thing.'

'Cremation paperwork? There must be loads of stuff.'

'If there is, I don't know where.'

Ryan sank his head against the back of the sofa. 'You've got to find it, Dad.' His voice sounded calmer than he felt.

'After all this time? Nah, I'd rather not.'

'Then, you'd better pray the forensic report doesn't tell us the bones are those of a four-year-old female. If Aaron Elliot says they are, we're in deeper shit than Mr Turd from Crapsville.'

**

Ryan didn't know how long it took him to walk home through the pouring rain.

He remembered passing The Travellers Rest so he must have got as far as Sunniside before heading home, but where else he'd been, he had no idea.

He was soaked through when he eventually arrived home. Kenzie flopped spark-out on the kitchen floor the moment Ryan opened the door.

The house soon bore the yeasty odour of wet dog. Ryan didn't care. All he wanted was a beer - and to sleep off the nightmarish day.

No sooner had he popped the tab on his can, his phone rang. He almost ignored it but, when he saw the caller's name, he decided to answer.

'Aal reet, James,' he said with as much enthusiasm as he could muster.

'You sound happy, mind,' James scoffed.

'Aye well. You could say it's been one of those days, mate.'

'Have you heard?'

Ryan sat up, suddenly alert. Had their father told the younger sibling about his sister?

'No,' he said, tentatively.

'He didn't tell you? Dad, I mean?'

Ryan sighed. 'James, it's been a shitty day. I can't be arsed to work out what you're talking about so just tell me straight out.'

'Right. Okay. Have you still got the ring?'

'I must be more pissed than I thought. What ring?'

'Gran's ring. The one she said we could have.'

'Course I've got it. She left it to me, remember.'

'I don't think she did. She left it to whoever needed it first.'

'I know she did, James. And I'm the eldest so I'll need it first.'

His brother laughed. 'Well, thanks to you, you don't. I need it.'

'*Thanks to me*? What you on about?'

'You told me I should surprise Muzzle. Do something nice to get her out of her moods. So, that's what I'm going to do.'

'Nah, this is still going over my head.'

'I need Gran's ring. I'm going to ask Muzzle if she'll marry me.'

Ryan knocked the beer can over. 'Shit!' he said, mopping ale from the cream sofa with a tissue.

'I reckon we both thought you and Hannah would be using it first. Who'd have guessed I'd be the one getting married before you.'

Ryan felt an unexpected pang of jealousy. 'She hasn't said yes yet and, to be honest, I'm not sure it's a good idea. It's early days and, well, she's a bit weird, isn't she?'

'Look, it's my choice. So, can I have the ring or not?'

'I suppose. I'm really busy at the mo, though, so I'll get it to you when I can.'

'Okay but try not to be long. I'm on pins here.'

Ryan hoped James didn't hear him say, 'Fucking hell' as they ended the call. He tossed his mobile down beside him. 'What a fucking day.'

That should be me and Hannah, he thought. *Heaven knows, we've had plenty of goes at it.*

Today had been the day from hell. He couldn't take any more. He messaged Rick Kinnear, told him he was unwell and wouldn't be in tomorrow, before he headed upstairs and, fully clothed, pulled the duvet over his head.

**

In Callaley Avenue, no-one was sleeping.

Marina Hickson swallowed a handful of tablets. Ivor carefully but deliberately switched the wine bottle to his side of the coffee table.

'That's enough. No more wine - and no more pills.'

'Ah come on, spoilsport. Don't be such a misery guts.' She prodded his midriff with a finger.

'I mean it, Marina. You never know when the adoption agency might call around. They said it would be some time in the next fortnight but they're not going to announce their visit in advance, are they? They'll turn up unexpectedly so we can't prepare for them. We don't want them to find you hungover or spaced out 'cos of your meds, do we?'

Rain rattled against the window as if someone had thrown a handful of pebbles at it. Marina waved a finger in the approximate direction of the garden.

'And a big hole in the garden where a skeleton's been hiding won't make them a teensy-weensy bit suspicious? What about the white sheeting to stop the neighbours seeing if anything else is lurking there? Nope, that's absolutely fine. The police tape across the front gate? Spotlights like the Utilita Arena out back? No, nothing for them to worry about there. No, of course not. As long as your wife isn't showing signs of enjoying herself, everything is fine and dandy.'

Ivor took hold of her by the wrists. 'I can find a lot more to tell them about, don't forget.'

'Ow. Get off. You're hurting me.'

'There was a time when you liked a bit of that.'

'Stop it. Okay, I admit, we had our fun.'

'*Had*' being the key word. We don't have much of that once you chose your drink and drugs before me, and who knows what else.'

'What do you mean by that?'

'Morris Chaplin, that's what I mean.'

**

Across the road, Nancy Douglas lifted a family photograph from its place on the wall. It was an old photograph. She was in Bournemouth, her brother to her right, his wife to her left. They looked so much younger. Probably because they were. In front of them, her nephew smiled broadly at the camera.

She stared into the eyes of her nephew. Despite the smile, they were dark and unrevealing. Like a shark's, she thought, even though he was still a slip of a lad. Yet, he'd grown into a fine man.

Since he moved up north, he'd do anything for her. He did all her odd jobs. A leaking tap? No bother, Auntie Nancy. Garden overgrown? I'll see to it, Auntie Nancy. Ceilings need a lick of paint? I'm your man, Auntie Nancy.

That's what family is all about, she thought.

That's why it was such a terrible shame.

**

Next door to the Hicksons, Nikki and Andy Reid snuggled up on the sofa, a Game Of Thrones episode playing out on the widescreen TV fixed to the wall.

'Don't you just love nights like these?' Nikki said, nuzzling his throat. 'All nice and cosy-warm listening to the wind and the rain outside. It makes me feel safe and secure.'

Andy played with her hair. 'Yeah, I know. I'd still prefer a summer's night, sitting in the garden with a cold beer, listening as the birds settle down for the night, though.'

'Mmm,' Nikki murmured, 'I wonder.'

'Wonder what?' Andy said.

'You know, if summer nights in the garden will ever be the same. Knowing what's been in there all this time?'

She felt Andy shrug. 'It won't bother me.'

Nikki moved away from him slightly so she could look into his eyes. 'Really? You don't think you'll feel any different?'

'Nah. I mean, it wasn't our garden, was it? And, secondly, they might have just found it, but it was there last year, and the year before, and the thought doesn't bother me. No, I still look forward to...' he coughed as he prepared a falsetto, '*Those sum-merr .... Nighhttts.*'

'Tell me more,' Nikki chided. They laughed before falling silent as their attention returned to the TV.

Peter Dinklage's character featured in close-up.

'I wonder what did happen to Stacey?' Nikki pondered out loud.

A few moments later, a thought crossed her mind.

'Andy?'

'Mmm?' he teased a strand of her hair around his hand.

'You said those bones had been in the garden for a couple of years.'

'At least,' he confirmed.

Still snuggled up to him, she asked quietly, 'How do you know?'

**

A few doors further along Callaley Avenue, a house sat in darkness save for the glow from a monitor screen.

Des Waddell gnawed at an already shorn fingernail. He glanced over his shoulder for the third time. The blinds were securely closed.

He stared blankly at the screen in front of him. He'd downloaded the images onto a memory stick, thought about destroying it, but couldn't bring himself to part with it. Instead, he peeled back an edge of carpet, slid the memory stick beneath it, and pulled the carpet firmly back in place.

Waddell prowled the lounge staring fixedly towards the point where he'd hidden the stick. Satisfied there was no hint of the carpet being displaced no matter what angle it was observed from, he returned to the sofa to ponder what to do next.

He wished he knew more about technology. He was confident he'd deleted the latest images from the laptop's files, he'd successfully erased his browsing history for the last God-knows-how-many years, removed all tabs and bookmarks from the sites he'd used, even looked up what the cloud thingy was to make sure it held none of his secrets, yet he was sure someone who knew what they were doing could trace his activities, somehow.

Someone like that bleedin' kid of a Detective; the one who'd stuck his nose in earlier in the day.

FOURTEEN

Marina Hickson walked across Butterfly Bridge. It was one place in the area she already knew, having traversed it with a hiking group she was part of many moons ago.

In fact, she felt an affinity with the Derwent Walk in general, its quiet waters, dappled shade, windswept hilltops where red kites circled overhead, and the smells of nature all around, acted almost as her personal feng shui.

This morning, the wind blew bitterly in her face - and she was grateful for it. It helped blow wine, pills and dark thoughts out her system.

The land on the south side of the bridge sloped down steeply to the narrow, normally serene, waters of the Derwent river. From there, a series of uneven steps gave access to a railway path built on a ledge which ran along the edge of the hill.

From Marina's current vantage point, access to the river was easier thanks to a small sandy beach which protruded from the thickly wooded area around Butterfly Bridge. She hunched into her jacket and watched the ripples coursing along the river's surface.

A meadow walk followed the riverbank, and Marina took it, her feet slipping and sliding in thick mud. She passed beneath the railway bridge where the meadow opened to reveal the dark waters of Clockburn Lake.

Marina stood atop the lake basin and imagined walking into the frigid water, feeling it seep through her clothes, numbing her body until her pain disappeared; until she simply disappeared beneath the surface.

She took a step forward. Trancelike, she took another. Then, a third. Soon, she was at the water's edge.

A spray of icy water hit her, jarring her back to reality. A second splash followed, and a series of high-pitched yelps rattled her eardrums. Two Labradors, one with a stick twice its size clamped between its jaws, paddled and snorted their way across the lake.

Marina heard a shrill whistle. A man, two fingers in his mouth, stood alongside her.

'Shelley! Marina!! - here girls. Come on.' He slapped his thighs to get the dogs attention. 'Sorry, love. Did they wet you?' the man asked.

'Did you just call one of your dog's Marina?'

'Aye. Her name was originally Crystal but I soon found she loved the water so I changed it when I registered her with the Kennel Club.' He stretched out an arm towards a dog frantically paddling towards the shore. 'That's her - the chocolate one with the branch in her gob.'

She smiled. 'Marina's my name, as well.'

'You don't carry sticks in your mush, do you?'

She laughed. 'No. Not often, anyway.'

The dogs emerged, their coats seeming to twirl in opposite directions to their bodies as they shook themselves.

Marina the dog ambled up to Marina the woman and dropped the stick at her feet. She nudged Marina Hickson with her snout, leaving a dark wet smudge and a trail of drool on her jeans.

The woman bent down, picked up the branch, and tossed it towards the lake. The dog bounded back to the water, tail swishing like a cheerleader's baton.

Marina watched her namesake spring through the rushes at the water's edge. 'Your dogs are full of life,' she smiled.

'That's what life's for, isn't it? Living?'

She turned towards the man. 'Thank you,' she said.

'What for?'

'For everything.'

She leant towards him and gave the astonished stranger a

peck on the cheek before she turned from Clockburn Lake and retraced her steps towards home.

Her eyes carried a new sense of purpose. She felt stronger, now. Tougher. It was as if she'd experienced an epiphany. Marina pulled down the hood of her coat, felt the wind whip her hair into a frenzy, and yelled 'Yesss!' to the skies.

There'd be no more wine, no more pills. She didn't need anything or anyone in her life. This - nature and life itself - was all she needed.

For Marina Hickson, a new dawn beckoned.

**

Eric Ross heard the door swing open. He saw a tall, straight backed young man with natural curly dark hair, look around his surroundings. The man seemed a little awkward, almost uncomfortable in alien surroundings.

'*The new bloke,*' Eric thought. 'You must be Treblecock,' he said.

The man shook his head yet smiled. 'It's Trebilcock, as in Sergeant Bilko,' he explained for what must have been the hundredth time since he'd moved to the north-east.

'I'm PC Eric Ross. I'll be working with you and Ry.. DS Jarrod.. on the case.'

'Pleased to meet you, so I am,' Trebilcock said, hand outstretched.

Eric's brow wrinkled. 'You're not from here, are you?'

'No, I be a Worzel, I be,' Trebilcock explained in an exaggerated Yokel accent. 'Cornwall,' he added.

'Oh. I'm sorry about that.'

Nigel let the comment pass. 'Where is Ryan?'

'He's not well. Passes on his apologies, and says he'll be in tomorrow.'

Trebilcock shrugged out of his coat. 'Let's grab a coffee, shall we? Where's the machine?'

Eric snorted. 'Machine? You mean the kettle? It's on the floor ower there. You'll find the coffee behind the blinds.'

'Okay. Milk in the fridge, is it?'

'Nee fridge, pal. There's powdered creamer in a plastic cup next to the coffee.'

'I don't think I'll have one. Let's get down to business, shall we?' Trebilcock took a seat next to Ross. 'I think you can start by showing me the files, telling me about the area, and perhaps we'll have a trip out to see where the bones were found.'

Eric hesitated. 'Happy with the first bit, but not sure we should be doing any investigating without the Sarge's say-so.'

'Yous don't need worry about anything like that. I just be 'avin a look around. I might even call in to see Ryan, if he's up to it. So, let's see those files, shall we?'

**

Ryan finally threw off the duvet around eleven-thirty. He did it reluctantly and only because he heard Kenzie whimper downstairs.

He let the dog into the garden, spent a few minutes playing pully on an old sock with him, and had a bit rough and tumble on the living room floor.

There was something magical about dogs. Ryan felt instantly better. Not great, obviously, but able to think straight.

He made a list of things to be done. Personal things, mainly, but *'personal'* and *'work'* tended to blur into one, these days.

Top of the list, Dad. He needed to check in on him. Ryan realised he'd been hard on him, and Norman would be hurting more than Ryan himself.

Next up, Aaron Elliot. If the doc could confirm the bones were male, or of an older child, or not a child's at all - say, a dwarf's - he could move on.

Which brought him to Rhianne. When all this was over, when he'd grown used to the idea of once having a sister he never had the opportunity to know, he'd want somewhere to visit her; to talk to her. At times like this, for example. She needed a proper memorial. A headstone to show she once walked on this planet. He'd speak to his Dad about it.

Hannah came next. He owed her an apology, too. She had been right to tell Danskin, right to advise Ryan he should have been straight in the first place, and right that they could trust Stephen Danskin. Right, pretty much as usual, about everything. Ryan allowed himself a wry smile as he remembered Eric Burdon's lyrics. Her intentions were good - it was he who had misunderstood them.

He tapped his pen against his teeth as he pondered what else to put on his list.

'James,' he wrote. Much as it pained him, he'd hunt out the ring. James, he realised, was someone else who'd been right.

Kenzie needed and deserved some of Ryan's time. He'd neglected the pup and felt bad about it. Kenzie went on the list.

Ryan ruffled the dog's neck and tickled him behind his ears while he thought.

There was one last thing to add. He wrote it beneath the other entries, then scrawled an arrow from the bottom of the list to the top.

'Coffee' the last entry read.

He forced himself to his feet just as his phone played The Blaydon Races.

Ryan glanced at the screen and sat down again.

'What can I do for you, Mrs Hickson?'

**

They were in the bedroom. The view from the window was panoramic, even though it was spread out beneath a metallic grey sky.

Blaydon tennis club and the Derwenthaugh fish pass lay to the east, Rowlands Gill and the grounds of the historic Gibside Estate to the west. Straight ahead, the hamlet of Winlaton Mill stood on a hillside across the River Derwent.

Ryan's eyes never reached the river. They were focussed on a patch of woodland between Callaley Avenue and the Derwent. The Foxhills, where his sister's ashes were spread.

'I haven't touched anything,' Marina Hickson was saying. 'Not with my fingers. I didn't want my prints on anything.'

'What? Oh, right. Good.' Ryan forced himself back to the present. 'Wait, it's your furniture. I'd expect it to have your prints on.'

Mrs Hickson stood before a chest of drawers the colour of Jason Tindall; a rich mahogany with a surface sheened like a spray-tanned ice rink.

One of the drawers stood part open.

'These drawers are my husband's. Everything in here is his,' she confirmed.

There was something different about the woman, Ryan thought. She seemed more poised. Confident, even.

'What am I looking for?'

'Have you any gloves so you don't leave YOUR prints anywhere? I used a tissue. I hope that's okay.'

Ryan pulled a pair of latex gloves from a pocket and wriggled his fingers into them. 'Voila,' he said, holding his hands aloft.

'Good. Come here.' She beckoned him towards her.

Ryan peered into the drawer. It had a divider in the centre. The left-hand side contained several pairs of rolled-up sports socks. 'There they are.' She pointed to the other side.

It housed various odds-and-sods. Cufflinks, tiepins, half a dozen pens, a book of stamps. 'What am I looking for?'

'You'll see. Please, help yourself.'

Ryan straightened. 'I don't have a warrant, Mrs Hickson. If these are your husband's possessions, I shouldn't look without his express permission.'

She pursed her lips. 'You might regret it if you don't.'

Ryan glanced over his shoulder to ensure Ivor Hickson hadn't abseiled through the window before gently disturbing the contents.

He found nothing unusual.

'I'll give you a clue, should I? They're in the back corner
103

underneath the drawer liner.'

The drawer wouldn't open fully. Ryan squeezed his fingers in and felt around. Sure enough, his fingers brushed against something.

He brought it out, held it up to the light, and whistled.

'There's another one in there,' Marina coaxed.

Ryan dipped his fingers back into the drawer. They emerged clutching a second small semi-cylindrical metallic object. It had a red, slightly concave, tip and a grey body. Both items were scarred and pitted.

By the look on the detective's face, Marina knew she'd been right. 'They are what I think they are, aren't they?'

Ryan dropped the objects into an evidence bag and secured it with the seal.

'Have you any idea why your husband might have something like this in his possession?'

She shook her head.

'No, Detective Sergeant. I have absolutely no idea why my husband would be storing used shotgun cartridges next to his socks.'

FIFTEEN

Ryan stopped dead in his tracks.

He was first to arrive at the Whickham station the following morning and was astonished to see the back wall of the office transformed into a makeshift incident board.

He glanced between the sheets of flipchart he'd been using and the meticulous display of maps, photographs, and dates - all intersected with coloured string - on the wall.

Ryan recognised the handwriting. Nigel Trebilcock. The set-up wasn't perfect but, as far as Ryan was aware, this was Treblecock's first attempt at setting up an incident board - and it was a bloody good attempt. More importantly, there were no photographs of any members of the Jarrod clan on the wall.

'Admiring my work, Ryan, are you?'

Ryan turned. 'Treblecock! Good to see you, mate. How you doing?'

'I'm fine. How are you? Oi hear you weren't too well yesterday.'

'Nah, I'm aal reet. Had a few things to sort out at yem. I was still on the case, mind, as well.'

Nigel nodded at the wall. 'What do you think?'

'Not bad, mate. There's a couple of things not quite right but considering you haven't done it before, and you've only the files to work from for background, it's bloody good.'

Nigel Trebilcock smiled. 'Thank you. Now oi've got your approval, yous just need to remember I'm Nigel. Yous can't call me Treblecock no more, says the Super.'

Suitably scolded, Ryan agreed. 'Aye, Danskin told us.'

'It's not all my own work, though. Eric did a proper job helping me get up to speed, he did. Oi like him. He's good.'

'Aye, but divvent tell him, for God's sake.' They laughed and, right on cue, Eric Ross joined them.

'Morning, Sarge. Feeling better?'

'Yes, but I've been through all that with Treble... with Nigel here, so let's move on and have a gander at this monstrosity on the wall. Hopefully, if you've done your job properly, we'll soon see where things stand. Now, I think it might help Eric and me if you ran through your understanding of the current position. Another perspective would be good, yeah?

Eric nodded his agreement and Ryan motioned for Nigel to take the floor in front of the wall.

'Just before you start,' Jarrod said, 'I want to point out a couple of things. Don't get hung up on it but a couple of the headings you've used - '*Victim*' and '*Possible Suspects*' - aren't strictly appropriate. Yes, there's been a death but until Aaron Elliot confirms otherwise, we shouldn't use either term. Reet, sorry - away you go, Nigel.'

'Fair point, Ryan. Anyways,' he said pointing to the erroneous '*Victim*' column, 'As we speak, it seems likely the bones are those of either Graham Waitrose,' he pointed to a photograph of cherubic looking boy, gap-toothed and freckled, bright blue eyes, and a mullet haircut - 'Or this young woman. Her name is Stacey and she is - or was - a traveller.'

Ryan was impressed Trebilcock had uncovered a photograph of the woman. Prominent forehead, flattened bridge to her nose, squared-off jaw - nothing to distinguish her from others with her condition.

Next to Stacey's image, Trebilcock had affixed a sheet of A4 paper containing a red question mark. 'We's must keep an open mind, of course. There may be others who aren't yet in the equation.'

Ryan swallowed hard as he thought, '*like Rhianne Jarrod, for instance.'*

He looked at the wall to hide his discomfort. 'Okay. Good work finding the photograph of Stacey, Nigel. Really good work. What do you make of our Persons of Interest?'

Trebilcock crossed out the word *'Suspects'* and retitled it *'PoI.'*

'Just now, I think we should focus on previous owners of the property, so I do.'

Ryan swallowed again but Trebilcock didn't seem to notice as he pointed to a series of photographs.

'Current owners, as we know, are an Ivor and Marina Hickson. They discovered the body but, until we know how long the bones have been there, oi think it unlikely be them. As you know, they've only just moved into the property.'

'I've a bit more to say about those two,' Ryan said, 'But I'll come back to it. Carry on,' he pointed a finger at Trebilcock then at the photographs of a couple beneath the Hicksons.

'Paul and Teresa-Claire Chevrier. They owned the property prior to the Hicksons. They aren't known to us. They have no children. Paul Chevrier is a chartered accountant in Stocksfield, where they now live.'

'We'll need to speak to them in due course but it doesn't seem to me that they've any involvement in illicit activities. Let's move on,' Ryan said.

'The Mowdens, Alan and Catherine. Two children, one of each. They're now resident in Greenwood, Nova Scotia. That's Canada.'

'I know where Nova Scotia is, cheers. Okay, let's leave them out of this for now. We'll never get approval for a trans-Atlantic investigation unless we have concrete evidence.' Ryan nodded towards the board. Eager to progress, he hurried Trebilcock on with a 'Next.'

The capricious north-east weather took a turn for the better as a shaft of sunlight speared through the blinds. Eric Ross closed the shutters. The incident wall fell into shade.

'Yous will loik these two. ' A red string ran from the photographs of a grey-haired man and a younger woman to the image of Graham Waitrose. 'This is Ronald Waitrose and his partner, Sophie Thackery.'

Ryan stared at the images. 'As soon as Elliot provides us with confirmation of the age of the bones, we get these two in for questioning. I doubt Waitrose will have killed his own son but you never know what goes on behind closed doors. More to the point, we know nowt about Thackery either so, if the remains fit the timeframe, I want them brought in.'

Ryan noticed the next set of images were linked by coloured thread to the photograph of the mysterious Stacey. 'Who's these two?'

'I've saved the best 'til last, so I have. Here we have Samson Boswell and Erin Goodwin.'

Ryan stared at a tattooed, shaven-headed man and a smiling woman wearing a turquoise headscarf and overworked lipstick. 'Where do they fit in?'

'They're the parents of a certain Stacey Boswell.' He pointed to Stacey's photograph in triumph.

Ryan gasped. 'You've traced them? Bloody hell, Nigel; that's fantastic work!'

Trebilcock wore an embarrassed smile. 'Wasn't me, Ry. Hannah Graves was up all night working on it. She found a Health and Safety report for an accident at the Town Moor fayre involving a Stacey Boswell. It were umpteen years ago and the name Stacey and the timescale struck a note wi' Hannah. She checked it out and discovered the report named three witnesses to the incident; two of which were Boswell and Goodwin. The report referred to them as '*Parents of Stacey Boswell.*'

'What was the nature of the accident?'

Trebilcock smiled. 'A woman fell down the stairs of Erin Goodwin's caravan after a tarot reading, and collided with Stacey Boswell who was making her way towards it. Stacey turned her ankle and needed St John's ambulance attention.'

'Routine, then.'

'Not exactly, no. You see, the woman claimed Boswell had been hiding behind a curtain and when the reading was over, he emerged to demand twice the agreed fee. The woman refused and claimed Boswell pushed her out the van into Stacey. When a duty officer arrived to take a statement, she changed her story. Said it was all her own fault because she hadn't been a' lookin' and fell down the stairs all on her own.'

'Boswell got to her in the meantime, you think?'

'Oi do, so I do.'

Eric Ross asked Nigel if Samson and Erin were still in the area.

'We don't know. Travellin' folk don't tend to advertise their whereabouts. They avoid authorities, often don't use schools or register to vote, and certainly don't pay council tax. Truth is, we don't know where they are and, more importantly, whether Stacey Boswell is still aloive.'

Trebilcock's gentle Cornish burr belied the significance of his last statement.

'I need a coffee,' Ryan said, 'Even if it's cheap Tesco shite. Let's break for ten and come back with a plan of action.'

Ryan hunted out a pack of Jammy Dodgers while Eric Ross made the drinks, which lived down to Trebilcock's expectations. Jarrod took advantage of the break to brief DCI Kinnear, who didn't seem particularly arsed until he knew for sure it was a murder investigation.

Ryan then took a large bite of humble pie. He rang Hannah Graves. She was owed both an apology and his gratitude for the unpaid work she'd done.

She got neither because she was unavailable, investigating a complex bank fraud involving scammers from Singapore.

He settled for messaging her. *'The girl done well. Thanks (and apologies) for everything, from your favourite nobhead.'*

He took a deep breath before returning to the case. 'Okay,' he began, 'Are we in agreement that we're not in a position to formally interview or identify a firm suspect until Aaron Elliot and co get back to us?'

Trebilcock and Ross nodded their assent.

'Reet. We can, though, speak to a few folks informally.'

'Where do we start, Ryan?' Trebilcock asked.

'I've already made a start. In addition to your list, there's couple of others I'm curious about. First off, there's a Des Waddell.' Ryan gave his colleagues a brief overview of his conversation with Waddell, and his background. He wrote his name on the board and asked Ross to hunt out a photograph to go alongside it.

'Do you want me to speak to him again?' Trebilcock asked.

'Nah, not yet. I tell you who you can look up, though. The Hicksons mentioned a plumbing firm they used to fix a leak after they bought the property but before they moved in. Tomkiss, the firm's called. They think they're based in Dunston. See if you can find out which of their employees did the work and have a quiet word with him.'

'Will do.'

'What can I do, Sarge?' Eric Ross asked.

Ryan thought. 'Ideally, I'd like to know more about Malcolm Waitrose and the lass he's with. They live in County Durham so we'll be reliant on the Prince Bishop force. Without a concrete case, I don't think they'll give us any resource.'

He tapped a marker pen against his forehead. Removed the top from it and wrote a name on the board.

Morris Chaplin.

'Eric, you have another look at this bloke, will you? On the QT, mind - I don't want him approached directly.'

Ross said he would.

'As for me, I'm gonna find mesel' an excuse to have another chat with Ivor Hickson.'

'Why's that?' Trebilcock asked. 'If you's don't mind me sayin', the timelines don't add up to the Hicksons being involved.'

Ryan gave a knowing smile. 'I'd tend to agree if it wasn't for these.' He held up a sealed evidence bag. Inside, two shotgun cartridges were clearly visible.

'It seems Ivor Hickson has a penchant for hiding used shotgun pellets in his sock drawer. Now, why would he be doing that? The bloke doesn't even hold a firearms license.'

SIXTEEN

Nigel Trebilcock remained a country boy at heart, which meant he retained an inherent dislike for major roads, avoiding them whenever possible.

He set the co-ordinates for Tomkiss Plumbing into his satnav and programmed the GPS to avoid the A1. The journey was one of little more than three miles - eight minutes, according to the ETA - yet, ten minutes later, Trebilcock was lost.

He'd journeyed along Market Lane past the Poacher's Pocket, through the village centre of Dunston, and followed the device's instructions down Ravensworth Road and Wellington Road, only to find himself at a dead end.

He pulled up against a set of concrete bollards and massaged his temples. Nigel had spent the short journey glaring into the sun, and white spots danced across his vision. He closed his eyes until the star-like images faded before he decided to ask a local for directions.

Fat lot of good she turned out to be, a shake of the head and a 'Nee idea, pet,' her only response.

The satnav told Trebilcock he was only a hundred yards from his destination, so he set his phone to Google maps and tried on foot.

The route took him around a block comprised of an odd conglomeration of businesses: a bakery, discount tyre outlet, community centre, and the Tudor Rose pub.

The musky, sulphide smells of the Rivers Team and Tyne merged in a fishy assault on Trebilcock's olfactory organs. Momentarily disoriented, he glanced up at the signage on a street corner. He was on Railway Street with Staithes Road, home to Tomkiss Plumbing, to his left.

Sandwiched between a florist and a Social Club, an unprepossessing building - more like a domestic garage than business premises - bore a hand painted sign: Tomkiss Plumbing.

Trebilcock stood back and observed the building. Brick built and in need of urgent pointing, the premises didn't offer a positive first impression. There were no windows to the front of the building, only a faded copper-coloured metal door of the up-and-over variety. There didn't appear to be any other means of entry.

Trebilcock knocked on the door. It made a tinny sound. Not the most secure of mechanisms, Trebilcock observed, which probably accounted for the array of CCTV cameras and the prominently displayed Verisure alarm equipment.

He knocked again. 'Hello?'

Silence.

'Hello? Is there anyone there?'

'Hold on. I'll be with you soon,' a man's voice replied.

Finally, Trebilcock heard the man grunt as he heaved on a spring-loaded pulley and the door opened.

The proprietor looked to be in his mid-thirties, though premature flecks of grey at his temples made aging him difficult. 'Can I help you?' the man asked.

Trebilcock produced his warrant card. 'DC Nigel Trebilcock, City and County Police.'

The man crossed his arms across his chest. 'Yeah?'

'I wonder if I could have a word? I'd like to know which of your employees were engaged on some damp-proofing renovation work in January. The property was on Callaley Avenue, Whickham.'

'That'll be me.'

Trebilcock was taken aback. 'You don't need check? It was a few months ago, so it was.'

'It was me.'

'You're sure?'

'Of course I'm sure. I don't have any employees. Can't afford 'em. I do it all myself.'

'I see. In that case, could I step inside a moment? I won't take up much of your time.'

The man stretched out an arm behind him. 'Be my guest.'

The door squealed as the man pulled it shut. The interior was thrust into darkness. Trebilcock once again saw himself blinking away spots of light until his eyes adjusted.

When he opened them again, the man had flicked on a fluorescent tube light. Trebilcock looked around. The place not only looked like a garage - it WAS a garage.

Against one wall, random pyramids of materials were piled precariously on top of one another. The other side wall was more organised. A metallic sentry-box sized cupboard wedged itself snugly in the apex with the rear wall. Four pallets lined up side-by-side next to it, each stocked with either WCs, sinks, baths, or shower trays.

The back wall consisted of a metal frame which held several boxes of nuts, bolts, washers and other fixing devices. Propped against the frame, an assortment of various-sized piping stood in random disorganisation.

Alongside the racking, a shadow board contained the tools of the plumbing trade while in the centre of the concrete floor, three work benches stood weighed down by items from the proprietor's latest job.

'Interesting set-up you have, Mr Tomkiss. I assume you're Mr Tomkiss.'

'Joseph Tomkiss.' He didn't offer Trebilcock his hand.

'Have you been in business long?'

'I started this place, what, seven or eight years ago. Perhaps a bit less. Not entirely sure, if I'm honest.'

'Oi'm sure your tax records will confirm.'

The man's face dropped.

'Don't worry. That's HMRC's business not police,'

Trebilcock smiled.

'Look,' Tomkiss said, 'I've a lot on. What's this all about?'

'Do you remember the job I'm talking about?'

'Off the top of my head, no. Tell me a bit more, and I'll tell YOU a bit more.'

'The house had stood empty for a few months. When the prospective owners visited it, there'd been a burst pipe and the leak brought the ceiling down. Like oi say, it was Callaley Avenue, in Whickham.'

Tomkiss thought for a moment. 'Yes, I do remember. I thought it a bit puzzling because they asked me to repair the ceiling. I can turn my hand to a few things but I'm a plumber by trade yet the biggest job was the ceiling.'

'I see. So, it struck you as odd that they employed you and not a builder?'

Joseph Tomkiss snorted a laugh. 'To be honest, it was a job and one I was happy to do. Money talks, yeah? Plus, it's not too unusual in this day and age. I guess they thought a one-size-fits-all approach would be cheaper for 'em.'

Trebilcock nodded. It made sense. 'What did you make of them? The owners, I mean.'

'Don't think I ever met them. If I remember right, the Estate Agent give me the keys and I got on with the job. The house was empty, you know, so if something's gone missing, it's nothing to do with me. Is that why you're here? A burglary?'

Nigel didn't provide an answer. 'How long did the job take?'

'Not sure. The leak I'd sort in less than half a day. Repairing the ceiling,' he shrugged, 'I dunno. Four or five days? I'm guessing, mind.'

'Did you see anyone else at the property while you were there?'

Tomkiss considered the question. 'Now you mention it, I did think the next-door neighbours were a nosey pair. The weather was Baltic but they spent a lot of time in the garden.

115

At least, the bloke did. I thought it a bit dodgy.'

'Define *a lot of time*. You'd be busy working, so oi imagine you wouldn't spend long checking what the neighbours were up to.'

Tomkiss gave Nigel a wink. 'Let's just say I took my time on the job. Time is money for me and if the owning cat was away, the temporary mouse would play.' As an afterthought, he added, 'Don't quote that to Trustpilot, will you?'

'That's not what I'm here for, sir.'

The man squinted through one eye. 'What ARE you here for, exactly?'

'I'm not at liberty to say, sir. While you were working there, was there anything you observed outside? In the garden, for example?'

'Not as I recall, no. There again, I was more curious about the bloke in next door's garden.'

'One last thing, if we need it, could we access your inventory for the materials you used, and your costs?'

The man straightened. 'Why?'

'You do have them?'

'Not here, no.'

'That wasn't my question.'

'Yes. I have them.'

'Thank you.' Trebilcock pointed to the work benches. 'I'll leave you to it. I appreciate your time, so I do.'

Trebilcock walked from the garage and heard the metal doors scream their resistance as they lowered shut.

Inside the ink-black interior, Joseph Tomkiss stood with his back to the door, eyes closed.

'Fuck,' he muttered.

**

'Thank you for coming in at such short notice. I know how valuable your time must be at present.' Ryan extended his hand and Ivor Hickson took it, briefly. 'Please, have a seat.'

They were in a cold interview room in the basement of Whickham Police Station. Ryan had made it as informal as he could, moving the table to one side and topping it with biscuits and a flask of coffee while setting two chairs at angles rather than facing each other.

He'd brought down a side table and put a couple of magazines on it, together with a photo of Ryan and Hannah taken at Aysgarth Falls which he'd printed from his phone images.

It still looked and felt like an interview room.

'That's no problem. I appreciate you asked me to call in on way back from work rather than drag me away from it. I'm still puzzled why you wanted me to come here, though. Couldn't you have spoken to Marina and I at home, like you have done in the past?'

Ryan made a face. 'Not really, Mr Hickson.'

'Oh. Okay, then. Now, am I here to listen to information from you, or to answer yet more of your questions?'

The inference was clear but Ryan chose to ignore it. 'It's part of our background information-gathering process, that's all. It's a rather delicate matter, though, which is why I thought it best to talk at the station.'

'I'm intrigued. I have to say, I'd have thought there'd be other folk more likely to help you than me. I've told you a dozen or more times we've only just moved in. We can't possibly have anything to do with those bones.'

Ryan offered a faint smile. 'We ARE speaking to other people, Mr Hickson. Like I say, we're collecting information from several sources.' He rose from the table and filled two plastic cups from the flask's contents. 'Milk and sugar? A biscuit, perhaps?'

Hickson declined. 'It's very strange a child can just disappear and turn up in an unmarked grave in my garden. I can well-believe you'll have quite a job on your hands, Detective Sergeant.'

'You'd be surprised how many strange things happen in my job, Mr Hickson.'

'So,' Hickson said, shifting his weight from buttock to buttock, 'What can I do for you?'

'It's about your wife, sir.'

He paled. 'Marina? Has something happened to her?'

'No, sorry. My bad. Nothing's happened. I just wonder if you could tell us a little more about her state of mind.'

Ivor Hickson flopped back in his chair. 'I never know from one day to the next, to be honest. It's like sharing a house with a Nile crocodile some days. One day she's the loving, caring woman I married, the next she's a completely different person.'

'I see. Is she bi-polar, if you don't mind me asking?'

'Not as such, no. She's been like that ever since she lost our baby. It did something to her, and I don't know if she'll ever recover. Look, what's this got to do with things, anyway?'

'I believe she's on medication?' Ryan asked, ignoring Hickson's question.

'Yes. Various sedatives, from time-to-time. Please, don't tell the adoption agency. It'll finish her if they find out.'

'This conversation is entirely private, I promise. Is there anything else I should know about Mrs Hickson?'

'Private, you say?'

Ryan nodded.

Ivor sucked in air. 'She drinks more than she should, especially with the tablets, an' all.'

'Has she always liked a drink?'

'No. Not until the miscarriage and the hysterectomy. That's when it started. When everything started, really. The tablets, the drinking...' He raised his eyes to meet Ryan's. 'The flings.'

Ryan's eyebrows elevated.

'You must have guessed, Detective. After all, you've met him at our house.'

'Chaplin?'

'The very same.'

'You welcomed your wife's lover into your house?'

He laughed bitterly. 'I wouldn't call it a welcome. The man's a shit. An arsehole. A fucking twat.' He glanced away. 'Sorry, but it's how I feel. And there's been others, though Marina doesn't know I know.'

Ryan chose his words carefully. 'How do you feel about that?'

'Ha! How do you think I feel? I wish the man was dead.'

'Do you feel mad enough to kill him?'

Ivor Hickson's face sagged. 'Chaplin's not dead, is he? Don't tell me that. Jesus, it wasn't me. I can account for every minute of every day.'

'No, sir. He's not dead. I'm just assessing your strength of feelings towards your wife.'

'I love her. When she's not in one of her phases, that is.'

'Does she lie?'

'She doesn't exactly admit to sleeping around, if that's what you mean.'

Ryan delayed his response until Hickson made eye contact. 'What about other things?'

'No. I don't believe she does lie, even when she's off on one.'

'I see.' Ryan reached for an item hidden behind the photograph of Hannah and him. 'In that case, you'll accept that these belong to you?'

Ryan held up the evidence bag containing the spent cartridges.

Ivor Hickson's eyes widened. 'Where the hell…?'

'They were found in your home. Marina found them. She was worried about you,' he lied, 'And asked us to make sure you were okay. That's why I called you at work.'

Hickson's mouth worked but no words emerged. 'Bless her. I'm sorry I worried her,' he eventually mumbled.

'So they do belong to you?'

'Yes.'

'Is that all you've got to say for yourself?'

'I shoot rabbits, for fuck's sake. For sport. When we lived by the Moor, I used to go out at night, when Marina was asleep, or drunk, and have a pop at some rabbits. Let off steam after a hard day, you know?'

'No, I don't, actually. Do you still have a shotgun now?'

Hickson bowed his head. 'Yes.'

'Why?'

'Same reason. I disappear into the fields behind Parkway and The Foxhills and let rip. Before you ask, no: I don't have a licence.'

'Mr Hickson, I already know that. I'll be applying for a court order to have your gun impounded. In the meantime, no more lamping. Understand?'

A light went on in Ryan's mind. He needed to backtrack on the conversation. Something Ivor had said about where he did his shooting at the couple's old home.

'After your wife's troubles, did she adopt any unusual activities or hobbies?'

'I'm not following.'

'Anything spiritual, perhaps?'

Hickson laughed. 'Ouija boards and such like so she could communicate with our miscarried child? No, Detective. Even at her worst, she was never into anything like that.'

Ryan sipped his coffee, eyes watching Ivor Hickson across the brim of his cup. 'You lived next to the Town Moor. Do you think your wife could have visited a fortune teller? A tarot reader, perhaps?

Ivor Hickson gave Ryan a curious stare.

'Mr Hickson, did Marina ever complain about being attacked or, more specifically, pushed out of a caravan at the Hoppings?'

SEVENTEEN

Hannah remained unavailable. Ryan sent her another message.

'Nobhead here again. Can you ring me asap? It's about the Roswell incident.' Bloody predictive messaging. He tried again. *'Boswell incident at the Hoppings. It's important. Ta.* x'

By the time Ryan arrived returned to the office, Nigel Trebilcock was back at his desk. They swapped updates, and agreed the significance of Ivor Hickson's revelation was far greater than anything Trebilcock had found at Tomkiss Plumbing. Nevertheless, Ryan scribbled the name of Andy Reid on a sheet of A4 as a reminder to ask about his interest in neighbouring gardens. He stuck the sheet to the wall.

Next, Ryan called Aaron Elliot, who was as grouchy as Ryan had ever known him.

'I told you Rufus would be in touch when he had something for you. Just leave it a couple more days THEN you can get back to me if you've still heard nothing. Now, I have a customer waiting. I must see to him. 'Bye, Sherlock.'

'Thanks for nowt,' Ryan mumbled to a dead line. 'Eric, did you get anywhere on Chaplin?'

'He's not on our books. He's not a therapist. He's definitely not Marina Hickson's stepbrother. Apart from that, nada.'

Ryan interlocked his fingers. 'Right. I think I'm done for the day. Another good day's work, guys. If we ever get the path lab's report in the next decade or so, we'll be good to go. Get yersels away and we'll start again tomorrow.'

Nigel and Eric weren't about to disagree and they scuttled off leaving Ryan to clear a tray of ring-marked cups.

'Sod it,' he said. He had more important things to do.

**

'I've brought wor tea, Dad. My way of apologising for being a shit yesterday.' He dropped two cartons of fish and chips on the kitchen bench, leaving Kenzie in a tortured foment, before popping open the living room door.

Norman Jarrod ran a finger beneath red-rimmed eyes. 'Thanks.' He blew his nose loudly and wiped away a residual bogey with the back of his hand.

'Ah, Dad. Sorry, man. I know it was a shock for me but I had nee right to speak to you the way I did.' He sat alongside his father on the sofa. Took his hand. Norman Jarrod crumpled before Ryan's eyes.

'I know you didn't, son. I know,' he eventually managed to splutter. 'I thought I was over it but talking about things has brought everything back again. All these years, and I'm still not ower it.'

'I suppose it's not summat you get over easily. I know it's not the same, but when Hannah told me she'd lost the baby she was carrying, I felt the same - and I'd never had a chance to form a bond so it must be ten-times worse for you.'

Norman sniffed. 'You know, I never thought of that. Hannah hadn't told you she was pregnant until she told you she wasn't. You didn't know you had a sister until I told you that you hadn't. It must have been tough for you, Ry. I'm sorry.'

'Honestly, Dad, I never thought of Hannah and me once when you told me about Rhianne. Don't beat yersel' up about that.'

They remained alongside each other, hand-in-hand, for a long time.

'James should know,' Norman said, quietly.

'Aye. He should. Do you want me to tell him?'

Norman shut his eyes but gave the slightest nod of his head.

They resumed their silence. Kenzie's panting reminded Ryan their food was still in the kitchen.

'Can you face owt to eat, Dad?'

'Oh hell, aye,' Norman replied.

'I'll get the plates.'

'No. Don't bother. We'll have it out the carton like we did when your Mam and me took you and James down to Cullercoats. You loved that chippy next to the arcade.' Norman's eyes began to water again.

'Shut up, you soft owld codger. Get your laughing tackle round the scran. You'll feel better for it, I promise.'

They devoured their fish supper deep in their own thoughts. While Kenzie lapped up the scraps of batter from the trays, Ryan wondered how his father would take what he was about to say.

'Dad, do you think we should get a headstone for her?'

Norman didn't answer.

'I just thought it'd be somewhere to go if we needed, I don't know, to think of Rhianne, or for you to remember her.'

Norman's mouth curled. 'Oh, I divvent know about that, like.'

'It's just when Spud died, I had him buried in the pet wood. It doesn't seem right a dog had a proper burial and Rhianne didn't.'

'We did what we thought was best,' Norman said, defensively.

'I didn't mean it as a criticism. I think she'd have loved the spot where you spread her ashes. But me and James, we've got nowhere to think about her.'

'Is it even legal? I mean, there's no body. There's not even an urn. Can you just put a headstone down wi' nowt under it?'

Norman had made a good point.

'I don't know, and we won't until we ask. What do you think?'

'I think I need to think, that's what I think.'

'Of course. I just thought we could maybe take Gran. She'd like that.'

'Look, don't play the emotional blackmail card. I said I'd think about it.'

Ryan held up his hands. 'Okay. That's fine. That's all I ask. Meantime, I'll make a few enquiries about whether it's kosher.'

Norman took Ryan's cheek in his hands. Gently, he twisted his head until they faced each other. 'No. Not yet. I'll let you know when I've decided. For now, you can tell James. Careful how you do it, yeah?'

Ryan's phone vibrated in his pocket. 'Sorry, Dad. This will be Hannah.'

He looked at the screen. He didn't recognise the number.

'Hello?' he asked. Then again, louder 'HELLO - who is this?'

The voice at the other end of the line was more timid than quiet, barely audible.

'Is that DS Jarrod?' Ryan managed to make out.

'Speaking.'

'I'm Dr Cavanagh.'

Ryan's mind raced but drew a blank. 'Do I know you?'

'I work with Dr Elliot.'

'Ah, Rufus. Of course. Is this a courtesy call, or do you have anything for me, mate?'

The voice may have been little more than a hesitant whisper, but there was no hiding its meaning. 'I'm not your mate. I'm a professional. I'm Dr Cavanagh to you, if you don't mind.'

Ryan removed the phone from his ear and gave it a 'Get you' look. 'Right, Dr Cavanagh - what do you want?'

'I'm calling to give you some information.'

'Has Aaron checked it over first?'

A frosty silence, then, 'Yes, Dr Elliot has seen my report, though I'm perfectly capable in my own right.'

It crossed Ryan's mind that Cavanagh may have a problem with people or communication, perhaps he was on the spectrum, which would explain his preference for corpses rather than patients. 'Please, Dr Cavanagh,' he said with emphasis, 'Do go on.'

'The remains found in Callaley Avenue showed no sign of hip deformity or progressive extension of the ribcage. Elbow mobility appears to be uninhibited and the arms and legs are proportionate to the rest of the skeleton.'

'Howay, man. Talk in proper English, will you?'

'You wanted my report so that's what I'm giving you, Detective Sergeant.'

Ryan bit his lip to avoid saying something he'd regret. 'What, exactly, is your report telling me?'

'The remains are not those of someone with achondroplasia. In terms you may understand, the body is not a dwarf.'

One victim ruled out, Ryan thought. *Progress at last.* 'How long have the remains been in situ?'

'Impossible to tell at this stage. I will need a much greater analysis to determine that with any surety.'

'Shit. Okay, is there anything else for me at this stage?'

'There is. Closer inspection of the skeletal remains showed the subject had a broader pelvic sciatic notch with a raised auricular surface.'

Ryan rolled his eyes. 'Which means?'

'The body is that of a young female.'

Ryan's eyelids slid shut. He was back to square one. The bones were neither those of Stacey Boswell nor Graham Waitrose.

'How old was the girl at the time of her death?'

'I don't have that information.'

Ryan hid his frustration. 'You don't have it *now*, or you won't ever have it?'

'I don't have it at present. I suspect it will need the expertise of Dr Elliot to determine that.'

'Could you give me your best guess, then?'

Rufus Cavanagh's voice remained calm, quiet, and detached. 'I could, but I won't. I - we - are not in the business of back-of-a-fag-packet guesstimates.'

Ryan realised he'd get no further. 'Thank you, Dr Cavanagh.'

Ryan ended the call. He remained silent while he worked the implications through his mind.

He turned to Norman Jarrod. 'Houston, we have a problem.'

'Oh aye?'

'Yes. I need to get up the loft. We've gotta find Rhianne's death certificate. Like, pronto.'

**

The stepladder fell short of the loft hatch. Ryan took his weight on his forearms and levered himself through the narrow opening as if performing a move on P-Bars.

Inside was cold, drafty, and pitch black. He felt around the dusty surface until his fingers brushed against a plug. He found the switch and flicked it downwards.

Nothing.

'Sod it.' He fumbled for his phone and clicked on its torchlight. Ryan swept the faint beam from side to side.

The cramped space was jam-packed with rolls of carpet offcuts, uninstalled installation foam, battered suitcases, a stack of old vinyl records, and a multitude of cardboard boxes. The boxes seemed as good a place as any to start.

He crouched low and manoeuvred himself between the joists. The only noise was a faint whimper from the foot of the stepladders where Kenzie sat, bemused by his master's disappearance.

Ryan opened the first box. It was full of crockery and utensils. He recognised some from his grandmother's. Others were of unknown origin. He lugged the box to one side and opened another.

Rammed with yellowing envelopes and stacks of paper, this was more hopeful. He brushed a cobweb from his hair and began sifting through the items.

Old bank statements and guarantees for long-since broken or lost household items lay on top. Ryan set them to one side.

He scratched the top of his head as something crawled through his hair.

He opened the next set of papers. Ryan swallowed hard. They were old love letters shared by his parents. He gave them a cursory glance but they were too personal, too uncomfortable, for him to read.

The next box offered nothing of significance. The other boxes were stacked behind the suitcases. He lifted the one closest to him and was surprised by its weight.

He lay it flat and decided to inspect the contents.

His heart jumped at the documents lying on top: certificates, bound together with a knot of white string.

Ryan allowed himself a smile. This was all he needed to exonerate his parents from any connection to the Callaley Avenue remains.

Of course, he knew there was no connection, but *'knowing'* and *'proving'* were different matters. Once he found Rhianne's death certificate amongst the bundle, he'd have his proof.

He untied the string with trembling fingers. The first item unfurled in his hands. It was his parents wedding certificate, beneath it lay their birth certificates.

His heart leapt at his next find. *'Certified Copy of an Entry of Death'*, the heading read.

'Yes!! Thank God,' he said aloud. Until he read on. As soon as he saw the word *'Carcinoma'* he knew he'd found his mother's Death Certificate.

Ryan's own birth certificate was next in line, then his brother's. Another surprise - James's certificate showed he'd been registered at birth as Norman James Jarrod. 'Well I never.'

The next find brought an unexpected pang of emotion. Rhianne's birth certificate. Somehow, its presence made everything seem real. He sat in solitude for a few moments before continuing his search.

'What? No. That can't be it.'

It was. There were no more certificates in the suitcase. All that remained were a collection of faded photograph albums. Filled with melancholy, Ryan flicked through them until he could see no more for the tears in his eyes.

Mam and Dad's wedding album. Childhood holidays with Ryan still in a pushchair. His first school photograph. An image of a tiny Ryan cradling a new-born James in his arms with his Mam watching them tenderly from a maternity ward bed. Doris Jarrod, his grandmother, with one boy either side of her at a time when her eyes sparkled with life, wisdom, and empathy.

Ryan wiped his eyes and sniffed noisily. This was harder than he'd expected. Much harder.

He opened another album and stared at it, wide-eyed. For the first time, he was seeing the short life of his sister. He saw her first as a babe in arms, then watched her grow into a pretty, blonde-haired girl. He knew from her smile she'd been a happy child, full of fun and, no doubt, mischief.

Ryan recognised the interior of the house in Callaley Avenue in some of the shots. He closed his eyes and held his head in his hands, but the reminder of recent events in the street spurred him on.

First, though, he wanted a photograph of Rhianne to keep for himself. He never took the torchlight or his eyes from the picture he'd selected as he unlatched the next suitcase.

Rhianne had the most captivating blue eyes, Ryan thought. Mesmeric, was the description which entered his mind.

He thought of Nancy Douglas's words. '*She had the most beautiful eyes.*' He set the photograph down beside him and shone the light towards the next suitcase as he opened the lid.

'Jesus Christ!' Ryan gasped. He scrabbled backwards, head rattling against the timbers, wooden splinters digging into his fingers from the floorboards. He didn't care. He just had to get away from the thing in the suitcase.

The girl wore a frill-collared blouse. Her chalk-white face bore large, glossy, blue eyes. Their unseeing stare remained trained on Ryan.

'Fuck. Fuck!! FUCK!!!'

'Ryan? Are you okay? What's going on up there?' Norman Jarrod's voice bellowed through the open hatch.

Ryan ripped his gaze from the monstrosity and turned towards the loft opening. The top of Norman's head poked through the gap.

Ryan glanced back at the suitcase - and saw the thing again.

'I'm aal reet. I think.' His voice came out weak and high-pitched.

'What's all the screaming about?'

'Nothing. I made a mistake, that's all. I'm done here now. I'm coming doon.'

Ryan flicked off his phone torch and the ghastly child-size porcelain doll disappeared into inky blackness.

EIGHTEEN

Ryan stretched out on the cream leather sofa in his house on The Drive, frustrated at his fruitless search and a little embarrassed at the doll incident, even though it truly was the stuff of nightmares.

He knew the skeleton had nothing to do with his family, and he knew it wouldn't be too difficult proving it. The trouble was, the easiest way to find proof was via his work equipment. To do that, he'd have to reveal his reason for looking into it and, by default, the family connection to Callaley Avenue.

Kenzie lay curled up in his bed alongside the sofa. Ryan reached down to toy with the pup's ears. The dog sat up, alert, then settled again with a double thump of his tail.

Ryan sighed. Much as it pained him, Rufus Cavanagh's findings left him with no option but to step back from the case. Explaining it to Kinnear would be difficult. He could trust Stephen Danskin but, really, he should tell Hannah first. After all, she was the first to warn him of the potential consequences.

For the fourth time that day, he called her. For the first time, she picked up.

'Hi Nobhead,' was her greeting. 'I was about to call you.'

'Really?'

'Aye. You wanted to know something about the Boswells.'

'Oh, that. I'd forgotten. It doesn't matter now. They're not in the equation anymore.'

'Hmm,' Hannah mused. 'You sound a bit flat. Is everything okay?'

'Nah, not really.'

'Howay, then: spit it out.'

'Where do I start? It's a bit complicated, to say the least.'

'Try me. I'm a good listener. Most of the time.'

Ryan snickered. 'Ta, but if you don't mind, I'd rather not go into it right now.'

'If you're sure.'

'Yeah, I'm sure.' After a pause, he said, 'I am sorry, you know.'

'You told me.'

'Not the same by message, though, is it? Seriously, I was wrong to say what I did. I'm sorry. There, I've said it again. Just…just don't make a meal of it, yeah?'

Hannah laughed. 'You win.'

'Hannah?'

'That's me.'

'Will you tell the DCI - both the DCIs - that I'm stepping away from the Callaley case?'

Hannah breathed in noisily. 'You're not, are you?'

'Aye. Listen, something's come up which means I shouldn't be involved until Aaron Elliot is able to confirm one or two things.'

'Are you sure you're okay?'

'Yes, man.'

'You're not in trouble?'

'Bloody hell, man. What's with all the questions? You wanted me to stand back days ago.'

'Hmm.'

'And stop saying 'Hmm', will you?'

'I will once you promise me something.'

'Go on,' he said, hesitatingly.

'When you say you'll stand back, you really will stand back. No going it alone or going rogue. It wouldn't be the first time, would it?'

'Aal reet. Point taken. No, I promise I won't. I think it'll only be a couple of days before Aaron tells me what I need - at least, I hope it is - then I'll be back on it.'

Hannah promised him she'd square it with Danskin, and she was sure he'd let Kinnear know in a way which didn't cast suspicion.

'Cheers, Hannah. I owe you a drink.'

'Just a drink? Is that all?'

Ryan laughed. 'We'll see.'

'I'll hold you to it, mind. Anyway, have you enough to occupy yourself with until Aaron comes up trumps for you?'

'Oh hell, aye. There's a few developments in the case I need to share with Treblecock and Eric before I step away, then there's some personal matters to attend to.'

'Such as?'

'Personal ones. That means private, comprendez?'

'*Ryan Jarrod - man of mystery*, eh? Okay, I take the hint. I'll butt out.'

'Thanks again, love.'

'What was that you called me?' she chided.

'You heard.'

'Yeah, I did. Thanks right back attcha, Ryan.'

She ended the call. Suddenly, life seemed better to Ryan.

**

The following day dawned as an archetypal Spring morning. Daffodils bent double in a blustery wind, isolated grey clouds whizzed across the sky as if by time-lapse photography, the sun shone at the same time as rain fell, and a rainbow arched over St Mary's Church in perfect symmetry.

Ryan didn't know why, but he felt good. Better than he should under the circumstances. His hand went to his jacket pocket where he touched the photograph of Rhianne.

That's why he felt good, he realised.

He hummed the eponymous James Brown song as he entered the office in Whickham Police Station, poured himself a cup of hot sludge, and waited for Trebilcock and Ross to arrive.

'Morning both,' he greeted them as they entered together.

'Somebody's in a good mood, so they are,' Trebilcock

commented, Styrofoam mug of proper coffee in hand.

'Don't know if that's good or bad,' Eric mumbled through his Co-Op breakfast sandwich.

'Okay,' Ryan announced. 'We have progress.'

He ripped the photo of Stacey Boswell from the wall. 'I've had an interim report from pathology. The remains aren't those of Stacey.'

Trebilcock raised his eyebrows in appreciation of the progress.

'Secondly,' Ryan continued, 'The bones are of a female child.' He stretched up the wall and removed Graham Waitrose's photograph.

'Where does that leave us, then? Eric asked.

'It leaves us with nee idea who's remains they are, that's where.'

'Balls,' Eric commented.

Trebilcock echoed the sentiment in his native Cornish tongue. 'Malbew!'

'Divvent worry, lads. Yes, it's disappointing - but it's also helpful. Assuming we are looking at a crime - and let's remember, we still don't know for sure that's the case - the fact it's not the Waitrose boy means there's no obvious motive for either Samson Boswell or Erin Goodwin or, for that matter, Stacey Boswell being involved.'

Ryan didn't remove their photographs from the wall but he did reposition them to one side. 'Slowly but surely, we're getting there.'

'Oi'm not sure we are, Ryan. All we've achieved is to make a big empty 'ole even bigger, if you arsk me.'

'In that case, I'll leave it up to you to fill some of the gaps while I'm away.'

'While you're what?'

'Away. Only for a couple of days, I reckon.'

Eric studied Ryan. 'You're off the case?' he said with meaning.

Ryan smiled his appreciation at Eric's subtleness. 'To an extent,' he said. 'I'll be chasing up the outstanding forensics and pathology information with Rufus Cavanagh and Aaron Elliot, and I've a few other things to do.'

'What about us?' Nigel asked.

'You're a big boy now, Nigel. See what more you can find out about the lot we've got left on the wall. You never know, any of them could still be connected to the case. The Hicksons, the Waddell fella, who knows - even your plumber might be worth a second look. You're in charge for the time being, but I'm always at the end of a phone if you need me.'

Ryan breezed out the office.

'And then he was gone,' Trebilcock said to himself.

**

On a whim, Ryan pulled a sharp right across traffic and meandered the Peugeot around the narrow confines of Church Chare.

Parked tight against a stone wall so he didn't block the road entirely, he squeezed out and made for the picturesque parish church of St Mary the Virgin. He didn't know what he was going to say, or who he was going to ask, but he'd made his mind up to ask something of someone.

Ryan circumnavigated the church before finding its heavy wooden double-doors. Was he supposed to knock? He had no idea, so he didn't.

The interior was larger than he expected. Rows of standard-issue pews, hued from hardwood oak, stretched across the church with a narrow walkway cutting through them. Set high in one wall, an impressive stained-glass window cascaded warm, kaleidoscopic colours across the nave, although the atmosphere within remained frigid.

An elderly woman sat hunched in a front-row pew, head bowed. Ryan didn't know who she was, but he guessed she wasn't the Vicar. Or Dean. Or whatever the bloke in charge was called.

A side door creaked open and a bespectacled man in a

brown corduroy suit entered. He cradled a pile of hymn books in his arms, which made him appear official enough for Ryan to approach.

Rather stiffly, the man told him he'd have to speak to the Reverend about his request. No, the Reverend wasn't in the building, he was out counselling a recently bereaved parishioner. Anyway, the man said he'd never heard of such a request before and doubted his Reverence would accede to it.

Feeling well-and-truly rebuffed, Ryan stepped out into the comparative warmth of the village square, wondering '*Where next?*' The Methodist Chapel, squeezed into a narrow slot further along Front Street adjacent to the Gibside Arms hotel, which Ryan always thought a strange location for a Methodist church, didn't have a graveyard, as far as he knew.

Blaydon had a cemetery. A large one, at that. And, he believed, it had an area set aside for plots dedicated to those who chose fire over earth. Did it have a church attached? He hadn't a clue.

Ryan found his car suitably ticketed by a traffic warden, but that was the least of his concerns as he made the short journey to Blaydon and its cemetery.

Inside the graveyard's wrought iron gates sat a cramped-looking stone bungalow. Even Ryan realised this wasn't a church. He began the steep climb up the cemetery's shaded paths and jumped when a gentle voice spoke to him.

'Good afternoon, young sir. It's a gorgeous afternoon, isn't it?' the voice said.

Ryan turned to witness a rotund, florid-faced man with a kindly smile. He was completely bald and, Ryan noticed, equally shorn of eyebrows.

The man reminded Jarrod of a Dickensian, pre-weight loss Matt Lucas but, more importantly, he wore a white dog collar around his neck.

Ryan introduced himself, explained his dilemma and, to his

astonishment, discovered the Reverend Murray Appleby thought the idea of a memorial to Rhianne a wonderful gesture.

So wonderful, Ryan found himself accepting an invitation to Saturday evening tea with Appleby to discuss the idea further.

Ryan smiled to himself when he thought what Norman Jarrod's reaction to the invite might be, but his smile receded when he considered his final duty of the day.

He brought his car keys from a trouser pocket with his right hand and patted his back pocket with his left.

The object was still there.

'One ring to bind them all,' he mused.

**

The route from Blaydon took Ryan over the Tyne's eighth - and least known - major crossing. Once across the Scotswood Bridge, the drive to Lemington lasted only a few minutes.

By the time he pulled up outside Muzzle's house on Hulne Terrace, Ryan had a well-developed strategy in mind: he'd wing it.

'Oh, it's you,' she said, answering his knock.

'Well, it's lovely to see you, too, Germaine.'

She looked around exaggeratedly. 'Nope. No-one called Germaine here.'

'Do I really have to call you Muzzle all the time?'

'That's my name.'

Ryan rolled his eyes before they settled back on his brother's girlfriend.

She wore heavy boots, tight black denim jeans held up with a faux-bullet belt, and a loose-fitting Elizabethan-style blouse complete with frilled cuffs and collar. With her white make-up, Ryan thought she bore a worrying resemblance to the doll in Norman Jarrod's attic.

Instead of inviting him inside, Muzzle stepped from the house and pulled the door shut behind her.

'Isn't he in?' Ryan asked.

'Yes, Jam Jar's in.'

Ryan tisked at the use of his brother's nickname. 'Can I see him, then?'

She stared at him with emotionless eyes and blank features. 'No.' Her voice was sullen and downbeat.

'Can I ask why not?'

She barked a bitter laugh. 'Do I look the marrying type?'

'Oh. He's asked you, then.'

'I got it out of him, yeah. He wasn't himself. All on edge. Eventually, he had to get it out of his system.'

'You said '*no*', I take it.' Ryan hoped his sense of relief didn't come over in his voice.

'Of course I said no. That's not something I want to do, ever. Understand?'

Ryan held his hands aloft. 'Nowt to do with me.'

Muzzle kept her cold eyes on Ryan, her face unreadable. 'He said it was your idea.'

'What? Now, had on a minute…'

The rays of the lowering sun sparkled off Muzzle's face-piercings in contrast to her gloomy visage. 'Are you calling him a liar?'

Ryan breathed in between pursed lips. 'All I said was he should do something to cheer you up. I meant buy you some flowers, take you out for the night, pay for a new tongue stud or whatever. I didn't expect him to ask you to marry him, for God's sake.'

'Why the hell would I need cheering up?'

'Because he said you were a bit miserable.'

Muzzle spat another laugh. 'Of course I was miserable. I like miserable. Miserable is what I do. I was miserable before and, Heaven knows, I'm miserable now.'

Ryan didn't know if she'd deliberately quoted Morrissey or not so he contained his smile. 'Okay. I get it. I didn't suggest he marry you, though.'

She cocked her head to one side. Smacked her lips together.

137

'Okay. I believe you. Now, will you leave me in misery?'

'Are you okay? I mean, not like you were before you met him, you know?'

'Like, a manic depressive, suicidal loon? No, not like that at all.'

'Good,' Ryan said, and meant it. 'What about James, though?'

'He'll get over it. He's more embarrassed than anything. We're still good, Jam Jar and me, if that's what you mean.'

'Good,' he repeated. Again, he meant it. '*I don't think now's the best time to break the news to him about an unknown sister,*' Ryan thought.

'Okay. I'll leave you to it. See you, Muzzle.'

The door closed in his face before he got a reply.

Ryan fingered the ring in his pocket as if he were a Baggins and it, his precious.

NINETEEN

The end of a long working day beckoned DCI Stephen Danskin towards the exit door. He had one final task to complete first.

Rick Kinnear was surprised to learn DS Jarrod had asked to temporarily stand down from duties at Whickham, but it didn't worry him. Jarrod's term of duty with Kinnear's team was almost over and the case he was working on - the unknown remains discovered in the garden of a pleasant suburb - hadn't been confirmed as a crime one week on from the find.

The only request he made was for Danskin to relay the news to Superintendent Sam Maynard.

Danskin poked his head around the Super's door. 'Can I have a word, ma'am?'

'Of course, Stephen. Take a seat.'

Stephen Danskin pulled the chair up to Maynard's desk. 'It's about DS Jarrod.'

Maynard set her pen down. 'Ryan? Is he okay?'

'Yeah, he's fine. Thing is, he's asked to be temporarily stood down from the case he's working on for Rick.'

Maynard looked surprised. 'That's not the Ryan Jarrod I know. What's the issue?'

Danskin paused. 'It's complicated. I don't know the full story but I understand he's only just learned he has a remote connection to the property where the remains were found.'

Maynard raised her eyebrows. 'Difficult position for him. What's the connection?'

'Ma'am, do you trust me?'

'Implicitly. Why?'

'Because Jarrod told me in confidence. It's personal and I'd prefer not to disclose it.'

'Curiouser and curiouser, said the cat.' Her eyes bore into Danskin. 'How remote a connection?'

'Very,' Danskin lied, 'But he felt it may present a conflict of interests.'

Sam Maynard rocked back and forth in her seat. 'I see.' She considered the revelation for a moment. 'Okay. I trust you and I trust Ryan. He's doing the right thing.'

Danskin breathed out in relief. 'Thank you, ma'am.' He stood to leave.

'Just a minute, Stephen. Ryan isn't your charge at present. What does Rick have to say on the matter?'

'He's cool, ma'am. That's why he suggested I should tell you, seeing as Jarrod will be reporting to me when he returns to Forth Street.'

'Okay. That makes sense. Keep me informed, though, Stephen. Ryan's one of our best and I don't want him sitting on his hands any longer than necessary.'

'Of course, ma'am.'

Danskin had no intention of keeping Maynard informed. He trusted Jarrod, but he also knew him.

Ryan Jarrod would be back on the case the moment he had an inkling his family were in the clear.

**

Joseph Tomkiss' last job of the day was an unpaid one. The job was simple, done as favour for an old customer. He was in the area anyway but he didn't hang around a moment longer than necessary. Once finished, he was in-and-out like a fart in a colander.

The plumber locked the door to his Athol Street flat behind him. He'd grabbed a Chinese from a local takeaway and forked the meal straight from its tinfoil carton with little enthusiasm.

He was tired, achy, and worried. The visit from the cop with the strange accent perturbed him. Was the job he did in

Whickham all those months ago just an excuse for DC Trebil-whats-it to gain entry to the lockup? Did the detective know half his gear was knock-off? Or should he really be concerned over events in Callaley Avenue?

Something or someone had prompted the cop's visit - and the fact he didn't know who, or what, troubled him.

There was one thing Tomkiss did know for sure: it was time he kept a profile as low as a snake's belly.

**

Marina Hickson felt as composed as she ever remembered.

She knew what had to be done. She knew it'd be painful and that it was only the beginning not the end, but she needed her life back. This was the only way she'd achieve it.

Marina switched off the table lamp and became swaddled in the warmth of night. Her smart watch flickered to life, briefly. She checked the time.

He was due home.

It'd soon be over.

**

Where Marina Hickson remained calm and composed, Andy Reid provided juxtaposition. He paced the darkened dining room of the house next door with the angst of a child who's pet hamster had passed away.

He looked through the window at the night's darkness; out to where he knew his garden lay in hiding.

'Damn Nikki and her fears', he thought. Until she'd mentioned the find next door, he'd put the consequences of the discovery out of his mind. Now, the thought of it very much dominated his reasoning.

'Things will never be the same again; our future has changed forever. Why did she have to say anything, the silly woman? Why?'

**

Des Waddell picked at a sore, both literal and metaphorical.

Dried blood flaked from the scab on his thumb while he ruminated on his past deeds. He wasn't proud of himself; he wished he had nothing to hide but hide he must.

He knew it would be prison for him this time if they ever found out. Des Waddell wasn't cut out for prison. He'd never survive. Prison would be his end of days.

Fresh blood oozed from the old wound as he wished events along the road hadn't brought him to the attention of the police. Again.

**

Across the avenue, Nancy Douglas squinted at the wall clock.

Nine-thirty.

She set down her knitting needles and three balls of lurid coloured wool so she could sip her nightly Ovaltine. She didn't like the stuff but it was her routine and, at her age, routines were important.

She cleared the mug into the kitchen, rinsed it, and nibbled a bourbon biscuit. All part of her routine.

Nancy checked the front door was locked, ensured the conservatory door was secure, and returned to the living room. Her nightly routine.

She made sure all was where it should be, straightened the family portrait on the wall, and tucked her knitting beneath the coffee table. Routine.

Nancy pulled the blackout curtains together, relieved to discover they met. She changed for bed, flicked off the bedside lamp, and opened the curtains again.

Nancy Douglas, invisible in the darkness of her bedroom, lay her hands on the windowsill and stared at the house across the road. The house of Marina Hickson.

Routine.

**

Away from Callaley Avenue, Norman Jarrod closed his eyes. He knew sleep wouldn't come. Not tonight. Would it ever?

Memories of Rhianne flooded his thoughts. Good times. Happy times. Sad times.

The best of times and the worst of times.

Norman pictured himself with Rhianne, gathering conkers

from beneath her favourite tree. Back home, Rhianne's mother would pickle them in vinegar, before threading string through them. Norman remembered Rhianne's squeal of delight whenever his conker split, and he heard her squeal in pain when the nut rapped against her wrist.

Those times were long gone and there was no going back.

Not now the skeleton was out the closet.

TWENTY

A blue VW pulled to a halt between streetlights outside the home of Des Waddell. The driver peered down the street. No-one saw him.

The house he watched lay as if silently asleep. The man in the VW curled his mouth. Something wasn't right.

He started the engine and the car crept towards its target. As he approached, he spotted a car parked on the driveway, part-hidden by a privet bush.

Marina Hickson was home and, he guessed, in bed.

He pulled towards the drive, dimmed the VW's headlights, and switched off the engine. The car coasted to a muted halt alongside Marina's vehicle.

Carefully, he tried the handle on the front door. It opened. The man crept inside and closed the door behind him, ensuring it made no sound.

The staircase loomed dark and forbidding in front of him. He thought about going straight to her bedroom, but he wasn't ready. Not yet.

He knew where the drinks cabinet stood, what optic housed which spirit, and where the crystal tumblers were kept. A voddie would help him unwind before he headed upstairs.

On tiptoe, he made for the lounge. Quietly, he opened the door. Just an inch at first, then further. He edged through the gap.

The man brought his hand to his eyes as light, harsh and unexpected, blinded him.

'What time do you call this?' Marina asked.

'For Christ's sake, woman. You nearly give me a heart attack. What are you playing at?'

'You're late.'

'So what? Look, I've got to make time up somehow. I've lost out on work because of this frigging house, not to mention looking after you.'

'Oh, of course. Ever the martyr, aren't you?'

'As it happens, I am, most of the time.'

'Apart from when you're belittling me.'

Ivor breathed in deeply. 'Helping you. That's what I'm doing. I'm helping you.'

'Are you? Are you really helping me?'

Now that he was over the initial shock of discovering Marina sitting in a darkened house, something struck him. Despite the argumentative words, his wife seemed different. Although there was nothing new in their disagreement, she seemed calm and controlled.

'I take it you've taken your tablets,' he concluded.

'As it happens, no. I've thrown them out.'

'You've what?'

'You heard. Washed them down the sink.'

'Drink, then. Is that it?'

She waved a hand in the direction of the drink's cabinet. 'What drink? There isn't any. It's gone to the same place.'

His jaw sagged. 'Not my twenty-one-year-old Aberfeldy, surely?'

'I said all of it.'

'That cost a hundred-and-eighty quid!'

'Oops. Sorry.'

'You mad bitch!' Ivor took a menacing step towards her.

Instead of cowering from him, she rose from her seat and faced up to him. 'A bitch, possibly. But not a mad one. Nor am I YOUR bitch. Not anymore.'

'Fucking Chaplin! He's welcome to you.' He backhanded her, Marina's head swinging to one side on impact.

She didn't cry. She didn't beg to be left alone. She didn't plead with him. Instead, she smiled.

'I don't need anyone.'

'You don't, do you? Little old pathetic, helpless Marina? The neurotic who wants everyone to sympathise with her. Women lose babies every day, man. There's childless women in every corner of the world. They'd all love a child of their own, but they're not obsessed by it.'

'Neither am I.'

'Ha! You've flipped again, haven't you? I've lived with your obsession for years. We're only in this fucking haunted house because of it.'

Marina lowered herself back to the sofa. She patted the seat next to her. 'Sit down, Ivor. Please, sit next to me.'

He raised his eyes. 'See what I mean? You've gone all nicey-nicey again.'

'SIT. DOWN!'

Ivor sat.

'You're not wrong. I have been obsessed. It's all I've thought about for years. Not any longer, though. Something happened today. Something that made me realise life is for living,' she said, quoting the stranger with the dogs by Clockburn Lake, 'And I haven't lived for a long, long time. A child isn't meant to be. If we adopted, it wouldn't be the same. I know that, now. So, from now on, I'm turning a new page.'

Ivor stared at her, disbelievingly. 'I'm not hearing this.'

'Then, you need to listen. It's time for a new chapter in my life...'

'Good,' he said, doubt written large in his voice.

'...Without you,' Marina said.

Ivor's jaw dropped.

'I don't need you,' she reinforced.

'Fucking Chaplin. I knew it! The bastard!'

'It's nothing to do with Morris.'

'There's another?'

She shook her head. 'No, there's no-one. I don't need a crutch...'

'A crutch? Is that what I am?'

Marina looked at him, genuine sadness in her eyes. 'Looking back over these last few years, yes - that's what you've been.'

'You...you...' he couldn't find the words.

'Your stuff is in the dining room. I'd like you to take it and go.'

'What the...?'

'The quicker it's over with, the sooner we get on with our lives.'

'I'm not going anywhere. It's my fucking house.'

Marina smiled. 'I'm sorry, Ivor, it's not. It's our house. At least, it is until it's sold. It's going on the market tomorrow. Don't worry, when it's sold, you'll get your share.'

Ivor desperately needed a slug of Aberfeldy, a hundred-and-eighty quid or not. But he didn't have any. He didn't have anything. Marina had seen to that.

'I'm not going anywhere. You can piss off to Chaplin's. I'm not moving.'

She brought something from behind a cushion. 'You are moving. See this? It's a restraining order drawn up by my solicitor.'

'A what? You're not right in the head. Why would you want one of those?'

She turned her face to one side. Pointed at the fading red mark on her cheek, then down to a tiny red light showing from the lower shelf of a bookcase.

'You hit me. We both know it's not the first time, either. I realised today it's YOU who turned me to drink, YOU the medication hid me from. It had nothing to do with children. I was hiding from you but I'm hiding no longer, Ivor Hickson. I'm not running, either. YOU are the one doing the running.'

She pointed again at the hidden camera and waved the formal letter in his face. 'I've got all the evidence I need to enforce this order.'

Ivor's mouth was stretched, lips drawn back; teeth exposed like an alpha male baboon. Except, he was no longer an alpha male.

'Like I said, your gear's all in the dining room. Now, go, won't you? Just go.'

**

Ivor Hickson loaded the bin bags and suitcases into his VW in a trance-like state. This couldn't be happening, surely. Not to him. Not to them.

All the shite he'd put up with over the years, yet it was he who was out on his arse.

He slammed the side window with the palms of his hands. Kneed the underside of the dashboard. Stomped his feet against the floor. Yelled a string of obscenities to himself.

With narrowed eyes, he took in the frontage of the house, his senses taking in every inch of it. His eyes came to rest on the front bedroom window.

In his mind, he saw Marina and the blubberous Morris Chaplin writhing beneath the covers, heard them mutter each other's names, listened to their orgasmic moans, and watched his wife roll off a satiated Morris Chaplin.

'Fucking bitch. Fuck fat bastard Chaplin. Sod the fucking house and the fucking thing in the back garden. Fuck them all.'

He closed his eyes and lay back against the headrest until it cradled his skull.

'Fuck the fucking skull!'

His fingers knotted around the steering wheel until his knuckles whitened. He realised he'd been holding his breath and let it out with a gasp.

His eyes opened wide and, for a moment, he imagined he'd seen a figure watching from an upstairs window across the street.

When he looked again, there was no-one there.

Ivor turned the ignition key and prepared to reverse onto Callaley Avenue for the final time. He looked over his shoulder but the view of the street was obscured by pile of belongings stacked high in front of the rear window.

He turned back towards the house. Switched off the engine. Opened the car door. He climbed out.

He climbed out because not all his belongings were with him.

Ivor Hickson made his way up the path leading to the rear of the house. He edged along the tall trees behind the back fence, and on towards the shed in the back garden graveyard.

He re-emerged moments later, a shotgun broken over his shoulder and a cache of cartridges in his pocket.

TWENTY-ONE

He watched the car drive off before cautiously making his way towards the house.

Through the windows, he saw the silhouette of someone moving around behind the curtains. The light in the front room extinguished at the same time as a new light illuminated a small pane of glass in the front door.

He assumed she was heading upstairs.

The man waited in the shadows. He cricked his neck as he waited for the stair light to switch off and the bedroom lamp go on. As soon as it did, the woman appeared in front of the window.

Heart pumping, the man crouched low until the woman reached up and wrenched the curtains together.

He waited a few moments in the cover of the darkened pathway at the side of the house. Satisfied he hadn't been seen, he hoisted his bag over his shoulder and slunk towards the rear of the house.

The man jumped at the sound of an owl hooting in the woods behind nearby houses. He waited for his pulse to settle before pulling the pen torch from his pocket as he made his way silently to the back garden.

He cupped his hand around the nib of the pen torch as he flicked it on. The light was faint, yet sufficient for his hand to take on an eerie, almost translucent appearance.

He aimed the torch at his feet and slowly removed his hand. Satisfied the beam wasn't noticeable, he pointed it towards the garden. The torch lit up an arc of little more than a couple of yards ahead of him.

As far as he could tell, the area was mostly lawn, sloping upwards and away from the house. He pointed his torch to his left-hand side. Shrubs framed the border with the neighbouring house, providing him a degree of cover in the area not shrouded by the white sheeting installed by the cops.

The intruder couldn't see as far as the rear of the garden, but he moved in the upward direction of it, keeping close to the cover of the hedge.

A creature, a cat or perhaps a small fox, scuttled in the undergrowth close to him. Automatically, he stepped away from it to his right and onto the lawn.

Instantly, a security light lit up.

'Balls!'

The light was solar-powered and, at this time of year, not particularly bright. Compared to his torch, though, it was as brilliant as a beacon.

He rolled into the cover of the shrubbery, a tympanic pulse thumping at his temples. The consequences of being discovered were unthinkable. He fixed his eyes on the rear door of the house.

To his relief, the door remained closed. No other light appeared at a back window. No-one called, 'Who's there?' like they would in a movie.

He closed his eyes for a moment and tempered his breathing. When he opened them again, the security light afforded him a clearer view of the garden than his feeble torch.

Tall, unruly Cypress-like trees protected the back fence. He saw the lawn near the back door had the beginnings of a terraced effect. One tier was complete; excavation of the second had barely begun. The work had come to an abrupt halt where…

The security light switched itself off. The garden disappeared into a black void.

But he'd seen it.

He swallowed hard, but he knew he must press on. The man repositioned his shoulder bag and inched towards, then along the edge of, the Leylandii trees.

The tree cover ended abruptly. He hoped he was close enough to the police sheeting on the western edge of the garden to remain hidden.

He switched his torch back on, sufficient to see an outer perimeter of brightly coloured tape. Inside the rectangular shaped cordon, he could just make out an inner cordon less than three yards square, bounded by white tape.

The man knew what lay inside.

'Oh crap.'

The harsh reality of the scene kicked him in the guts. He began to have second thoughts. He shouldn't be here. Shouldn't be doing this.

He flicked off the pen torch and hunkered down. The weight of his backpack as he lowered himself jarred him back to reality.

He'd come this far. He had no option, now. He had to go through with it.

The man lowered himself flat on his belly and crawled towards the mound of earth dug from the hole.

The lawn was damp, yet he stayed prone to ensure he didn't trigger the security light again. He mightn't be so lucky second time around.

In the darkness, he wasn't sure of the direction in which he crawled. He knew he must be close, but how close? Dare he use the torch again?

He fumbled for it in his pocket. Found the switch. The beam came on. And saw it illuminate the bottom of a muddy trench over which his head loomed.

'Bloody hell!'

The man had been inches for tumbling into the shallow grave.

He stared into the stark, bleak hole for a full minute. The thought of what had been down there made his flesh creep.

He shuddered violently.

A twig snapped in the night behind him. He jumped. Raised himself to his knees. The security light came on. He spun towards it, then back towards the source of the sound.

A figure loomed over him, silhouetted and all-the-more threatening because of it.

The only weapon he had to defend himself with was a four-inch pen torch. He didn't even have time to use that.

Strong arms hauled him to his feet. Clasped him so he couldn't move. He wriggled and thrashed, but there was no escaping the grip.

'Don't. Fucking. Struggle,' a voice whispered in his ear, low and menacing.

'*This is it,*' he thought. '*It's over. I'm done for.*'

'Stop struggling, and I'll let you go, okay?'

'*There's hope yet,*' he realised.

He stopped panicking. In turn, he stopped struggling.

He felt the pressure on him ease, just a little. He took a deep breath.

'That's better,' his assailant said.

The security light extinguished when their movement stopped. He realised he hadn't taken a good look at his opponent. In the dark night shadows, he knew the opportunity had flown.

'Now,' the newcomer said, 'What the bloody hell are you doing in this garden?' the man asked Des Waddell.

**

Waddell tried to muster a sense of false bravado. 'I could ask the same thing about you.'

'You could, but I think I've got more of a right to be here than you.'

'Ah, shit. You're a cop?'

'I might be.'

'Ah shit.'

Waddell still couldn't see much of the other man - he'd brought out a torch of his own and it shone blindingly into Waddell's eyes - but he knew he was taller, younger, and stronger than he.

Waddell's hand wrapped around his pen torch before he realised it was futile. It'd have no effect on the guy and, on top of everything else, he didn't want 'Assault on a Police Officer' as an addition to the charge sheet.

'You are?' the man asked.

'Des Waddell - but I'm sure you already know that.'

He did know, but he wasn't going to let Waddell know. The poor sod looked as if he might wet himself. He could use that to his advantage.

'And you were sneaking around in the dark, why?'

Waddell swallowed hard. Frantically tried to think of an excuse which might, just might, stand up.

'I...I was just curious. You know, to find out what had really gone on here. You know what the news is like, full of half-truths and such like.' He realised he was gabbling so forced himself to stop talking.

The cop remained silent, compelling Waddell to speak again.

'I bet you could tell me what happened. Then, I could go back home, y'know, forget aboot it all.'

'I can't discuss that with you.'

'No. Of course not. Sorry. I shouldn't have asked. Sorry.'

'You seem nervous,' the cop declared.

'I am. You know, being jumped like that. Wouldn't you?'

'It's not that you've something to hide, is it?'

'No. Not at all. Definitely not.'

The cop stayed silent. Waddell restrained himself this time. The whispered tones of the night filled the silence.

The cop continued to shine the torch into Waddell's eyes. 'What have you got in your backpack?'

Des Waddell withered in full sight. The game was up. He had one last chance. It was a hopeless one, but he had to give it a go.

'Reet. Okay. This is going to sound ludicrous, but I've got some rubbish I want to get rid of.'

The cop laughed. 'You're right. It does sound ludicrous.'

'I'll prove it.' Waddell lowered his backpack and unclipped the straps. He tipped out a load of smashed up metal, damaged circuit boards, and a sheet of glass.

For a split-second, the torchlight flashed onto the junk then back to Waddell's face.

'I don't drive,' Waddell continued. 'I can't get to the tip. Me bin's overflowing. Daft as it sounds, I thought I'd hoy it in the hole and cover it up with soil.'

'That's interfering with a crime scene, I hope you know.'

'*Shit. Another charge,*' he realised. 'I understand that, now. I'm sorry. Good job you stopped me. It wouldn't be a good look, I suppose.'

The light again left Waddell's face momentarily and shone on the discarded contents of the backpack.

Beam back on Waddell, the cop spoke again. 'Mr Waddell, those appear to be the remains of a computer. Am I wrong?'

Waddell took a deep breath. 'I'm saying nowt. And you'll find nowt on it, anyway. It's shot to shit.'

'I can see you made sure of that.'

'Aye, well. Sorry about that,' Waddell sneered.

'Okay, then. On your way.'

Des Waddell's mouth opened. 'You're letting me go?'

'I am.'

Waddell breathed rapidly.

'Thank you.'

'There isn't a great deal I can do about it anyway,' the cop laughed, turning his torch on himself.

Waddell gasped. 'You bastard!'

It wasn't a cop.

'It's that fucking neighbourhood watch guy. What's the nosey bugger called, again?'

Des Waddell searched his memory banks.

'Reid, that's the sod's name. Andy Reid.'

TWENTY-TWO

Morning sun warmed the conservatory as Nigel Trebilcock took a seat on a padded wicker chair.

'Thank you, Mrs Douglas,' he said. 'This be a lovely view you have from here.'

'It is. I don't often use the conservatory. I find it too cold in winter and stifling hot in summer. This time of year, it's just right.'

Nigel looked out over green fields and distant pastureland. On a hillside far away, horses grazed benignly in fields alongside a silver streaked Thornley Burn. For a moment, he was whisked back to the county he called home, serene tranquillity as opposed to brash urban noise.

'Could I offer you some tea? A currant bun, perhaps?'

'Tea would be just perfect. Thank you.'

Trebilcock dragged himself away from the panorama and followed Nancy into the kitchen.

'Make yourself useful,' she said. 'Milk is in the fridge behind you. Sugar in the drawer next to it.

He pulled out a carton of UHT milk and put it on the bench between Mrs Douglas and himself. 'Oi don't take sugar, I don't.'

'Nor me, but I like to have some in for guests. Your colleague likes his sugar.'

'DS Jarrod, or PC Ross?'

'The good looking one.'

'That be Jarrod.'

She poured boiling water into two China cups and dipped a tea bag in each. 'He reminds me of somebody but I can't think where from. Is he not working today?'

'No, Mrs Douglas. He's taking a few days off.'

'Pity. I like him. Not that I don't like you, of course,' she smiled. 'No offence.'

'None taken,' he assured her.

'Let's take these in the living room, shall we? I struggle to reach my cup on the table in the conservatory.'

Trebilcock agreed, with some reluctance. 'Thank you for your call last night, Mrs Douglas. It was very public spirited of you.'

She gave a dismissive wave. 'Nothing of the sort. My generation do that sort of thing. Always have done, always will. We like to keep an eye out for each other.'

Trebilcock sipped from a steaming cup. Despite the UHT milk, she made a good cuppa. 'Mmm. If your currant buns are as good as your tea, oi might regret turning your offer down.'

The woman beamed.

'Oi thought I'd call in to have a word. We despatched a car last night to make sure there wasn't any trouble. The officers saw nothing unusual in the area. We'd normally leave it at that, but seein' what's gone on lately in these parts, I thought I'd come see you myself. So, what exactly happened last night?'

'I was just getting ready for bed when I heard a bit of a ruckus going on outside.' She waved a blue-veined arm in the rough direction of the window.

Nigel caught a glimpse of the living room around him as he followed her signal. His eyes settled on the house opposite. 'Was it Mr and Mrs Hickson?'

'Aye. They were having a right ding-dong.'

'Do you know what the argument was about?'

'Oh no. I'm not the nosey type. Not me.'

Nancy Douglas smiled and Nigel couldn't decide if it was innocent or ironic. 'Then what?' he asked. He shivered uncontrollably. 'Brr.'

'Are you cold?'

'No.'

'What was that, then? You look like you've seen a ghost. Are you feeling ill?'

'Oi'm fine. Don't know what 'appened. Think someone walked over my grave, so's they did.'

'Your blood sugars must be down. Perhaps you should have a bun, after all.'

He chuckled. 'No, I'm fine.' He shook himself down. 'So, what happened next?'

'Ivor - that's Mr Hickson - drove off.'

'Anything else?'

She shook her head. 'Not that I can think of.'

He drained his cup. 'That was lovely, Mrs Douglas. Please, if you see anything else, don't hesitate to call. It's folk like you we police rely on.'

'Nice of you to say so, and I certainly shall. Thanks for calling by - oh, and tell young Mr Jarrod I said hello, won't you? I'm sure I know his name from somewhere, you know.' She shook her head. 'Age does funny things to the memory.'

'I'll see myself out, Mrs Douglas. Thanks again. I'll make sure a patrol car pops down the avenue once or twice tonight, just to ensure everything's fine.'

'That's very kind of you, officer.'

'No problem. You be sure to take care, won't you, Mrs Douglas?'

On the doorstep, Nigel Trebilcock looked up at the house opposite. He thought about having a word with the Hicksons, but a domestic dispute wasn't something for a detective to get involved with, especially on a Saturday.

Nigel shivered again. He had the odd sense he'd missed something. Something significant.

**

'That wasn't so bad after all, was it?' Ryan said to Norman Jarrod.

'I suppose not. Mind, I'm glad he had to change the time to this morning. I wasn't looking forward to cucumber sandwiches and crumpets.'

Ryan laughed. 'Nor me, to be honest. What did you make of Reverend Appleby?'

'You know, I thought he was a canny bloke. For a vicar, like.' Norman took off his tie as they walked and opened the top button of his shirt.

'What do you mean, *'For a vicar?'* Men of the cloth are meant to be nice blokes.'

'Aye but they're all preachy and *'strike you down with thunder'* and aal that shite.'

'Oh, and you'd know that, of course.'

They walked along Shibdon Road, towards the cemetery where Ryan had left his car.

'I could do with a pint, son. Fancy one?'

Ryan wasn't fussed but realised discussing Rhianne with a stranger must have been difficult for Norman. 'Where were you thinking?'

'The Bisley's just along the road back where we've come from.'

'Hadawayandshite. I'm not going there.'

'Why? There's nowt wrong with it.'

'Normally, no - but I think we're a bit overdressed for it, even if you have taken your tie off. Listen, there's a micropub not far from it. Let's give that a go, okay?'

Norman shrugged. 'Suit yersel.'

As it happens, Norman was delighted with his son's choice. He slugged back a Barista Stout while Ryan sipped a pint of Dunston Rocket.

'I think we should go for it, son,' he said at length.

Ryan wasn't sure if he meant another pint or the memorial they'd discussed with Murray Appleby, so he asked.

'The headstone, you knacker-heed. I wasn't sure about it but the more I think about it, the more I like the idea. I'm not particularly arsed, mind, but for your and James's sakes.'

'If you're sure. Don't worry about the cost. I'll pay.'

'Hadaway, man. No, I'm just a bit surprised Murray Appleby's happy to go with it.'

Ryan smacked his lips and held his pint up to the light. 'Nice,' was his verdict. 'Anyway, like you said, *he's a canny bloke'*. There's only one problem, though.'

'Which is?'

'James. He still doesn't know.'

Ryan's phone vibrated in his pocket. 'I'll just take this,' he said to Norman.

'Aaron, mate. You've finally decided to speak to me.'

'Indeed I have.'

'Good. I'll get more sense out of you than your apprentice. He's a bit retentive, isn't he?'

'You're on speaker phone here, Ryan,' Elliot said, alerting Jarrod to Cavanagh's presence.

Ryan smiled to himself. 'So, what have you got for me?'

'I have a more accurate age-range for your garden friend.'

Ryan felt his heart thump against his ribcage. 'Please, tell more.'

'I can give you the age with a two-year margin of error.'

'How old, man?'

'Eight.'

Ryan did the maths. The child was between six and ten. Although he never doubted it, there was now clear evidence the remains weren't those of Rhianne.

Which meant he was back on the case.

'Great work, Aaron.'

'It's Dr Cavanagh you need thank. He's the one who's done all the work on her. I've checked all the findings personally and fully corroborate his conclusions. Your victim was eight years old, give or take.'

Ryan let Elliot's words form in his brain. 'You said *'victim.'* Does that mean you have a cause of death?'

'I'm afraid not. On the balance of probabilities, though, I'd suggest the body of an unknown eight-year-old found buried in a garden indicates death was not due to natural causes.'

Ryan inhaled. 'Thanks, Aaron. Oh, and thanks to you, too, Dr Cavanagh.'

He just about heard the junior pathologist whisper, 'My pleasure,' before Aaron Elliot spoke again.

'If it's of any comfort to you, now we have the preliminary findings I'll be taking over the case from hereon. Once I have more information, I'll let you know.'

'One more quick thing before you go: how long was the body in the ground?'

'Don't quote me but given the comparative shallowness of burial and the absence of a significant presence of insect or bacterial life, '*Not long*' is the best I can do for you at present.'

'Brilliant. Thanks, Aaron.'

He terminated the call.

'Do you want the good news or the bad news?' Ryan asked his father.

'Stop arsing about and tell us, man,'

'The good news is we have forensic proof it isn't Rhianne. Also good is the fact that it means I'm back on the case.'

'And the bad?'

Ryan eyed his father.

'Because I'm back on the case, how do you feel about telling wor James about Rhianne?'

Norman made a horse-like noise. 'Bollocks.'

'Is that a '*yes, bollocks*' or a '*no, bollocks*'?'

'Aye. I'll do it. I'll be seeing him at the revenge mission ower the Mancs at St James' tomorrow. I'll tell him ower a pint. Let's hope we win to put him in a decent fettle, aye?'

Ryan wasn't listening. He'd turned his mind to other things.

Things like, if the skeleton was only recently buried, where the hell had the body been kept until then?

TWENTY-THREE

With the cause of death still uncertain, the name of the girl unknown, and the nature of any crime yet to be determined, there was no urgency for Ryan to return to the station. Instead, he spent Saturday evening and Sunday morning at home going over facts, probabilities, and, finally, possibilities.

By mid-afternoon Sunday, he'd made as much headway as he could. As it was Norman's turn to use their shared season ticket, Ryan considered watching the match on Sky. He caught the tail end of the early kick off before he thought of something better.

She answered on the third ring.

'Ah, if it isn't Nobhead himself,' Hannah joked, a smile in her voice. 'I wondered if you'd ever get round to calling me.'

'Wonder no longer. That drink I mentioned - how are you fixed for, say, forty minutes time?'

'Well, if you'll take me as I am, that'll be okay. If you want me glammed up like a supermodel, best make it forty-five minutes.'

Ryan laughed. 'Okay. How does Bar Blanc sound?'

'Osborne Road? That'll mean supermodel me. What about ordinary me and The Lonsdale?'

'It'll be rammed, mind, with the match on.'

'Supermodel me it is, then. See you in Bar Blanc.'

'Champion. I'll feed Kenzie and let him do his business then set off. I'll be on the bus and Metro because we might need a few drinks when you hear what I've got to tell you.'

'I'm intrigued. Tell me more.'

'Later, alligator.'

The thought of seeing Hannah lightened his mood. The anticipation of seeing a glammed-up Hannah meant he practically ran to the bus stop in his eagerness to get to her.

**

Bar Blanc sat within Whites Hotel, a three-minute walk from Jesmond Metro station. Hannah was already there when he arrived, occupying a shell-like bucket seat at a table-for-two up against a gaudy cerise-coloured divider.

She'd sprayed glitter on her curls and wore a short, tight-fighting gold coloured dress which perfectly complemented her tanned legs.

Hannah stood and gave Ryan a wave whilst beckoning him towards the seat alongside her.

'Sorry you've had to make do with ordinary me, after all,' she apologised.

'Kidda, if that's ordinary, bring it on.'

They kissed and took their seats, Ryan somehow avoided staring at her legs as she crossed them and smoothed down her dress.

She'd already set their drinks on the table; a trendy bottled lager for him and a fishbowl-sized glass of white wine for her.

'It's been a while since we did this,' he said. 'Too long.'

'Did what?' she teased.

'Like, a date.'

'Oh, is that what this is? Here's me thinking you were simply returning a favour.'

Ryan felt strangely nervous, almost like he had on their first date, what was it, almost six years ago or more? How had he forgotten? His hand shook slightly as he raised the bottle to his lips. They began speaking at the same time. Laughed. 'You first,' they said together. Laughed again.

They exchanged small talk. He got in another round of drinks at ludicrous cost. He slid his arm around her shoulders.

'I'm feeling honoured,' Hannah said, 'You choosing me over the match, an' all.'

'No contest,' he smiled while risking a peek at his smart watch to check for any score updates. 'Besides, I'm celebrating. I'm okay to get back on the case.'

'Wow! You live a really boring life if that's all you've got to celebrate.'

He coughed as he choked on his lager. Hannah thumped his back. Beer dribbled from his nose. They laughed again.

'You never told me what the fuss was all about, anyway,' she reminded him.

He played for time, taking a more controlled sip of beer.

'You're an only child, Hannah. Ever wondered what it'd be like to have a brother or sister?'

'Okay. A bit random, but okay. No, not really. I mean, I've barely got a Mam or Dad, let alone any siblings. In fact, Stephen's about the only thing I have got. He's been brilliant with me since I was a kid but, with working together, it's not really a father and daughter - or step-daughter - relationship.'

He gave a tight smile.

'Where's this going, Ry? Is there something up with James?'

He looked at her earnestly. 'If I tell you something, promise me you'll keep it a secret.'

She gave a half-smile, not knowing if he was about to say something serious or madcap.

'I've a sister as well as a brother.'

'What?' She set her fishbowl down with a thud.

'Aye, I've just found out I had a sister.'

'Where is she?'

'No, I said HAD a sister. She's dead. I never even knew her.'

'Bloody hell, Ry.'

He teared up. Blamed it on the drink but he was only onto his third. 'Aye. Don't say owt to anybody because wor kid doesn't even know yet.' He glanced at his watch. Ran a hand through his hair. 'But he will do soon.'

Hannah didn't know what to say, so she settled for, 'Fucking hell.'

Ryan wiped his eyes with a round, paper drip mat. It left his face wetter than before.

'That was a waste of time,' he said, tossing the scrunched paper over his shoulder.

They giggled, self-consciously this time.

'How did she die? I mean, you don't have to tell me but…'

'Nah. Not yet, Hannah. It's a bit raw. She was only four when she died…'

Hannah clicked her fingers. 'Oh Ry - that's why you stepped away from the case, wasn't it?'

He nodded.

'So, I'm guessing you've found out it wasn't her in the garden, which is the reason you're back on the job?'

'You'd make a bloody good cop if you tried hard enough,' Ryan joked.

She took his hand in hers. Placed it on her thigh.

'Let's get out of here. I've plenty booze in my apartment. Let's go there. It's quieter, more private, and a helluva lot cheaper. Let's get pissed out of our brains.'

'Pissed sounds good. Howay then, lass. What are we waiting for?'

**

Somebody else was pissed.

It had been a good week business-wise for Joseph Tomkiss and he was more than happy to share his profits with the landlord of the Dun Cow.

He'd arranged to meet Darren Haley at one o'clock but Tomkiss had been propping up the bar since opening time. When the local scrap metal dealer finally arrived, Tomkiss was already several sheets to the wind.

He'd heard that there was a time scrap merchants paid their customers for taking away their rubbish, not the other way around. Tomkiss knew he'd overpaid the man, but he didn't give a toss. He just wanted it gone.

Shortly before five, Joseph Tomkiss bid his farewells to Haley and stepped from the Dun Cow straight onto Dunston's busy Ellison Road.

He stopped dead as the fresh air hit him while getting his bearings and, somehow, staggered an S-shape route onto Ravensworth Road without being hit by traffic.

Tomkiss meandered his way towards home, singing all the wrong lyrics to 'If I Were A Rich Man.' He stopped at the junction with Kent Road, hugging a Give Way sign while gathering his breath.

He made it as far as the old Medical Centre before doubling over the wall and vomiting thickly. He spat out clotted filth and dragged his sleeve across his mouth.

'Fuck's sake,' he swore. He stood up straight. Swayed slightly. He opened his eyes wide then blinked several times until the street stopped moving. 'Jesus.'

A kid on a pushbike sped towards him. The bike reared up like something from the Calgary Stampede as its rider pulled a wheelie.

'Get out my way,' Tomkiss shouted, swatting at the kid as if he were a fly.

The lad responded with a cheerful, 'Grumpy git.'

Tomkiss was at the junction with Wallace Street when the lad's mate appeared out of nowhere.

He was on a skateboard, arms outstretched, when he saw the drunkard step in front of him. The youngster tipped the leading edge of the skateboard upwards and made to grab it as he jumped a dismount.

He missed.

The board careered into Joseph Tomkiss. Already unsteady on his feet, the impact knocked him sideways. His turned his ankle on the kerb.

'Stupid fucking idi...'

Tomkiss didn't finish the sentence before the street began moving again. This time, in large circular loops.

He didn't feel a thing until he landed flat on his back.

The brake lights of the blue car which had sent him flying flared momentarily, before it sped from the scene.

When Joseph Tomkiss looked down, he was grateful for the alcohol in his system. It helped deaden the pain.

Both his legs faced the wrong way.

TWENTY-FOUR

Trebilcock and Eric Ross hunched over a shared PC monitor, papers and images strewn across the adjacent desk.

Trebilcock pointed to something on the screen and PC Ross scribbled a line of notes on a post-it. He wandered to the incident wall, stuck it on an appropriate space alongside Morris Chaplin's photograph, and returned. Trebilcock's eyes flitted between the screen and a sheathe of papers on his desk.

Neither saw Ryan make his entrance.

'Morning all.'

His two colleagues jumped.

'What are you doing here, Sarge?' Ross asked.

'Ah well, I'm back on the case.'

'Already?'

'You sound disappointed, Nige.'

'Not at all. I just be surprised,' he said in his BFG accent.

'Have you had clearance?'

'Of course. Hannah sorted it with Danskin last night.'

'Welcome back aboard, Cap'n,' Ross joked.

'Right, tell us where you're at and I'll tell you what I've found.'

Eric spoke first, explaining Morris Chaplin was a childhood chorister who was excommunicated - he apologised for not knowing the correct term - for having a wank beneath his cassock during a rendition of '*All Things Bright and Beautiful*.'

When the laughter died down, Eric told Ryan it was the only blemish until the domestic abuse accusation which never came to court. Other than that, there wasn't a hint of a black mark.

'What have you got for me, Treblecock?' He saw the DC's glare. 'Sorry. What have you got for me *Nigel*?' he said with emphasis.

'A bit of a do on Friday evening. Nancy Douglas said she witnessed a row between the Hicksons. Quite vocal, so she says. A marked car toured the estate but found nothing odd. Oi spoke to Mrs Douglas Saturday morn'. There doesn't seem to have been anything in it.'

'Did you have a word with the Hicksons?'

'No. It seemed to me as if it were a domestic incident. There'd been no complaint by either of the Hicksons so's I let it lie.'

'Aye, you probably did the right thing. I'll have a word next time I'm up there.'

'Funny thing is, I gets this strange feelin' when I left old Nancy's house.'

'So?'

Trebilcock shrugged. 'Nothing. Just a feelin' with it happenin' on a Friday. There's an ol' saying we 'ave in Cornwall. It goes, *'Friday for sorrow; Saturday see your lover tomorrow.'*

'Superstitious bollocks if ever I heard it,' Ryan said, whilst noting he did see his lover the day after Saturday.

'You said you had something for us,' Eric interrupted.

'Aye. Most of this,' he pointed to the wall, 'Is history.'

'What?' Trebilcock and Ross said in unison.

'I've got confirmation from Aaron Elliot. The skeleton is that of an eight-year-old girl. That rules out just about everybody on the wall. What's more, the remains haven't been in the garden for long. Not long enough to decompose in situ, leastways.'

Trebilcock let the statement sink in. 'So she was kept somewhere all those years?'

'Seems like it.'

'Jesus.'

'Aye. So, looks like we must start all over again, as the song says.'

'Sarge?'

'Yes, Eric?'

'TI think it was mentioned once before but that means the girl's clothes weren't in the ground with her. Which means they are - or were - somewhere else.'

Ryan breathed in deeply. 'Great point, Eric. Okay - I want you two to run through misper records for anyone within a ten-mile radius. Any kids between the ages of six and ten, who remain unaccounted for, I want their names on my desk by the time I get back.'

'Where are you off to this time?'

'If the kid's clothes were removed before burial, there's a certain someone I want a word with.'

**

'Oh for fuck's sake. What now?'

'I'd like a word if you don't mind, Mr Waddell.'

'And if I do mind?'

'I'll be having a word, regardless.'

Des Waddell clicked his tongue against the roof of his mouth. 'Come in then, why don't you?'

Ryan looked around the dark grimy room. It looked almost exactly as it had last time he'd been in it. Almost.

'Well?' Waddell asked, clearly irritated.

'In your own words, tell me about the images you downloaded.'

'*Shit. He knows*', Waddell thought, until he realised Jarrod was referring to the images for which he was convicted, not those previously stored on the smashed-up computer hidden in the makeshift grave.

'I told you last time. Innocent ones. The kind your grandad probably looked at under the bedclothes in H&E magazine.'

Ryan hadn't a clue what the man was on about.

'How old were the children on the photographs?'

171

'Bloody hell, man. I didn't index the bloody photos. How should I know how old the kids were? Sodding hell, I told you this was years ago, man.'

'*Roughly* how old, would you say?'

'I dunno.'

'Thirteen? Fourteen? Younger?

Waddell mumbled, 'Younger.'

'Eight, perhaps?'

'I divvent know, man.'

'Before puberty, though?'

Waddell lowered his eyes. 'Some of them.'

'How old were they, Mr Waddell?'

'Look, this is all owld hat. I'm not like that anymore. I've paid my dues.' His eyes slid towards the spot under the carpet where the memory stick lay. 'Give us a break.'

'How old?'

'Probably aboot eight or nine, aal reet? Satisfied now, are you?'

'Mr Waddell, I'd like you to come to the station.'

'Eh?'

'To give us a sample.'

Des Waddell paled. Began to tremble. 'What sort of sample?'

'Just a throat swab, for DNA purposes.'

'DN…now, had on…'

'Purely routine. Call it a chance to prove your innocence.'

'Innocence of what?'

Ryan waited until Waddell's eyes met his.

'Oh, I don't know. How about murder?'

**

Des Waddell said he'd be at the Front Street station first thing tomorrow, which was soon enough for Ryan. Jarrod didn't even know if it was possible for Dr Elliot to extract DNA from old bones but it'd been fun scaring the shit out of the creepy old pervert.

Ryan was about to return to see how Trebilcock and Ross were getting on when he remembered he'd said he'd call on the Hicksons.

He relived the memories of sharing Hannah's bed as he sauntered along the avenue, a distracted smile on his face. Before he reached the Hickson place, a man's voice stopped Ryan in his tracks.

'Ah, Detective Sergeant, you'll be here about the other night, I presume?'

'Sorry?'

'The other night,' Andy Reid said.

'Oh. You mean the argument?'

'Nah. I know nothing about any argument. I meant the weirdo down the road.'

With a sigh, Ryan veered left towards the Reid residence. 'I haven't a clue what you mean, Mr Reid.'

'Ah. Sorry. I assumed that's why you were here.'

'Okay. Do I need hear this? If not. I'll keep on gannin'; if I do, you'd better invite me in.'

Ryan remained standing while Andy Reid told of his encounter with Des Waddell.

'Des Waddell was in the Hickson's garden? Beside where the remains were found?'

'Yeah. I mean, he was virtually INSIDE the hole.'

Ryan's eyebrows narrowed. 'Doing what, exactly?'

'He said he was going to use it as landfill. He had some rubbish to dump, would you believe?'

'Not really, no. What kind of rubbish?'

Andy Reid almost told him, then thought better of it. The police might offer a reward for information. He'd seen them do that on Crimewatch. No, he decided he'd hang onto that little snippet of information rather than show all his cards.

'I don't know, I'm afraid.'

'Thank you, Mr Reid. I'll investigate what you've told me,' at the same time as thinking, *'And I'll have Waddell's arse for breakfast when he shows up tomorrow.'*

**

Marina Hickson appeared calm and relaxed as she greeted Ryan on her doorstep.

'Can I get you a drink, Detective Sergeant? I'm sure you can bend the rules now and again.'

She rested her hand on his wrist. *'My God, she's not flirting with me, is she?'* He shook his head. 'No thank you, Mrs Hickson. It's just a courtesy call to see how you and your husband are doing. You know, with the trauma an' all.'

'I'm absolutely fine. Never better,' she beamed.

'Has she been drinking again?' He couldn't smell alcohol. *'Doubled up her tablets, possibly?'*

'How are you coping with your meds? Are they helping you?'

'I don't need them. I'm on my own regime now. No drink, no medication, just me and the rest of my life.'

'How about Mr Hickson? I see his car's not on the drive. At work, I'm guessing.'

Marina gave an almost hysterical laugh. 'I don't give a shit where he is, Detective Sergeant. He's gone. Left.'

'I'm sorry to hear that. I can see if we can get some counselling for you, if it would help.'

'Ha! Counselling, schmounselling. No, you misunderstand me. I've given him the boot. I came to my senses. HE was the cause of all my troubles, not my miscarriage, not my hysterectomy; just Ivor-bloody-Hickson. And now, he's gone. I'm free as a bird.' She flapped her arms above her head.

'And mad as a hatter,' Ryan thought.

'Before you ask, it's nothing to do with Morris Chaplin, either. I won't be seeing any more of him, for sure.'

Ryan wished he had accepted that drink. 'As long as you're okay, I'll be off. Oh, I don't suppose you noticed anything odd in your garden last night, did you?'

'Like a witch's coven, you mean? Not the damned UFO again, surely?' She screeched with laughter. 'No, nothing happened outside. All the action was in here.'

She rubbed her cheek.

'He hit me, you know, Detective Sergeant. Ivor, I mean. He hit me quite hard. That's why I told him to go.'

'And he did, just like that?'

She pointed to the bookshelf camera. 'He didn't have much choice in the end.'

'You set him up?'

'I couldn't possibly say,' she smiled.

'Did you fix the surveillance stuff up all by yourself?'

She laughed. 'No, not me. My handyman did it for me.'

He looked at her quizzically.

'You naughty boy. Nothing like that. He's done a few jobs for me, that's all. A neighbour recommended him. He's very…handy.'

Ryan resisted rolling his eyes. If this was her *never better,* he was beginning to understand how taxing things must have been for Ivor Hickson, though he would never, ever condone his or any other man's violence against a woman.

'Yes,' she continued, 'If you're too busy to do any handiwork for yourself, I can thoroughly recommend him.'

'Thank you,' he felt obliged to say.

'No problem, Detective Sergeant. If you need him, just ask Nancy Douglas across the street. She's got his number.'

TWENTY-FIVE

Ryan Jarrod couldn't ask Nancy Douglas for his number because she wasn't at home.

With his brain as fogged as the Tyne, he made his way back to Front Street in the hope of better news from Trebilcock and Ross.

He was sorely disappointed.

'I've been onto Ravi Sangar at Forth Street. He's pulled together an algorithm filter or whatever he called it for me. Me 'n' Eric ran misper through it and we drew a blank, so we did. All are accounted for, either found alive or, God rest their souls, dead and identified by a parent or guardian. The only exception be the Waitrose lad but we know he's not our victim.'

'Seriously? He's the only one unaccounted for? How far back did you go?'

'Five years.'

Ryan made a sucking noise. If Elliot was right, and he usually was, five years should have been enough.

'Looker, we're at a dead end here until we come up with a name for the lass. I'm buggered if I'm gonna hand this over to HQ. This is our case. Besides, Ravi's one of the best digital forensic officers there is. If he hasn't been able to help, I doubt anyone else will.'

'So where do we go from here, boss?

Ryan scratched his forehead. 'Nationwide.'

'What?'

'We go nationwide.'

'In what sense?'

'How many senses are there, man? We have a body. That means someone at some point, somewhere, went missing and remains unaccounted for. We'll find them. Make a list and go through it, name-by-name.'

Trebilcock looked blank. 'You're 'avin my arse, so you are. Tell me you're 'avin' my arse, Ryan.'

'Nope.'

'Eric, make me a cup of that shitty coffee, will you? I needs it, for sure.'

Ross laughed. 'That bad?'

'Yes, that bad. Do you know how many people go missing in the UK each year?' Trebilcock explained. 'Multiply it by five, and we'll be stuck 'ere 'til next year. Probably the year after.'

'You're wrong, Nigel. We don't multiply it by five.'

'Thank the Lord.'

'We multiply it by twenty.'

'Piss off. No way. Why?'

'The body hasn't been in the ground long, but Elliot said for full decomposition to occur, some corpses take up to thirty-five years, depending on where they're kept. You should be thankful I'm only asking for twenty and not the full whack.'

The kettle stopped bubbling and its click was audible in the shocked silence. Eric filled three plastic cups and brought them back to where they sat.

Nigel slurped noisily. 'I needs that, I do. It tastes bloody good so's I must be desperate.'

'I really don't think the task is as bad as you think,' Ryan said whilst thumping away on a keyboard.

'I'm all ears.' Trebilcock didn't sound convinced.

'Okay. Let's do the maths. One-hundred-and-seventy thousand folk go missing each year for sure, but we're not interested in adults. We're looking for kids, remember?'

'How many are children?'

'Sixty-five thousand.'

'Praise the Lord,' Trebilcock said, making jazz hands. 'Only sixty-five thousand. We'll only be here 'til Christmas, then.'

Ryan's computer screen finally loaded. He swung it so it was visible to Ross and Trebilcock.

'What am I looking at?' Eric asked.

'It's the UKMPU Data Report.' He saw Eric's glazed look. 'The UK Missing Persons Data Unit report.'

'Ah. Got it.'

'Good. Now, it breaks the statistics down to minute detail. See,' he pointed at a table in the report, 'Most missing children are barely children at all. Teenagers off to find the bright lights, poor buggers. Fewer than eight thousand are under the age of eleven.'

Trebilcock nodded his head, slowly.

'Filter the table even more, and we see the number of misper in our age category comes in at around five thousand. Even better, 96% of the little buggers turn up. That means, nationally, an average of one-hundred-and-seventy-eight children in our victim's age range remain missing.'

'Fascinating,' Eric said.

'It is, Mr Spock. And it gets better.' He scrolled down the tables. 'It says here, boys make up 60% of the long-term missing. We're looking at 40% of one-hundred-and-seventy-eight.'

Ryan allowed himself a smug smile.

'So, gentlemen: we have reduced our workload down to a total of seventy-one each year. I think that's just about manageable, don't you?'

'Oi do, indeed' said Trebilcock. 'Who the hell needs Ravi Sangar when we've got Chase on the case?'

They chuckled.

Trebilcock held up his plastic beaker. 'Eric, make me another cup, won't you? Oi'm getting a taste for this muck.'

'As soon as it's boiled,' Ryan ordered, 'All three of us are on this until we have a list. I'll start with years minus twenty to fourteen. Eric, you pick up unlucky-for-some until eight. Nige - you're from current date down to year seven.'

Ryan clapped his hands and rubbed the palms together.

'You know, sometimes I even amaze myself.'

**

By four pm, Ryan didn't feel quite so amazed.

It was slow, mind-numbing work, referencing and cross-referencing databases, ringing forces around the country for follow-up information, checking photographs, even recording the weights of the missing girls in case Aaron Elliot was able to give an estimate of it.

They looked for anything which might prove useful, took screenshots, printed reams of sheets containing names and addresses until the printer jammed, then they started handwriting the information.

At four-thirty, Ryan set down his pen.

'We're having a break. All of us. I don't know about you, but I'm going boss-eyed ower this and I don't want us to miss owt. Let's come back at five and swap notes for the last hour before we call it a day. We might have missed something so another set of eyes looking it over can't do any harm.'

Trebilcock went for a wander along the Highway in the direction of the old riding school, Ross sat on a bench in the station's grounds with a sandwich and a Yorkie bar, while Ryan headed towards the village.

He took a seat on the village green, his back to St Mary's, and called Hannah. He should have known. She was out on a case.

He dialled another number. 'Hiya, it's me. Listen, it's going to be another late one. Can you do the duties with Kenzie again for me? Oh, and have you heard owt from James today?'

'Yes to the first - I like the company - and no to the second, not today. I reckon he'll have the hangover from Hell. He had more than a skinfull after our little chat after the match.'

Ryan squinted into the sun. He hadn't noticed how glorious the day had turned out. 'Any second thoughts on how he took the news?'

'Not really. He wasn't a happy bunny at being kept oot the loop, but I got the impression he wasn't ower upset. It might have been the beer, probably the fact we gave Man U a good twonking but, whichever it was, I don't think he was as bothered as us two.'

'Okay. It might hit him later, though. I think his heed's probably on Muzzle at the minute so let me know if you think he's going downhill.'

'Aye, nee bother, son.'

Ryan drank in the early evening sun on the way back to the station. He swatted at the swarms of midges which hovered under cover of overhanging trees.

His head itched like crazy by the time he returned to the office. Trebilcock was already there, drinking another coffee, while Ross arrived a couple of minutes later.

'Right, I'll have a gander at your notes, Eric, while you look over Trebilcock's. Nigel - you take mine. Shout if you see something interesting.'

They sat in a silence broken only by the sound of shuffling paper and the occasional *'Anything yet?'* and its negative replies.

Ryan checked his watch. Quarter to six. He stretched and yawned, sweat pooling in his armpits. He fanned himself with a sheet of paper. When he set it down, one entry hit him straight away.

'Eric, I thought you'd already done all the local cases.'

'Aye, we have. All accounted for.'

'What's this one doing on the national list, then? It's a seven-year-old called Sian. Your notes says she disappeared from Lemington, assumed snatched by her absent father eight years ago.'

'I remember seeing that. It wasn't local, though. Let's have a look.'

Ryan handed him the paper.

'Nah, that's me lousy handwriting, Sarge. It's Lymington, not Lemington. Sorry.'

Ryan tutted. 'Okay, but be careful in future, right? We don't want to go off on a wrong track.'

'Yes, boss.' Eric's phone rang. 'Eric Ross,' he answered.

Ryan and Trebilcock returned to their paperwork while Ross moved to the back of the room.

'Bloody hell, lads. You're not gonna believe this,' Eric called.

'What is it?'

'It's Chaplin.'

'What about him?'

'He's dead.'

**

The converted barn stood in a remote farm not far from Eccles Hall near the westernmost edge of Earsdon village.

Despite its remoteness, Ryan and Trebilcock had no problem finding the location. They spotted the blue lights flashing brashly against the sky's muted reds and pinks from a mile away as daylight faded like Morris Chaplin.

The narrow road morphed into a rutted track then a potholed lane before ending in a paved courtyard.

The lights of the patrol cars picked out the silver haired scalp of DI Lyall Parker. Ryan and Trebilcock made straight for him.

'Good to see you again, laddie,' Parker greeted Ryan.

'You too, Lyall. It's been too long.' Ryan tilted his head towards the stone barn. 'He's in there, I take it.'

Lyall Parker nodded grimly. 'Aye, he is, that.'

'How'd he die?'

'The hole in his chest gives us a wee clue. Shot - and from close range.'

'We'll get ourselves inside, then.'

Parker took Ryan gently by the wrist. 'A word to the wise, first. This is oor case so don't go interfering. We called you in as a courtesy because the databases told us he was a PoI in your investigation; that's all, ye ken?'

'Sure, Lyall. You come in with us. Show us what's what.'

They followed Parker into the double-fronted stone building. They were barely through the door when they saw the bulk of Chaplin illuminated by the harsh flash of a forensic photographer's camera.

Chaplin lay on his back with a cherry-red bloom across the front of his white shirt.

'Aye, I'd say that's been pretty close range,' Ryan said. 'Have you spoken with his ex-wife? The one who accused him of beating her up? She's gotta be a suspect.'

Parker shook his head. 'No to both.'

'Shouldn't someone be bringing her in for questioning?'

'It's our case, remember?'

'Sorry. Force of habit.'

'Besides, we know who did it.'

'Already?'

'Aye.' He dipped his head towards the adjacent kitchen. 'You might want to look in there.'

Ryan and Trebilcock exchanged glances, shrugged, and stepped into the kitchen.

'Bugger me,' Ryan whispered.

The copper-like stench of blood permeated their senses, though Trebilcock barely noticed. His eyes were glued to the faceless corpse spread across the stone floor. The Cornishman gagged on bile.

Ryan swallowed hard, then dragged his eyes from the corpse to the kitchen floor and the gore which still dripped from surrounding work surfaces like a leaking tap.

'We don't have a motive for the killer's actions, nor an ID,' Parker explained. 'The fact he's blown half his own head off has slowed us down on the identification front.'

Ryan raised his eyes to the ceiling and where a chalk mark, numbered 4A, circled an indentation in the ceiling. A yellow triangle, marked 4B, stood alongside a bloodied object on the floor. Ryan recognised it straight away.

'I know his motive and his identity.'

'What? How come?'

He pointed to the '4B' marker. 'I've seen those cartridges before. They belong to a guy called Ivor Hickson. That's what's left of him, there. Chaplin's been shagging his wife.'

TWENTY-SIX

Whilst Ryan had no doubt who the faceless man on Chaplin's kitchen floor was, he had to wait overnight for the forensic team to complete their work before a formal identification was possible.

Although identifying a man with half a head and no facial features wasn't the easiest of tasks, the fact Ivor Hickson's car was found barely a mile away across open fields, in the car park of the Cannon Inn, still packed with his belongings, was a giveaway clue.

A relative's formal identification was still a requirement and a wedding ring and a watch were useful accessories. Ryan had both in his pocket as he climbed the steps leading to the house he had come to know so well.

Marina Hickson wore make up and a dressing gown as she invited Ryan inside with a 'People will begin to talk about us.' When the detective didn't respond, Marina adopted a frown.

'Mrs Hickson, please, sit down.'

'You know who the body in the garden was, don't you?'

'No. Not yet.'

'Oh. Right. You've got that look on your face, that's all.'

Ryan kept the look on his face as he said, 'You need to prepare yourself for some bad news.'

Marina fidgeted with the cord of her dressing gown. 'Oh God - what?'

Remembering Marina's history of mental health problems, he started with the lesser blow.

'It's about your friend, Morris Chaplin. There's no easy way of saying this. I'm afraid he's dead.'

Marina gasped. 'Oh no. Poor Morris.' She stared straight ahead as she spoke. 'It'll have been his heart. I always told him he needed to lose weight.' She shook her head. 'Poor man. Well, thank you for telling me. I appreciate it.'

'I'm afraid there's more.'

'What do you mean?'

'Morris wasn't alone when he died. He was with your husband...'

'Jesus!'

'... and I'm sorry to say Mr Hickson died with him.'

Marina's eyes rolled back. She began to pass out until Ryan steadied her. 'Can I get you something, Mrs Hickson?'

'No. No. I can't believe it. Not Ivor.' Her breath came in short spurts as if awaiting the midwife's order to push. 'Ivor and Morris? Why were they together? I don't understand. No, it's not Ivor.'

'Mrs Hickson, could you tell me if you recognise these items?' He withdrew a polythene bag from his pocket. It contained a watch and a ring.

Marina didn't need speak for Ryan to know the answer. Mrs Hickson's mouth formed a circle which she filled with her fingers.

'Marina, do these belong to your husband?'

'Yes,' she whispered.

Tears welled in her eyes. She wiped them away with the back of a hand.

'Can I see him, just to be sure?'

Ryan's mouth formed a narrow line. 'I'm afraid not.'

'Surely I can see him? I might have given him the push but we were still married. I've a right to see him.'

'I'm sorry, I strongly advise against it.'

'I'm a big girl now. See, I haven't reached for the bottle, swallowed a load of pills, or broken into hysterics. I'm in control of myself,' she said, returning to her weird breathing exercise.

185

'Mrs Hickson, Ivor shot Morris Chaplin dead then turned the gun onto himself.'

Marina's eyes widened. 'Ivor shot Morris? And suicide? No. That can't be right.' She looked towards the ceiling. 'Sweet Jesus.'

'I'm sorry for your loss. I'll send a female officer over to stay with you. Is there anyone else I can tell?'

'No. There's no-one,' she said, sadly.

'I'll see myself out. My colleague will be with you very soon.' With sincerity, he added, 'I am really sorry to break such bad news to you.'

As he left, he heard Marina say, 'Looks like I'll need Nancy's handyman more than ever, now.'

To Ryan, Marina Hickson sounded almost cheerful.

'*She's crazy, for sure,*' he thought.

**

Back at the station, Ryan despatched a female family support officer to care for Marina Hickson and entered the office to hear the end of Trebilcock's brief to Eric Ross.

'Bloody hell. Glad I wasn't there, I tell you.'

'It weren't a pretty sight, for sure,' Trebilcock said.

'His wife wanted to see him, an' all,' Ryan added. 'I told her not to.' He walked to the wall and peeled off two photographs, which he repositioned to one side.

Ivor and Marina Hickson.

'Although we can't rule them out completely, I think it's even more unlikely now that either of these two, or Chaplin for that matter, have owt to do with the girl in the garden.' Ryan looked at the wall. 'We're getting there, slowly but surely.'

His eyes fixed on the image of Des Waddell. 'When this sod gets here, we should be close to ruling him in or out. Until then, I want us to go back to the lists we made yesterday and see if we can come up with some sort of priority order of who the remains might be.'

A uniformed officer interrupted proceedings. 'Des Waddell's at reception. Do you want one of the lads to take the DNA sample?'

'Not bloody likely. I'll take it. I want to see what's in his eyes. Nigel, Eric - you run over those lists. I've got a bloke to see.'

**

Ryan smacked on a pair of gloves. 'Okay Mr Waddell, this is quite straightforward. It'll feel just like a Covid test.'

Ryan rammed the swab against the back of Waddell's throat.

'Ow. Fucking hell, man,' he gagged.

'Oops. Was I a bit vicious? Sorry.' He rubbed the swab tip against a petri dish and handed it to a similarly gloved officer who labelled it. She left them alone.

'Is that it? I can gan yem now?' Waddell asked.

'Not on your nelly, pal. I've got a few questions for you.'

'Aw, man. What now? I've answered every bloody question you've asked.'

'You have. Except this one: what were you doing in the garden of Ivor and Marina Hickson?'

Waddell blinked rapidly. 'I don't know what you mean.'

Ryan sat back. 'I think you do, Mr Waddell.'

'I don't.'

'Look, stop playing me like I'm a knacker. We have it on good authority that you were seen at the spot where the remains of a child were discovered.'

Waddell swallowed hard.

'A girl we know was eight years old. I repeat - eight years old. You told me you made images of naked girls of that age. Now, why were you in that garden?'

'No comment.'

'Fine, have it your way. Just remember we have a sample of your DNA. We'll be running checks on it.''

Waddell made a face like a cat licking wasabi. 'You're not recording this interview, are you?'

'Not yet, but it can be arranged if you wish to consult a solicitor.'

'Aal reet, then. You want the truth? I'll give you the truth. I've been looking at kiddie porn again. A bit more than the last lot I got done for.'

'I see.' Ryan leant towards Waddell. 'What do you mean by *'more'*?'

'Stronger. A bit…I dunno, nastier, I suppose.'

Ryan maintained a silence although he really wanted to smash Des Waddell's teeth down his throat.

Waddell relented. 'I was getting rid of the stuff, that's what I was doing.'

'In the illegal grave of a little girl.'

'I'm not proud of myself. I just can't stop looking at the stuff. I don't even enjoy it.'

'The way I look at it, ' Ryan said, 'You either make a statement here-and-now confessing to making pornographic images of minors, or I charge you with it along with trespass and anything else I can think of until such a time as we get the results back on your DNA.'

Des Waddell cried like a baby. 'Give me a pen. I'll make a statement. One thing you should know, though. You'll find none of me DNA on the poor kid. I might look at 'em but, I swear, I never touch 'em. Never have, never will.'

He met Ryan's eyes for the first time.

'I swear I've got bugger all to do with them bones.'

**

Ryan didn't want to believe him - but he did.

'Balls,' he said to himself after the custody sergeant took Waddell's statement and led the man away.

Still, he had to follow up on the DNA.

'Sorry to trouble you, Aaron, but I need to ask you something.'

'You're lucky to catch me, Sherlock. I'm just taking a break for five.'

'Are you working on my case?'

'No. I've got a lovely young lady on my table who seems to have poisoned herself. I've let Rufus have the pleasure of finishing her off.'

Ryan winced at the doc's impersonal terms, then realised it was probably the only way Aaron ever got through a day in the mortuary.

'I'll cut to the chase: is it possible to extract DNA from a skeleton?'

'Yep. Not as easy as you'd think, but it is.'

'What about someone else's DNA?'

'Ah-ha. I see what you're getting at. No. After all this time, it wouldn't be possible to identify your little girl's killer. '

'Thought not. Shame.'

'There is a chance whoever moved her to the burial spot may have left something. I can't guarantee it without a thorough inspection, though.'

'You could check?'

'I could.'

Ryan screwed his eyes tight. 'I don't suppose you could determine if the girl was shot, could you?'

'There won't be any residue from the bullet but, if it hit bone, there's every possibility we'll be able to show what caused the bone damage. Having said that, Rufus or I would have spotted any major splintering.'

Ryan felt a surge of hope. 'When you get round to looking at her, you'll check that for me, won't you?'

Aaron Elliot tutted. 'I'm disappointed in you for even thinking I'd be so lapse as to miss something like that.'

Ryan chortled. 'Aye. Sorry. Good man. Cheers.'

'As a matter of fact, we'll know soon enough. Your girl's name is first up on tomorrow's schedule.'

TWENTY-SEVEN

Back in the office, Des Waddell's photograph remained firmly in place on the wall as Ryan asked for an update from Trebilcock and Ross.

The Cornishman's response wasn't encouraging. 'It's not easy tryin' to prioritise a list when we don't know what priorities we're lookin' for.'

'The way we decided to do it was start with those whose ages fit spot-on the eight-year-old mark,' Ross added. 'So far, I've got six…'

'…and I've one less.'

Ryan puffed out his cheeks. 'It's a start, I suppose.' He pondered for a moment. 'Right. Let's put some faces to the names you've got. Print out the last known pictures of the eleven you've come up with. I'll leave you to do that, Eric. You focus on the lists again,' he told Trebilcock. 'Oh - and their last known locations would help, an' all.'

Trebilcock shifted through some papers before holding one aloft. 'Already got 'em, so I have.'

'Good work. Let's see.'

Ryan snatched the sheet from his colleague and scanned the list.

Two were from Yorkshire: Doncaster, and Huddersfield; two from the Birmingham area, and two from the Met's domain, Brixton and Deptford.

Ryan racked his brains for anything which struck a chord. Nothing did so he returned to the list.

That left Largs, Cromer, Lymington, Accrington and, finally, Kidsgrove.

'Listen, we could go on for ever adding to the list. Let's take a deep dive into the ones we have so far before we look at any others. Get their photos and key facts on the wall. We'll rule them out one-by-one.'

'Sounds like a plan,' Ross said above the clicks and whirrs of the printer.

'Aaron Elliot said he was having a good look at wor lass first thing. Might be as well to wait until then before we make a start as I'm thinking his report could rule some out for us.'

Trebilcock opened the lid of the biscuit tin and grabbed a handful of custard creams. 'What do we do until then?'

'You can get your backside back up to Callaley Avenue. Just have a general scout around. Have another word with some of the locals if you think it'd help. Leave Marina Hickson out of it, though. She's seen enough of us lot, I reckon.'

Trebilcock mumbled something incomprehensible through a mouthful of crumbs.

'What aboot me, Sarge?'

'You stay here and man the fort because I'll be building a charge against our friendly neighbourhood paedo. I'll grab a couple of PCs to give us a hand.'

'Good luck with that. You've nee chance. They're tied up on a hit and run in Dunston.'

'You've just talked yourself into a job with me. We'll do it from here so we can keep an ear out for the phones.'

Ryan checked the wall-clock.

This time tomorrow, he'd have Aaron Elliot's report on his desk.

This time tomorrow, he might know the identity of the bones in Callaley Avenue.

This time tomorrow, he may know the killer.

Or this time tomorrow, he could be no further forward.

**

Although the road was more Nightmare on Elm Street than Miracle on 34th Street, Nigel Trebilcock had become increasingly fond of Callaley Avenue.

Its views, its tranquillity, the pleasant-looking houses many with the rarity of a front garden as opposed to the paved driveway which had become the depressing norm, all served to make the location one in which he could happily settle.

Right on cue, he spotted an Estate Agent's van outside a residence, its driver planting a 'For Sale' sign in one of the gardens he so admired. Even if Trebilcock could afford it, he wouldn't be making an offer.

Not on this house. Not the one currently occupied by Marina Hickson.

He stopped in his tracks. *'That's all a bit soon, in't it?'* he thought. Still, he had his instructions. *'Don't disturb Marina Hickson,'* Jarrod had told him. He wouldn't, but he would report back to Jarrod.

One thing he didn't like about Callaley Avenue, or anywhere else in the region, was the unpredictable weather. No two days were ever the same and, in the early afternoon of the day, ominous grey clouds threatened more than mizzle.

There wasn't much doing on Callaley Avenue for him today. Trebilcock flipped up the hood of his light coat and, head down, sunk his hands into his pockets.

'You look like you could do with another cup of tea,' a female voice said.

Trebilcock glanced across the street in time to see Nancy Douglas fasten the ties around a plastic rain hat as her taxi splashed off.

She looked terrible.

'You's get yourself in. You leaves those shopping bags to me,' he said. 'I'll bring 'em in for you.'

'That's very kind. I'll put the brew on. Perhaps you'd like a currant bun this time, as well.'

'Oh go on then, you've convinced me, so you have.'

Trebilcock followed Nancy Douglas into the house then through into the kitchen. He set her two carrier bags of shopping onto a bench.

Nancy looked haggard. Older than her years, with pronounced sacs of loose flesh beneath her eyes. 'You sit yourself down, Mrs Douglas. I'll make the tea.'

'Ooh. Thank you. I'm feeling quite jiggered. I can't do as much as I used to.'

Trebilcock moved Nancy's knitting aside and placed her cup on the coffee table. He sat opposite her. 'You don't look too well, if I may say so.'

'Don't worry about me. I've had a busy few days, that's all.'

The energy and mischievous edge to her voice was no longer present.

'Do you want to tell me about it?'

'Not really.' The reply was terse and out of character.

'Oh. Righty-oh, then. It don't matter.'

Nancy rubbed her brow then pinched the bridge of her nose. 'I'm sorry. That was uncalled for.'

'Not at all, Mrs Douglas. May I say something, though?'

Nancy inclined her head.

'Oi think you may be doing too much. You should get your shopping delivered.'

'I wouldn't know how to work that webernet thing,' she said, dismissively.

'Then get someone to do it for you. A neighbour, perhaps?'

Nancy wrinkled her brow as she looked across the street.

'Looks like I'll be getting some new neighbours soon. I see Mr and Mrs Hickson are on the move already. I suppose it must have been a shock to them, the thing in their garden, I mean.'

Trebilcock considered mentioning Ivor Hickson's demise but thought better of it. It wasn't his place. Instead, he glanced around Nancy Douglas's living room.

'Your house looks in fair condition but you need someone to look after it for you. Do I remember you's sayin' your nephew helps out?'

Nancy sighed. 'Yes.'

'Good. As long as you've got someone.'

'We all need someone, Detective. No matter how much we deny it, we all need someone.' She looked at Trebilcock with sad eyes. 'Do you have anyone?'

'Me? My family are at yon end of the country but yes, I have.'

'That's where my brother is.'

'Yes, you told me. Bournemouth, I think you said.'

'That area, aye. At my age, it's too far.'

She yawned. 'I think I'll take forty winks. Would you mind?'

Trebilcock set down his cup. 'No. Not at all. Oi should have noticed. You knows where I am if you need anything, don't you?'

The woman was already asleep.

Nigel took the cups through to the kitchen before letting himself out.

Back in the dank, miserable air, Trebilcock shivered.

He wasn't cold.

He had the same odd feeling he'd encountered last time he'd been inside Nancy Douglas's place.

**

At the end of a long and largely futile shift, Ryan walked Kenzie along Washingwell Lane and onto the public right of way through the fields beyond.

He unleashed the German Shepherd dog and let him run free. Inquisitive though he was, Kenzie didn't venture far from his master, even when the petrichor scent of recent rain tempted him into the hedgerow.

The rain had stopped but the long grass remained sodden. Ryan's feet were soon wet through and, long before he reached his intended destination of The Highwayman, he about turned and made for home.

Normally, such a venture would clear his mind and, somewhere in his thoughts, he'd find a pathway through his case. Not this time. This time, with only a few days until his return to Forth Street, he was no nearer solving the puzzle.

Ryan opted for a lazy night in front of the TV in the hope its blandness might spark him into a revelation. Instead, it left him more frustrated.

Emilia Fox stood over a grey corpse laid out in her lab. She gave a running commentary on the procedure as she pulled out the cadaver's organs and weighed them on a set of lab scales. A young Jewish trainee in checked shirt and burgundy beanie watched from behind a glass screen; he Rufus to Emilia's Aaron.

Of course, *Silent Witness* was drama, not real life. Within five minutes, they'd identified the victim and established cause of death. In real life, Aaron Elliot was nowhere near discovering either after nearly three weeks.

'Tomorrow is another day', Ryan remembered as he fought off desperation.

TWENTY-EIGHT

Tomorrow brought with it the overcast and damp skies of the day before.

Ryan's spirits were equally downbeat. He'd spent a restless night fearing he'd be beaten by time on the case, then worrying about the fact he still hadn't heard from James, and finally realising how much he missed Hannah.

He arrived at Front Street feeling thoroughly pissed off with life, the universe, and everything.

'Mornin' Sarge' Ross greeted him, cheerily.

'You think so, do you? What's good about it, like?'

'It's just a saying.'

'Well divvent say it. I'm not in the mood.'

Eric had been about to show Ryan the photographs he'd found of the missing and their associated information. He thought better of it.

'Where's Trebilcock?'

'Out.'

'I can see that, man. Out where?'

Ross hesitated.

'Well?'

'He's delivering flowers.'

'He's WHAT?'

'Delivering flowers. To that Nancy Douglas woman. He said she's not herself.'

'I give up.' Ryan flung his hands in the air. 'Right. We're expecting a call from Dr Elliot this morning. I don't want to be interrupted before then. You just get on with stuff.'

Eric wasn't going to argue. He went for the head down-arse up invisibility cloak approach, even if he wasn't sure what Ryan referred to as *'stuff'*.

As the minutes turned to hours, the grouchier Ryan became. Eric remained invisible and Trebilcock, when he finally deigned to appear, began preparing a handover for his and Jarrod's return to Forth Street.

When the call did come, Ryan almost leapt from his seat.

'What you got, Aaron?'

'It's Dr Cavanagh here,' a deadpan voice corrected.

'Okay. What have YOU got, then?'

'Nothing yet. Dr Elliot asked me to let you know he's checking one final thing and hopes to have the results to you in about an hour.'

'*About* an hour, or an hour?'

'I'm only telling you what Dr Elliot asked me to report, Detective Sergeant. Those were his words, not mine.'

'Look, I know we didn't get off to the best of starts...'

'I was perfectly fine but you're correct: YOU didn't.'

Ryan bit his tongue. Literally. He wiped his finger across its tip and it came away red. 'I was going to thank you for the assistance you've given me and Aaron...'

'...Dr Elliot...'

'...Me and Aaron on the case, and to apologise for being off with you. But I'm not going to bother now because I have concluded you're a tit. Now, get Aaron to ring me as soon as.'

He ended the call with a, 'What a tosser.'

**

Ryan considered calling Hannah but thought better of it. In his current mood, he'd say the wrong thing, he just knew it. Instead, he rang his brother's girlfriend. She would give as good as she got.

'How's James doing?'

'Jam Jar is just fine.'

'How about you, *GERMAINE*?' He used Muzzle's real name deliberately.

'She's pissed off at not being called Muzzle.'

'Apart from that?'

'Not bad, Ryan. How are you?'

Ryan nearly dropped the phone with shock at Muzzle asking after his welfare.

'You know. Getting there, I suppose. But I've had longer to get used to it than James has.'

'Look, I don't want this to sound mean, but I don't think he's ower bothered about having a sister. If he'd known her, it might be different. As things stand, he's still more embarrassed about even thinking I'd welcome his frigging stupid marriage proposal.'

Ryan replied in kind. 'Look, I don't want to be mean, but I think you should appreciate the fact he thinks enough of you to ask you in the first place.'

Muzzle stayed silent. Finally, she said, 'I do appreciate it. It was still fucking stupid, though.'

Fortunately for her, she ended the call before he could respond. No sooner had the conversation ended than his phone rang.

'I accept your apology,' he said.

'Pardon?'

'Oh. Sorry. I thought you were someone else. Who is this?'

'You have three guesses.'

'Ah Aaron, man.'

'You named that tune in one.'

'Have you got summat?'

'Do you know, I strongly believe I have.'

'Had on a minute. I'll put you on speaker.'

He waved an arm to attract Trebilcock and Ross's attention. 'It's Elliot. He's got something.'

They hurried over.

'First on the DNA front: I'm afraid that's the bad news. We found no trace of any DNA on the remains. We did find a minute trace of Fe_2O_3. That's iron oxide - or rust to most of us. Wherever the girl was kept before burial, it contained, or was made of, metal. '

Ryan puffed his cheeks. 'It'll be difficult to get a conviction without DNA but I'm not surprised, I have to say. Mind, the rust presence could be useful. Do we have a cause of death? Without it, we have no crime. At least, not a major one.'

'I'm pretty sure I do.'

'Shotgun wounds? Please, let it be a shotgun.'

All three stared at the phone expectantly.

'No evidence of that, I'm afraid,' Dr Elliot informed them.

'Bollocks.'

'Ah, Hell.'

'That's a buggeration, that is.'

With Ivor Hickson an ever more unlikely suspect, Ryan was losing hope of ever solving the case. 'Was she murdered at all?' he asked.

'That's a very good question, and one I can't give a legally binding answer to - although I can give you a clear indication.'

'Howay, then. What did you find?'

'Okay. Now, bear with me on this. When we have skeletal remains, over time we tend to see some distortion in the plane of the bones. You see, without muscle mass and tendons to keep them in place, bones have an annoying habit of moving out of position. Are you following me?'

All three nodded their heads before they realised Elliot couldn't see them. 'So far, yes,' Ryan eventually said.

'Good. Well, this case is no exception. The skeleton was broadly in the right shape but the ulna and radius, for example, weren't in alignment with the humerus. Now, as I say, that's to be expected. The same goes for some of the bones of the hands and feet.'

Ryan tried to swallow down his impatience. He glanced at Trebilcock and noticed his face redden as he held his breath.

Eric Ross moved his hand in a circular motion; a 'hurry up' gesture.

'Similarly, several vertebrae on our girl were dislodged. A number, but not all. You see, I noticed the atlas and axis appeared fused.'

'Talk to us as if we're the idiots we are, Aaron.'

Dr Elliot took his time as he thought of a layman's way of putting it. 'Okay. The atlas and axis are the top two vertebrae of the spinal column. One supports the weight of the skull, the other allows the head to rotate from side to side. In the case of our victim, there was almost no flexibility whatsoever.'

'Which means?'

'It means, she most likely died of a broken neck.'

Trebilcock breathed at last. Ross gave a smile of triumph. Only Jarrod remained puzzled.

'Had on a minute. You said the neck was fused. Surely if she'd broken her neck, it would be the absolute opposite of fused?'

Elliot laughed. 'You are very astute, Sherlock. That's why I like you so much.'

'Right. So, if she broke her neck, how come her neck isn't, err, broken?'

'This is where you get the closest to proof of murder you'll get. Our killer, assuming we do have one, disguised the fact the girl's neck was broken.'

'Disguised? How?'

'The bones have been sealed together by a thin layer of a milky-white adhesive.'

All three let out an audible gasp. Murder, most foul, this was.

'And the killer knew what he was doing. The material he or she used doesn't set rock hard. This meant when the remains were lifted from the site, there would have been some very minor movement of the skull. If it had been completely rigid, I'd have noticed it immediately.'

'This is great stuff, Aaron. Our perpetrator isn't any old thug,' Ryan mused.

Elliot was speaking again. 'Have any of you heard of a substance called Triethoxyoctylsilane?'

'Hadaway. Not likely. I can't even say it never mind owt else.'

Elliot continued unabated, clearly excited by his discovery. 'It's a sealant found in products such as Fernox. Specifically, Fernox LS-X. It's what was found between the girl's uppermost vertebrae.'

'Right. How easy would it be to find the specific batch of this Fernox stuff? Is it a common product? I've never heard of it.'

Trebilcock and Ross shook their heads. They didn't know of it, either.

'After this time, I'm afraid it would be impossible to determine the specific details of the batch it came from. As for being common, it depends on who you are.'

'Meaning?'

'You can get it from Screwfix, but it's a trade product in the main. I would say you're looking at your killer being a joiner, boiler maintenance engineer, heating technician, or plumber.'

Jarrod, Trebilcock, and Ross stood with mouths agape.

They had their man.

'Joseph Tomkiss!'

TWENTY-NINE

Ryan set up an urgent teleconference. DCIs Kinnear and Danskin listened intently as Ryan detailed recent key developments and, particularly, Aaron Elliot's findings.

'All three of you have done a magnificent job, lads. You should be proud of yersel,' Kinnear praised.

Stephen Danskin's appreciation came more in his tone of voice than his words. 'Are you needing any support from my lot? You can have any resource you want.'

Ryan almost suggested Hannah Graves just so he could see her, but he worried she'd be a distraction. Plus, the third person listening in from Forth Street HQ wouldn't agree.

'No, sir. We'll be fine. Trebilcock and me can handle it, and Eric will round up a squad of uniform to help with the knock. All I need is for the Super to get me a warrant for Tomkiss's home and business addresses. Ma'am, could you prepare it urgently, please?'

'It'll be my pleasure, Ryan. It's the least I can do for you.'

'How soon?'

'I'm halfway through it already.'

'You should know her by now, Jarrod,' Danskin laughed.

'Do we have the ID of the girl yet?' Rick Kinnear asked.

'I'm afraid not, sir. But I bet you we will once we bring Tomkiss in.'

'He's not known to us, is he?' Superintendent Maynard asked.

'No, which is a bit odd for a crime like this. I'd expect him to be on our books somewhere.'

'I agree. Very unusual. Now, you're certain you don't need support from either Stephen or Rick? I don't want Tomkiss slipping through our fingers.'

'No, ma'am. I'm quite sure we can handle it.' He temporarily muted the call. 'Nee bugger's gonna take our glory away, lads,' he told Trebilcock and Ross, who gave a thumbs-up response.

Ryan heard the clink of fingers working a keyboard. He rejoined the conversation. 'Where are we with the warrant, ma'am?'

'I've just pinged it over via e-mail. I've used my electronic signature so that means it isn't Magistrate-approved. You need to tread warily. Do nothing to jeopardise the warrant's validity. Understand?'

'Nee fear of that, ma'am.' Ryan checked his secure e-mail. The warrant was there. He pressed print. 'The warrant's here. Ross will get a troop together and we'll do a simultaneous raid on the premises.'

'Go get 'im,' Sam Maynard said before she ended the conference.

**

Precisely thirty-five minutes later, police vans sealed off both ends of Athol Street, discretely hidden from view from the mid-street property rented by Joseph Tomkiss.

Behind the van at the Seymour Street limit of the road, Ryan struggled into a stab vest. Eric Ross did the same, while the occupants of the van already wore them.

Ryan clicked on the radio. 'We're all ready at this end, Nigel. How about you?'

'Same here. Ready to go on your word.'

Trebilcock was stationed at the junction of Railway Street and Staithes Road, preventing access or egress. Mobile units served a similar purpose at the Collingwood Terrace and Cormorant Drive junctions.

'Take up positions,' Ryan said into the radio.

He gave a nod of his head towards an officer holding 'the big red key' - an enforcer battering ram - in his grasp. The man climbed out the van followed by three of his colleagues. Two other officers appeared at the far end of the street.

Slowly, quietly, they inched along the wall towards Tomkiss's residence.

A similar act played out around the garage unit workshop.

'Ready, Ryan,' Trebilcock whispered. 'I've alerted Verisure. They've disarmed all alarms and surveillance. He won't have an inklin' we're here.'

Ryan took a gulp of air. 'My count. On three.'

He glanced at his party. They stood tense and, behind their face shields, grim-faced.

'One.'

'Two.'

'Three. GO. GO. GO!!!'

**

The thin door splintered like matchwood on the Enforcer's impact. Ryan pulled away wooden shards and climbed through the gap. Ross and the others raced in behind.

'Police!'

'POLICE! DON'T MOVE!!'

'Get down!'

'Stay where you are!'

The demands may have been contradictory but it wasn't important. The aim was to make as much racket as possible to scare the shit out of the man inside.

Except, there was no man inside.

Uniform officers searched every room, one-by-one. Each incursion was followed by an announcement of 'Clear' until only the bathroom remained.

Ryan gave the signal.

A shoulder crushed the door.

It wasn't necessary. A turn of the handle would have been sufficient.

Joseph Tomkiss wasn't cowering in the grubby bath; his eyes weren't peering over the rim of a stained toilet bowl.

Joseph Tomkiss wasn't at home.

Ryan leant against a wall.

'Shit.'

**

The metal door of Tomkiss Plumbing took longer to break through.

Once inside, Trebilcock led the chorus of confusing commands.

The result was the same. The garage-style lock up was deserted. Men stationed at the rear confirmed no-one had exited the building.

Trebilcock tried the handle. It was locked. Even if Tomkiss had fled out the back exit, unseen, there's no way he would have lingered long enough to lock up after him.

Tomkiss wasn't there, either.

Nigel Trebilcock knew Tomkiss wasn't one for paperwork - too many dodgy dealings for that - but he must have a diary or a ledger somewhere. Something which would indicate which job he was undertaking - and, more importantly, where it was.

The place was the same unruly mess it had been on his last visit. Everything had its place and nothing in its place. Nigel Trebilcock remembered the upright filing cabinet. If Tomkiss kept a record of his jobs, that's where it would be.

Trebilcock turned towards the spot where it stood, only to find a blank space.

And a rectangular smear of rust where it had once been.

'That be just bleddy 'ansom,' Trebilcock cursed.

His squad filed out of the unit, leaving Trebilcock alone. He took a long look around. Nothing had changed since his last visit, he was sure. Nothing except for the missing stationery cabinet.

He had a thought but, before he could carry through with it, Ryan's voice crackled over the radio.

'Please don't tell me you haven't drawn a blank an' all,' Jarrod said.

'No signs of him, Ryan. I was just about to ask Verisure to review any stored footage of the lock up. See if there's anything on there.'

He heard Ryan breathe out. 'It's all we've got. May as well give it a gan.'

'There's one thing, though. There was a cabinet in here last time. It's gone now.'

'So?'

'It was a tall cabinet. And it was a rusty one, so it was.'

'Like, tall enough to store a body you mean?'

'A small one, for sure.'

Ryan vibrated his lips. 'Okay. Let's get back to the station. See if we can make sense of owt.'

'We needs to know who the girl was.'

'You're not wrong, Nigel. We need a breakthrough, that's for sure. Otherwise, we've cocked this up. Big style.'

**

Ryan ran through the failed raids with his three senior officers. They weren't impressed but Ryan was relieved to know they didn't apportion blame; only offered him sage advice.

'For the record, Jarrod, I suggest running some surveillance to ensure your suspected target is at home before ordering a raid in future. It happens to us all at some point. Let's make sure you learn from it, yeah?' Danskin observed.

'Sir.'

'Good thinking to ask for the surveillance footage, though,' Maynard comforted.

'That was Trebilcock's idea, ma'am. We should have preliminary results within the hour.'

'Good. We'll have a retrospective magisterial approval on the warrant by then. Once it comes through, we'll get forensics away testing the rust samples. If we can prove the samples match those found by Elliot, we know for sure Tomkiss is our man. We just need locate him, that's all.'

'Ma'am, we're going to review what we know against our potential victims. If we can somehow link Tomkiss to any of them, we'll have a strong enough case to present to CPS.'

'I agree, Ryan. So, what are you waiting for?'

'Nowt, ma'am. All three of us are on it. We'll get there, I promise you.'

'I hope so, Jarrod,' Danskin said. 'You're back here in two days. I don't want a failure as a member of my team.'

Ryan knew the DCI well enough to know he was joking.

Trouble is, Danskin was right. If Ryan didn't crack the case, he'd feel he was a failure, whether anyone else thought it or not.

There was no way Ryan Jarrod was returning to Forth Street as a failure.

**

The threesome pored over the lists of the missing once more. They came up with an eight-year-old from Ripon, another from Pembroke Dock, and a father and daughter combo from Bristol.

They now had fourteen in total.

'Right. That's enough. I said when we had eleven we should take stock of them before moving on. We've fourteen now. Let's stop there before we get bogged down.'

'Makes sense to me,' Eric agreed.

'Nige?'

Trebilcock looked into space. 'There's something naggin' me. Something I should be seein'.'

'Does that mean you think we should continue?'

'No. The opposite. I think we already have what we need. We're just not seein's it.'

Ryan poured three cups of liquid crap and handed one each to his colleagues. He screwed his face as he sipped his own.

'I tell you what, I'll look over the girls from the big cities, London, Birmingham, and the three Yorkies. Nigel - are you aal reet with the Scots and Welsh lass? Add on the Lymington and Bristol ones seeing as there from doon your way…'

'…Gives or takes a couple of hundred miles.'

'You're okay with them, though?'

'I am.'

'That leaves you with the rest, Eric. Cromer, Accrington, and Kidsgrove. Bit of a hotchpotch but there's only three of 'em.'

'Aye, I can handle that. No idea where Kidsgrove is, mind.'

'It's not important but it's doon Stoke way, as it happens. Right. Crack on, lads. While uniform hunt for Tomkiss, I want us on this until we get a handle on our victim.'

Thirty minutes in and Trebilcock took a call. His face told Ryan all he needed to know.

'There's been no activity in-or-out of Tomkiss Plumbing for three days.'

'Aw man. Looks like he's a step ahead of us.'

They resumed their research for another fifteen minutes until Ryan called for an update. In almost an hour, they'd ruled out a grand total of zero.

'We're getting nowhere here,' he said, the desperation clear in his voice.

'I've got a head like an ant in a beehive,' Trebilcock agreed. He popped out a couple of paracetamol and wandered to the windowsill where a lukewarm bottle of water had been standing in the heat.

He pulled a face as he swigged from it.

Eric continued to pore over the files. Ryan stared at the information on the wall in the hope the answer would hit him in the face.

Trebilcock walked over to join him. He took another gulp of water - and jettisoned a stream of it from his mouth.

'You okay, Nigel?' Ryan asked as Trebilcock coughed and spluttered beside him.

After he stopped choking, Trebilcock smiled broadly. 'Never better,' he said.

He waved the water bottle at the wall.

'I just realised I not only know whose bones they are; I also know their connection to Tomkiss.'

THIRTY

Technology at the Whickham station was little better than what could be found at an average sixth form college.

Ryan guessed it didn't matter much because Whickham didn't have a Ravi Sangar-type amongst its team. The kit the station did have was adequate for the requirements of the staff working there, and more than sufficient for Ryan to pull together a PowerPoint presentation.

Ryan and Eric Ross cleared the information, maps, and photographs from the office wall. Jarrod took several photographs first in case they needed to reconstruct it but he knew it wouldn't be necessary.

Deep down, he was confident they had their man.

Ryan projected the slides against the wall and he and Trebilcock ran through them in preparation for a videoconference with Danskin and Kinnear. They agreed on a couple of tweaks and waited for the two DCIs to join the conference.

Ryan believed they had all the evidence needed for an arrest but Trebilcock insisted they get senior approval first. Jarrod agreed mainly because the puzzle wasn't quite complete. He hoped Eric Ross would soon return with the final piece.

Their screens flickered to life as Danskin and Kinnear joined the conference from Forth Street.

'I take it you have some good news for us, lads,' Danskin assumed. 'It's almost midnight so it'd better be worth it.'

Nearly midnight? Ryan felt nonplussed. He had no idea it was so late. Still, he answered his DCI's question with an 'Aye, we have. We're sure we know not only the cause of death and the killer; we also now have a name for our victim.'

'Is it enough to bring a charge?' Kinnear asked.

'We believe so, sir, but that's why we've called this conference.'

'Aal reet: what you got for us?'

Ryan pressed a few buttons on his keyboard. The footage of the DCI's disappeared, to be replaced by a still image of an angelic-faced young girl.

'I'm sharing my screen with you,' Ryan explained. 'What can you see at your end?'

Danskin's voice came back hushed and reverential. 'Ah man, she's a lovely bairn. Is that our victim?'

Confident in the knowledge the IT was working, Ryan let Trebilcock explain.

'It is. She was eight-years old when she disappeared from home. Her name's Sian Rumney.'

'Should we know that name?'

'No. Sian's not from our patch. She went missing from Lymington with her father, Thomas Rumney.'

With a click of the mouse, Ryan brought up the next slide, the picture of Sian's father which Ryan had clipped from the wall. 'This is him.'

'Are you telling me Thomas Rumney did a flit with Sian to our neck of the woods?' Danskin asked.

'Yes.'

'Why?'

'Rumney split from the girl's mother under acrimonious circumstances. The mother denied Rumney access to his daughter. In turn, he stopped paying maintenance. The CSA got involved and imposed a Detachment of Earnings Order on him, which pissed Rumney off a tad.'

'I can imagine.'

'Anyways, the father was still registered with Sian's school as an authorised person so he was able to turn up at the premises, collect her early on the pretence of a fake dental appointment, and bugger off.'

'As easy as that?'

'As easy as that.'

'Why did they come here?'

'We think because it's about as far away from Lymington as he could get.'

The conversation hushed while Danskin and Kinnear assimilated the information.

'Okay,' Kinnear asked. 'Where does Tomkiss come into the picture?'

Ryan was ready for that one. He clicked the mouse and the face of Joseph Tomkiss appeared on screen.

'You'll recognise this as Joseph Tomkiss, owner of Tomkiss Plumbing.'

'Yep. The guy who killed Sian Rumney, you believe.'

'We don't *believe* he did. We're *sure* he did,' Ryan reaffirmed.

He clicked the mouse to animate the presentation. An image of Thomas Rumney slid into place alongside Joseph Tomkiss.

'Bloody hell,' Danskin swore.

'Aye. Rumney and Tomkiss are one-and-the-same person. He's clean shaven now, dyed his hair and changed its style from neat and tidy to wild and rugged, donned coloured contact lenses, and aged naturally - but it's him. A change of name can't disguise that fact.'

Danskin groaned like a Scooby Doo ghost. 'But it was enough for you to overlook it.'

'That's not fair, Stephen,' Rick Kinnear interjected. 'They had no reason to link a lass from Lymington to one in Dunston, or wherever they lived at the time. I think the lads have done brilliant to make the connection at all. I mean, they didn't know how long ago this Sian went missing - and how many kids disappear each year? Must be hundreds.'

'Of that age, a hundred-and-seventy-eight,' Ryan said confidently.

Ryan imagined Danskin reconsidering his impulsive comment. He pictured him running his hand over the crown of his head, slowly nodding, then saying…

'Rick's right. I should be congratulating you, Jarrod.'

'Thanks but it was Nigel who made the connection. He deserves the praise.'

Trebilcock played it down. 'We're a team, Ryan; so's we are.'

'I think you've more than enough to bring Tomkiss, or Rumney, or whatever he's called, in for questioning, but not enough for an arrest just yet,' Danskin decided.

'I suppose it's the lack of motive, is it?'

'Dead reet, Jarrod. Why would he break his own kidda's neck after going to all that bother to bring her here with him?'

Ryan shrugged. 'You have a point, sir.'

'Aye, I do. So, bring him in. Keep him there 'til you find a motive. Squeeze his knackers until they pop like balloons if you must - just go get him.'

Ryan sighed. 'That's the problem, though, isn't it?'

'What is?'

'He's not at home. He's not at work. We don't know where the hell he is.'

Danskin spoke through gritted teeth. 'Then I suggest you do some detecting, Detective Sergeant Jarrod.'

'I've got PC Ross looking for him as we speak but me and Trebilcock will join him straight away.'

'What are you waiting for, then? Stop talking to us two and do something more important.'

Just as Ryan was about to end the conference, Stephen Danskin spoke again.

'For what it's worth, with the resources you've had, I think the three of you have done a stonkin' job. Well done.'

Ryan closed the video conference.

'Y'know, I can never tell whether he's happy or not.'

**

By two-fifteen, they were running on empty.

They had no CCTV footage of Tomkiss, didn't know if he was driving a vehicle and, if so, what make or model. Without that information, the ANPR system which captured the movement of vehicles via registration plate recognition couldn't assist.

They checked with local taxi firms. None had a booking under either name. Ryan was aware the man could have flagged down a cab without making a reservation, but it was impossible to check with every driver of every cab of every taxi firm.

Ryan unearthed a rumour on social media that Tomkiss had been seen getting rat-arsed at the Dun Cow a couple of days ago so, if true, he hadn't long been missing. A bit of gossip wasn't enough to rouse the landlord in the middle of the night, so they'd wait until daylight.

They ran checks on recent housing lets in case he'd moved into another property. There was no record of a Tomkiss or a Rumney renting a property locally in the last month.

The threesome already knew there were no clues to his whereabouts in his Athol Street flat or his workplace. With that in mind, Ryan suggested they call it a night.

Trebilcock agreed. Eric Ross wanted to plough on. He was over-ruled.

They left an almost-deserted station and agreed to reconvene at seven-thirty. At least they'd have a few hours in a comfortable bed to rejuvenate themselves. Or Eric and Ryan would.

Nigel Trebilcock suggested kipping down on Ryan's sofa to cut down on travelling time. Ryan was quick to agree. They were asleep within half an hour.

Within another hour, Ryan was awake again.

Somewhere in the distance, he heard music. It stopped. As he closed his eyes again, it restarted.

Ryan recognised the tune, this time. It was The Blaydon Races.

His phone was ringing.

'Jarrod,' he yawned.

The voice on the other end was euphoric.

'I've found him, Sarge!' Eric yelled. 'I know exactly where he is, and he's not gannin' anywhere anytime soon.'

'Does that mean I can go back to kip?'

'If you must,' Ross laughed.

Ryan rubbed his eyes. 'Hang on, where are you?'

'I'm at the station. I knew I'd never sleep so I thought I might as well go back in and get on with it.'

'Bugger sleep,' Ryan said. 'I'm on my way doon.'

As an afterthought, he added, 'And feel free to disobey an order anytime you like, PC Ross.'

THIRTY-ONE

Trebilcock was less enamoured at being roused so soon. He walked with his head to one side like a man carrying a plank over his shoulder as he massaged the crick in his neck.

'Oi hope for your sake this is worth it. I be teasy as 'n' adder if you woke me up for nothin'.'

Ryan held the door open for Trebilcock by way of apology.

Eric Ross looked up, dark sacks under his eyes emphasising their red rims. 'What kept you?' he smiled.

Before Trebilcock could launch into a tirade, Ryan asked Eric what he'd found.

'It was a last resort, really. I decided I'd ring around some hospitals in case Tomkiss had chucked a wobbly or owt. Most of 'em didn't have anyone on the switchboard or, if they had, they were asleep on the job...'

'Oi knows the feelin',' Trebilcock moaned.

'I managed to get through to the QE, though. They didn't have any record of admitting a Joseph Tomkiss or Thomas Rumney.'

'I hopes that's the bad news and not the good 'un.'

Again, Eric ignored the grouchy Cornishman. 'After a little guesswork from me, though, they told me they had recently admitted a bloke by the name of Joseph Rumney.'

Ryan whistled. 'And you think he could've been playing about with his name again?'

Eric nodded. 'I did but I wanted to be sure so I ran the name *Joseph Rumney* through our records.'

'You have him on file?'

Eric wobbled a hand and grimaced. 'Not exactly.'

'What did you find, Eric?' Trebilcock asked with growing impatience.

'Right. Do you remember a few days back I said we were short of back-up?'

Ryan dragged a hand beneath his chin. 'Not really .. oh, was that something about a hit and run? Was that the one?'

'That's it. Turns out the bloke that was hit gave his name to the ambulance crew as Joseph Rumney. Wor lads spoke to him in hospital but he told them to bugger off.'

'Shouldn't that have made 'em more suspicious?'

'Not really. He claimed it was all his fault. That he was pissed - we know he'd been in The Dun Cow - and he stepped into the path of the car. Of course, it's still a live investigation but without a reg number or any witnesses willing to come forward, it'll be a long haul.'

'Why call himself Joseph Rumney?' Trebilcock asked.

Ryan had the answer. 'He knew he'd already come to your attention so he wouldn't want to give the name Joseph Tomkiss. I guess Rumney was the next obvious name to come to him and, I dare say, he never in a million years would he have thought we'd make a link between the bones and Sian and him.'

Ryan looked through the window. It wasn't yet dawn but the sky showed the first signs of brightness.

'Okay, we need a bit of kip. Like Eric said, our man isn't going anywhere in a hurry. Let the hospital staff get on with their work for now and we'll get him in the morning.'

He pointed a finger towards Eric. 'Get some sleep. I mean it, this time. Let's reconvene here at nine-thirty. I don't want anyone else bringing him in. This is our case. He's all wors.'

**

The journey from Whickham police station to Gateshead's Queen Elizabeth hospital was only five miles but, thanks to the hideous tailbacks caused by the A1 upgrade between

Team Valley and The Angel, it took them the best part of half-an-hour.

Somewhere between Joicey Road and Sheriff's Highway, they agreed on their strategy. Ryan would lead the interview, with Eric witnessing it. Trebilcock, being the only one of the three who Joseph Tomkiss, or Thomas Rumney, would recognise, was to stay out of view and only appear to apply the coup de grace should their suspect continue with the Joseph Rumney nonsense.

They showed their ID at reception and a security guard escorted them to a private room. 'Stay here,' Ryan ordered. The security didn't know if the order was directed at him or Trebilcock, so both remained outside.

Ryan opened the door and strode in.

'About bloody time I had some more painkillers. I'm in agony here,' the bedridden man complained.

Ryan studied him. Both legs were encased in plaster, raised above heart height by a pulley contraption. Beneath the thin bedclothes, Ryan could see the man's hips and pelvis were similarly plastered.

Eric had been right - he was going nowhere fast.

'Come on then, doc. Give me those...' He stopped as he noticed the uniformed PC Ross.

'What the fuck?'

Ryan produced his warrant card. 'I'm Detective Sergeant Ryan Jarrod, City and County Police. This is my colleague, PC Eric Ross.'

'What do you want?'

'The truth, for starters.'

'I told you I don't want to press charges. I was drunk. It was my fault. There's nothing more to it. Now, leave me alone.'

'I'm not here about your accident, Mr Rumney.' Ryan didn't smile, didn't frown, remained deadpan, as he added, 'Mr THOMAS Rumney, that is.'

Rumney played the innocent, but it was too late. His eyes had given him away. 'You've got yourself mixed-up. My name's Joseph.'

'As in Joseph Tomkiss, you mean?'

'Shit.'

'And very deep shit it is.'

Rumney tried to recover his position. 'I'm saying nothing. You've got the wrong man. Honestly, you're puffing air here. I don't know who you think I am, or what I've done, but you're wrong.'

They were interrupted by Trebilcock before Ryan could continue. 'Not yet,' Ryan hissed, shielding Trebilcock from Rumney's view.

'He's got a visitor,' Trebilcock whispered.

'I don't care if it's the Pope. No visitors. Not now. What are you thinking, man?'

'I'm thinking the visitor is more important than the Pope, so I am.'

'What?'

'Look who's it is.'

Trebilcock stepped aside.

'I think our time's up, Thomas' the visitor said. 'We need to come clean. For Sian's sake, it's time.'

Nancy Douglas shuffled in and took the grey padded visitor chair.

**

'It was an accident,' Rumney told a shell-shocked Ryan. 'She was my daughter. I loved the bones of her,' he winced at his phraseology. 'I'd never do anything to harm her.'

Ryan took a deep breath. Rumney's words were almost a replica of those used by Norman Jarrod when he'd accused his father of burying Rhianne.

'I need you to tell me, in your own words, exactly what happened.'

'Sian and I were spending time together. Precious time, you know? We'd been apart for too long and were making up for lost time. I'd taken on a new identity, enrolled Sian in a school up here as Sian Tomkiss, and we were just, like, having fun. Like father and daughter should.'

'What sort of things did you do, Mr Rumney?'

'Simple things. The best things. I took her to Longsands beach, played in the park, went for walks in the woods. Nothing flashy - I'd only just started my business and had come up here without a penny to my name - but they were good things, you know? Good for me and my girl. That's all I wanted; to be with her.' He brushed away a tear.

'Why did you kill her?'

'I didn't!'

'Mr Rumney, we have forensic evidence which shows your daughter died of a broken neck, and you attempted to disguise the cause of death. You hoped you'd get away with it, didn't you?'

Nancy Douglas glared up at Ryan. She didn't speak, just shook her head at his ignorance, as Thomas Rumney protested his innocence.

'Of course I did! But I didn't kill her. Not murder.'

Ryan glanced at Trebilcock, then Eric Ross. Satisfied Eric was taking a full set of notes, he asked Rumney, 'Why hide her body if you didn't murder her?'

'Isn't it obvious? Because she wasn't supposed to be with me! Sian and Thomas Rumney had disappeared into thin air. We were Sian and Joseph Tomkiss. I'd lost enough. I didn't want to lose my liberty as well. I thought if I kept it secret, no-one would be any the wiser.'

'What did you tell her school to explain Sian's absence?'

'That I'd found a job in Scotland and Sian was coming with me. I thanked them for their kindness during the short time they'd taught her, and that was the end of it.'

Ryan remained silent. His mind twisted between pity for the man if he was telling the truth, anger if he was spreading more bullshit, shock at the callous way he'd covered his tracks - and with a degree of grudging respect for the way he'd covered up his tracks.

Ryan was less sure of Nancy Douglas's role in it all. He gambled on an educated guess.

'Where do you come into things, *Auntie Nancy*? That is who you are, isn't it? This is your nephew, the plumber you recommended to Ivor and Marina Hickson, isn't it?'

Nancy Douglas didn't turn her eyes from Ryan's stare. 'It is,' she said, simply.

Trebilcock spoke. 'I gets it now. All the time I was drinking tea with you, I has this feelin' I be missin' something. It was there all the time, in plain sight.'

Both Ryan and Nancy Douglas looked confused.

'The photograph on your wall. The one with your brother you's said was taken in Bournemouth. It wasn't Bournemouth, was it? It was Lymington. Only about twenty-odd miles apart, I'd be guessin'. Thomas be on that picture, but he be in his teens. I didn't recognise him straight off but I knew I'd seen something not right; I just didn't recognise what it be.'

Ryan was impressed. *'So much for superstitious bollocks'*, he thought.

Nancy Douglas smiled. 'I like both you boys,' she said to Trebilcock and Ryan. 'You're good at your job, and you're good men. But so is my Thomas. You'll see that he is. Just let him finish his story.'

Ryan fixed his gaze back on the man strung up like a snared fox.

'I'm waiting, Mr Rumney. Trust me, I'm waiting.'

THIRTY-TWO

'It was the October school holidays. God, seven years ago. Seems like yesterday and a lifetime away, both at once. Anyway, me and Sian were spending the day at Auntie Nancy's. The day was unseasonably warm. The sun had been out all day but was just beginning to set. Its rays sprinkled through the branches, the leaves a mix of rusts, golds, reds, and browns. Lovely colours, they were.'

Rumney's hospital room had fallen silent. Everyone hung on the man's words. Tears glistened in the eyes of Nancy Douglas and rolled down the cheeks of her nephew as he remembered the last few hours of his daughter's life.

'Beneath the trees, fallen leaves covered the ground in the same autumnal colours. Sian saw something glint amongst the fallen foliage. *'Look Daddy,'* she said, *'I've found a fifty-pence.'* I put on a pirate's voice. *'Thar be treasure buried thar,'* I joked.'

For a second, Trebilcock thought he was taking the piss out of his accent but he was too immersed in Rumney's confession to complain.

'Let's dig for treasure, Daddy,' my little girl squealed. So, that's what we pretended to do. We ran our hands through the leaves. Tossed them in the air and waited for them to rain back down on our heads, like Dianne Keaton and Queen Latifah did with banknotes in Mad Money.'

Ryan didn't know the movie but he could picture the scene, nonetheless.

'But we didn't find any more treasure. We sifted through the leaves for a good ten minutes or more, but there wasn't any lost coins. Instead, we started unearthing chestnuts. Lots of them. I juggled with four or five. Sian laughed 'til tears ran down her face.'

Ryan swallowed hard at imaginary scenes of Rhianne and his Dad doing exactly the same thing, possibly in the very same spot.

'By the time we'd finished, we had mud under our fingernails and our hands were wet with mulch from the damp leaves at the bottom of the pile.'

Rumney's head sagged. Ryan saw the man's shoulders heave and heard his breath come out in sobs. 'That's when it happened.'

Ryan wanted Rumney to come out with it himself, but the man was too overcome with emotion. Ryan had to prompt him.

'What did happen, Mr Rumney?'

It took several minutes for Rumney to compose himself. His body shuddered so much the chains holding his smashed legs aloft rattled.

Thomas raised his eyes to the ceiling, as if searching for his little girl in the Heavens.

'Sian shouted '*I'm so happy!*' She ran towards me with her hands held out. '*I love you Daddy!*' she squealed. She jumped into my arms and I caught her by the hands.'

Rumney looked down. Shook his head. 'I'd done it dozens of times before. I caught my little girl and spun her through the air, faster and faster. Sian loved it. She laughed and squealed in delight. '*Faster, Daddy. Go faster.*' So, I did.'

Rumney couldn't continue. He reached for a plastic cup of water to compose himself but his hand shook so much he spilled the contents over his gown.

'I'm sorry, Mr Rumney. I need you to finish telling us.' Ryan WAS genuinely sorry. All the time, he was witnessing at first hand the anguish Norman Jarrod must have felt.

Rumney nodded. 'I'm okay. Like I said, I'd lifted my little girl from the ground by swinging her around just as I'd done loads of times. I'd never done it with wet hands before, though.'

Self-consciously, as if reliving the moment, he wiped both palms on his hospital gown.

'I didn't even feel my grip loosen. One moment, I had the weight of my little girl in my hands; the next, I was holding nothing but fresh air.'

Rumney met Ryan's eyes.

'And I saw my Sian fly head-first into a horse-chestnut tree barely four paces away.' Rumney clenched his eyes shut yet tears leaked through his eyelashes. 'I can still hear the crack as she hit the tree.'

His voice came out eery and high-pitched. 'Sian hit the ground. She jerked violently, two, maybe three times. And then, she was quiet. Everything was quiet. The birds stopped singing; I think even the traffic noise stopped. Everything stopped - including my little girl's heart.'

'Thank you, Mr Rumney. I can't begin to imagine how hard that must have been for you. I appreciate it. We'll leave you to gather yourself.'

Ryan looked towards a broken Nancy Douglas. 'Really, Nancy. I'm sorry I had to put you both through that.'

'You were only doing your job,' she whispered. 'I can tell you're genuinely sorry. Thank you. It helps.'

Ryan looked uncomfortable. 'I'll give you some time together before I come back.'

He motioned with his head for Trebilcock and Ross to step outside.

The noise and bustle of the busy hospital corridor seemed a world away from the solitude of Thomas Rumney's room.

**

There was a Costa on Level 2 of the Emergency Care Centre and Ryan despatched Eric to bring them some decent coffee and a few cookies and muffins to up their sugar levels.

Once he'd gone, Ryan dismissed the hospital security guard. Blinking against the harsh glare of sunlight reflecting off the corridor's white walls, Ryan turned to Trebilcock.

'What do you think?'

'He's either telling the truth or should be up for a BAFTA.'

'Yeah. I believe him. Not only because of his reactions but also the way Nancy behaved. They couldn't have rehearsed that between them.'

'Good point.'

Ryan exhaled through his nose. 'I actually feel sorry for him.'

'That be a first.'

Ryan gazed into the distance. 'It's not, actually. Remember the Byker Wall incident?'

Trebilcock screwed his face. 'Oh yeah. The property scam.'

Ryan tipped his head. 'Aye. The lass involved in that - I sympathised with her, an' all.'

After a silence, Trebilcock asked, 'What now?'

There were a couple of seats wedged against the wall outside the general ward. Ryan took one. Trebilcock joined him. 'Well, first off, we perk worsel up with some caffeine, if Eric eventually finds his way back. That'll give Rumney and Nancy some time together.'

'And then?'

'Then, we start all over again. It's inevitable the poor sod will be charged with *'Preventing the lawful and decent burial of a dead body'* and, quite probably, *'Obstructing a Coroner by preventing an inquest.'* Together, I reckon he's in for a custodial. We've no choice but question him about it.'

Trebilcock whistled. 'And that's before we even thinks about manslaughter, perverting course of justice; not to mention dodgy paperwork for his plumbing business.'

They considered the consequences of Rumney's actions. 'It's sad but I reckon he's going away for a canny spell. As if the poor bugger hasn't suffered enough already.'

Trebilcock shook his head. 'You wouldn't believe what's gone in that street, would you? I means, lovely setting. I could see myself living there one day.'

'You'll be spoilt for choice. The Hickson place is up for grabs, Waddell's going down for his pervy stuff so that's another one up for sale, and we don't know about Nancy Douglas yet.'

'Put like that, I'm not sure Oi fancy livin' there no more.'

A breathless Eric returned with an eggbox-like tray holding three Styrofoam mugs in his hands and a bag of goodies beneath an arm.

'Sorry, lads. The queue was humongous.'

Ryan gulped his coffee while Trebilcock savoured his with an orgasmic look on his face.

'Speaking of ol' Nancy, what do you think she's looking at?' Trebilcock pondered.

'Perverting the course', I reckon. Hopefully she'll get a lenient judge and a humane and sympathetic CPS barrister up against her.'

Eric munched on a double-chocolate cookie. 'These are lush. Do you lads want summat?'

'Not yet. But divvent even think of scoffing the lot. You stay here, Eric.' Ryan looked at Trebilcock. 'Howay, let's get this ower with.'

**

They passed through the general ward and entered Rumney's room at the same time as a nurse exited.

'How are we feeling now, Mr Rumney?' Ryan asked.

'Like shite, how do you think I bloody feel?'

'The painkillers will soon kick in.'

'My legs are the least of my worries.'

Despite the nature of Rumney's words, Ryan could tell the man was less emotional.

'We need to ask you a few more questions about the events immediately after Sian's accident.' He used the word advisedly. 'What happened straight after?'

Rumney groaned. 'My van was parked not five minutes away. I brought it as close as I could, down a track, then I picked up my little girl and carried her to it. I didn't stop to think if anyone saw me. Luckily for me, nobody did.'

Rumney spoke as if he was a third party. Perhaps it was the only way he could handle it.

'I sat there, crying and shaking, for nearly an hour. Might have been more, might have been less.'

'Then what?'

Rumney couldn't make eye contact. 'Then, I came up with a plan. I knew it wasn't fair to take her to Auntie Nancy, so I took her to the only other place I could think of - my lock-up.'

'In daylight?'

He shook his head. 'No. Well, I drove there in a sort of twilight world of my own but I waited until it was gone three in the morning before I took her round back and carried her in as if she was a bit of my plumbing.'

Rumney winced at the memory.

'Once inside, I didn't know what to do. I mean, I couldn't just leave her there on the floor, could I?'

'Where did you keep Sian?' Trebilcock asked, although he'd already guessed.

'I had an old stationery cupboard. One of those upright things. I cleared it out. Most of the stuff in there was rubbish anyway. Empty boxes, that sort of thing. Once it was empty, I...I...'

'Take your time, Mr Rumney.'

'I stood her up in it, locked the door, and left her.'

'What? You left your daughter's body in a cupboard for seven years?' Ryan was quickly losing sympathy for Rumney.

'Why do you think I had all that security at the lock-up? Certainly not because there was anything worth stealing. It was all to protect my Sian from being found by anyone. Who knows what they might do to her?'

'*He's bloody mad,*' Ryan thought.

'I know what you're thinking, but it kept her close to me. I'd even talk to her sometimes. It might sound weird, but I found it, I dunno...comforting, I suppose.'

Ryan looked at Trebilcock who shrugged his shoulders. 'Mr Rumney, when bodies...'

'...I know, I know. The smell. It was bloody awful but my workplace stinks of all sorts of things anyway. Glues, adhesives, it's close to the Teams Gut which stinks to high heaven at the best of times. That all helped disguise it.'

Trebilcock shivered. Ryan shook his head. Rumney stared at nothing.

'When did you decide to remove Sian?'

'It was my idea.'

Heads spun towards Nancy Douglas.

'When I heard the house opposite needed repairs done, and that the owners weren't going to be living there, I thought Sian could come home to me. I'd look after her. So, I recommended Thomas to them.'

Ryan wanted to say, '*You're all bloody mad*,' but he remained professional. 'Did you use your van to move her?'

Rumney looked at Ryan as if he was an idiot. 'No, I got on a bus with her,' he mocked.

'This isn't a laughing matter, Mr Rumney,' Ryan said.

'You don't have to tell me. This is my daughter we're talking about. My only child.'

Ryan thought it best to say nothing. He waited for Rumney to speak again.

'Yes, I used my van. There was nothing unusual about it being there. I was on a job and the neighbours had seen me coming and going with my tools. The nosey bugger next door was at the window most of the time but not in the middle of the night. I reversed the van onto the drive and lifted Sian straight into the house.'

'At what point did you choose to disguise her broken neck?' The words sounded cruel and callous because they WERE cruel and callous.

Rumney shook his head. 'It wasn't deliberate. I mean, it wasn't calculated. When I lifted her into the house...'

For the first time in the second interview, Rumney began to weep. He took a sip of water without spilling it before continuing.

'Her head almost fell off. I couldn't have my Sian like that so I used a sealant to fix it in place. I didn't do it to hide how she died. I never expected her to be found.'

'When did you bury her?'

'I'm not sure, exactly. I worked on the job for a couple of days then, at night, I'd do a bit of digging. The trees at the back block out most of the view from the street at that end, and I tried to dig where I thought the fella next door couldn't see.'

'And you moved the bones from the house and buried them.'

Rumney nodded. 'Then, I filled the hole in. I'd made sure I kept most of the turf intact so when I covered Sian up, I replaced the turf. You really couldn't tell the ground had been disturbed.'

'*Hell's teeth. He sounds proud of himself,*' Ryan thought.

Nigel Trebilcock asked the next question. 'What happened to the cupboard where you kept Sian? When I searched your premises, it weren't there.'

Rumney gave a grim smile. 'See, as soon as you turned up the first time, I knew you'd coming looking for me again. I got rid of it.'

'Where?'

'I don't know. I sold it. To a scrap man. Probably crushed to bits now. That's how I ended up in here. I got pissed in the pub thinking I was in the clear, and some bugger ploughed into me on my way home. Bloody typical.'

He laughed humourlessly.

Ryan gave Trebilcock a nod and Nigel left the room.

229

'My colleague will be back in a moment with PC Ross who will read you your rights and arrest you. You'll remain here under guard until you're fit enough to be moved into custody before trial.'

Thomas Rumney nodded. 'Can I ask you something?'

'Go on.'

'Will Sian get a proper burial now? Something peaceful? That's what I'd like for her.'

Ryan blinked through watery eyes as he thought of Norman, Rhianne, and their request to Reverend Murray Appleby.

'I'll make sure she does,' Nancy Douglas replied. 'If I'm allowed?' She looked pleadingly at Ryan.

'That will depend on the courts, Nancy, but I'd like to think so.'

'Will I be charged, too?'

'You will.'

'I see. Thank you for your kindness.' She looked at Ryan quizzically. 'You have the look of your father, you know, when he was younger.'

Ryan's jaw dropped.

'Yes, I realised the other day where I recognised you from. Except, it wasn't you I recognised. You weren't even born then. I saw your father in you.'

Ryan coughed and tried to put Nancy's observation behind him.

'Mrs Douglas, I can understand why Thomas did what he did, sort of. But why did you get involved in covering up Sian's death?'

She reached up and took her nephew's hand.

'Because Thomas is family, that's why. We're nothing without family.'

She smiled up at Ryan.

'You should know that, with you having an elder sister. I hope she's doing well.'

THIRTY-THREE

SEVEN WEEKS LATER

A breeze rustled the verdant leaves of an overhanging tree. The last daffodils of spring wilted in small borders while a sweet fragrance of burgeoning summer flowers hung in the air, teasing with the senses.

The plot lay in a shaded part of the cemetery, close to the lodge and slightly apart from the main graveyard which, unlike life, seemed to run forever.

Ryan listened to traffic rumble by only yards away yet, somehow, the sound was muted. Almost reverential. He stepped backwards a pace or two until he stood alongside Norman Jarrod. Hannah laid her hand on Ryan's shoulder and he reached up to cover it with his own.

James moved ahead of him and placed his flowers on the plot. A butterfly flitted from posey to wreath and back again. A bee hovered lazily above the petals of a flower before daring to hunt for the treasure within.

When James retreated, Muzzle took his hand and almost smiled. She seemed more comfortable with death and the dead than she did life and the living.

Ryan turned away from the plot, towards the footpath skirting the manicured lawns. Doris Jarrod sat in a wheelchair, rug on her lap. She seemed at ease, almost as if she understood where she was and what she was witnessing.

She looked straight at Ryan and smiled. Or was it his imagination?

The Reverend Murray Appleby crouched beside her, his hand tenderly holding hers. He nodded towards Ryan.

'Just a minute, Hannah,' he whispered.

When he saw Ryan approach, Appleby struggled to his feet. Ryan extended his hand and Murray Appleby took it in both of his.

'Thank you for this,' Ryan said. 'It means a lot.'

'It's my pleasure. I had to twist a few arms - gently and metaphorically, of course - but we all deserve to be remembered. Life may be frenetic but it's so fleeting. We deserve our peace when it's our time to pass over.'

Ryan thought of Sian Rumney. 'We do, indeed,' he said. Ryan turned towards Doris Jarrod. 'Not too cold, Gran?'

Doris glanced up at him. 'I'm fine, Norman.'

Murray Appleby smiled sympathetically. 'You're doing just fine, aren't you, my dear?' the clergyman said to Doris.

'Yes thank you,' she replied.

'Look,' Ryan said, 'We're gannin to the pub after this if you'd like to join us.'

Murray Appleby smiled. 'Ah, I'd love to but not when I'm on duty. I'm like you when it comes to that.'

Ryan chuckled. 'Thank you again,' he said before retaking his place beside the headstone.

Hannah slipped her arm through his. 'You okay?'

Ryan thought for a moment. 'Do you know, I am. I feel more at ease than I have for yonks. It's odd.'

He looked at the headstone. A simple, black marble rectangle with a brass vase set into its top. The inscription, etched in gold lettering, was minimal.

'Rhianne Jarrod
Much loved daughter and sister
Taken too early
Aged Four Years.'

Hannah leant into Ryan and whispered into his ear. 'I've got something to tell you.'

He raised an eyebrow.

'Later,' she teased.

Ryan checked on his father and brother. They were fine. He wasn't sure about Muzzle but, if she wasn't fine, she probably preferred it that way.

'Howay,' Norman said, 'Let's have a drink on Rhianne. She's back with us.'

The party moved away. Ryan moved with them, then stopped when he noticed Hannah was still by the headstone. He moved back to her.

'Penny for them,' he said.

Hannah smiled, the dimple in her cheek blossoming like one of the flowers by the plot. 'I was just thinking, that's all.'

'Thinking what?'

'I like the name. Rhianne - it's got a nice ring to it.'

'Aye, I guess.'

'There's no guessing about it. It's a lovely name; part Ryan, part Hannah.'

She kissed him on the cheek.

'Perhaps if it's a girl, we should call her Rhianne.'

Ryan spun to face her, open-mouthed.

'Your face!' she giggled.

He heard a voice in his head. *'Don't let me be misunderstood,'* it sang.

Hannah nodded her head. Smiled at him.

'Yep, it's amazing what a session at Bar Blanc and a bit of afternoon delight can do, isn't it?' she said.

****

COMING NEXT FROM

COLIN YOUNGMAN:

THE
GRAVEYARD
SHIFT

A Ryan Jarrod Novel

'Horror movies aren't real. Are they?'

Acknowledgement:

To you - for taking the time to read Bones of Callaley. Your interest and support mean the world to me.

If you enjoyed this, the eighth Ryan Jarrod novel, please tell your family, friends, and colleagues. Word of mouth is an author's best friend so the more people who know, the greater my appreciation.

I welcome reviews of your experience, either on Amazon or Goodreads. Alternatively, you can 'Rate' the book after you finish reading on most Kindle devices, if you'd prefer.

If you'd like to be among the first to hear news about the next book in the series, or to discover release dates in advance, you can follow me by:

Clicking the 'Follow' button on my Amazon Author page
https://www.amazon.co.uk/Colin-Youngman/e/B01H9CNHQK

OR

Liking/ following me on:
Facebook: @colin.youngman.author

Thanks again for your interest in my work.

Colin

About the author:

Colin had his first written work published at the age of 9 when a contribution to children's comic *Sparky* brought him the rich rewards of a 10/- Postal Order and a transistor radio.

He was smitten by the writing bug and has gone on to have his work feature in publications for young adults, sports magazines, national newspapers, and travel guides before he moved to his first love: fiction.

Colin previously worked as a senior executive in the public sector. He lives in Northumberland, north-east England, and is an avid supporter of Newcastle United (don't laugh), a keen follower of Durham County Cricket Club, and has a family interest in British Gymnastics and the City of Newcastle Gymnastics Academy.

You can read his other work (e-book and paperback) exclusive to Amazon:

The Tower (Ryan Jarrod Book Seven)
Low Light (Ryan Jarrod Book Six)
Operation Sage (Ryan Jarrod Book Five)
High Level (Ryan Jarrod Book Four)
The Lighthouse Keeper (Ryan Jarrod Book Three)
The Girl On The Quay (Ryan Jarrod Book Two)
The Angel Falls (Ryan Jarrod Book One)

The Doom Brae Witch
Alley Rat
DEAD Heat
Twists (An anthology of novelettes)
****

Colin Youngman

Printed in Great Britain
by Amazon

21840624R00138